STAR TREK

VOLUME 1

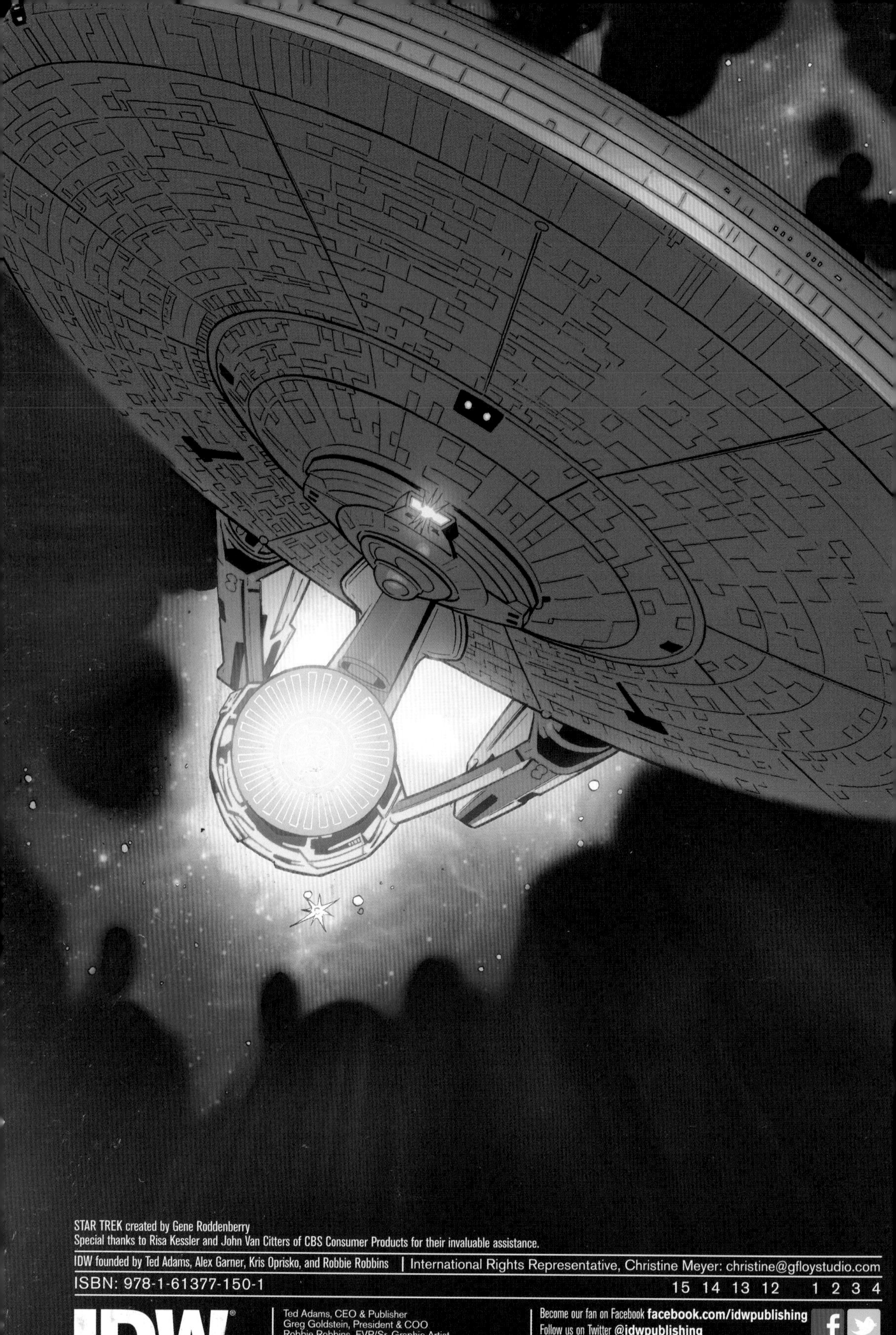

STAR TREK created by Gene Roddenberry
Special thanks to Risa Kessler and John Van Citters of CBS Consumer Products for their invaluable assistance.

IDW founded by Ted Adams, Alex Garner, Kris Oprisko, and Robbie Robbins | International Rights Representative, Christine Meyer: christine@gfloystudio.com

ISBN: 978-1-61377-150-1

15 14 13 12   1 2 3 4

IDW®

Ted Adams, CEO & Publisher
Greg Goldstein, President & COO
Robbie Robbins, EVP/Sr. Graphic Artist
Chris Ryall, Chief Creative Officer/Editor-in-Chief
Matthew Ruzicka, CPA, Chief Financial Officer
Alan Payne, VP of Sales

Become our fan on Facebook **facebook.com/idwpublishing**
Follow us on Twitter **@idwpublishing**
Check us out on YouTube **youtube.com/idwpublishing**
www.IDWPUBLISHING.com

Originally published as STAR TREK Issues #1–4.

STAR TREK

VOLUME 1

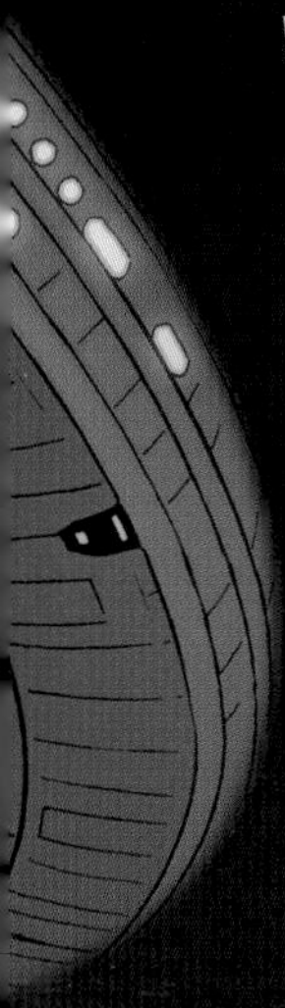

Written by
MIKE JOHNSON

Art by
STEPHEN MOLNAR
and JOE PHILLIPS

Colors by
JOHN RAUCH

Creative Consultant
ROBERTO ORCI

Letters by
NEIL UYETAKE

Series Edits by
SCOTT DUNBIER

Collection Cover by Tim Bradstreet, Colors by Grant Goleash
Collection Edits by Justin Eisinger and Alonzo Simon
Collection Design by Chris Mowry

Based on the original teleplays of *Where No Man Has Gone Before* by Samuel A. Peeples
and *The Galileo Seven* by Oliver Crawford and Shimon Wincleberg

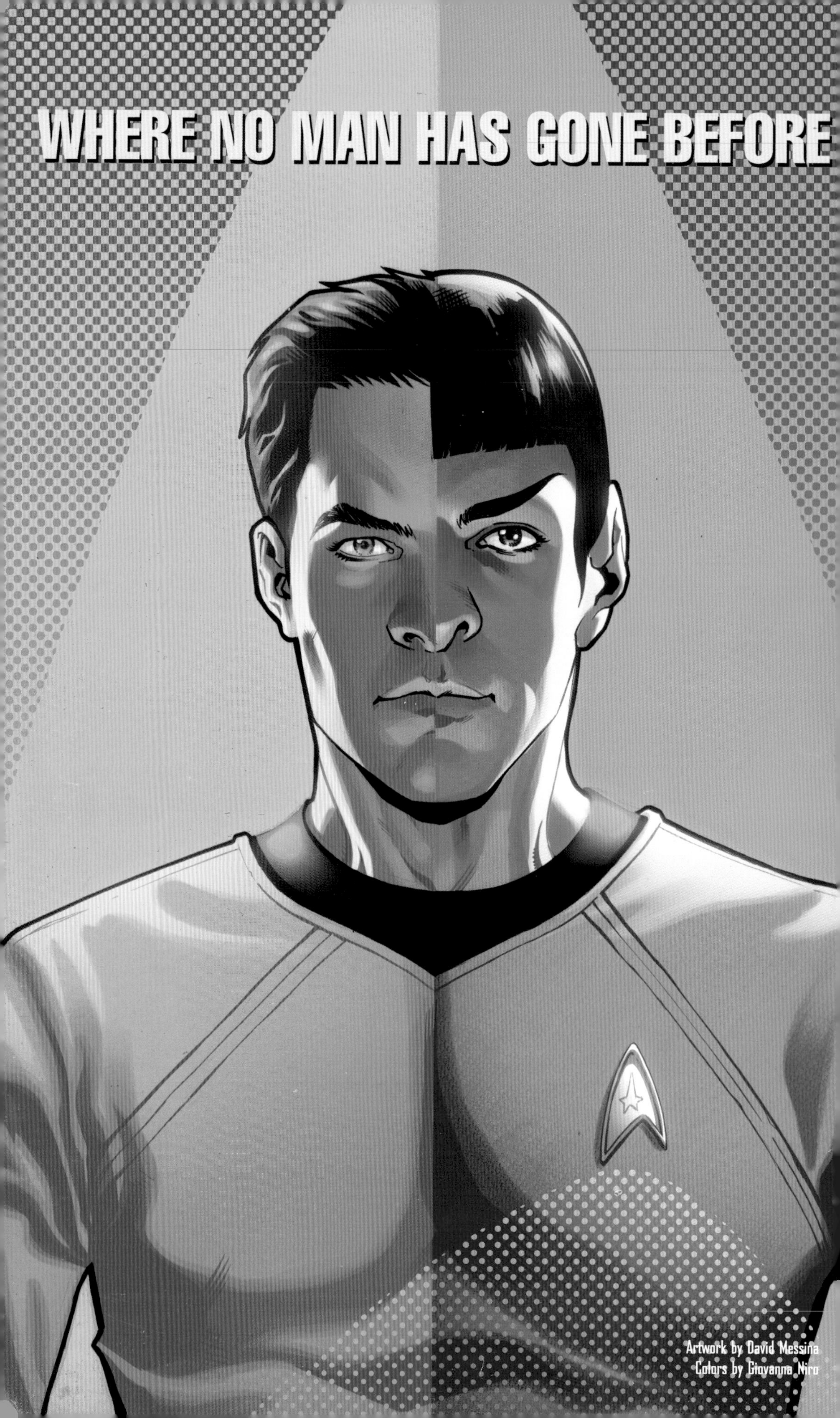
WHERE NO MAN HAS GONE BEFORE
Artwork by David Messina
Colors by Giovanna Niro

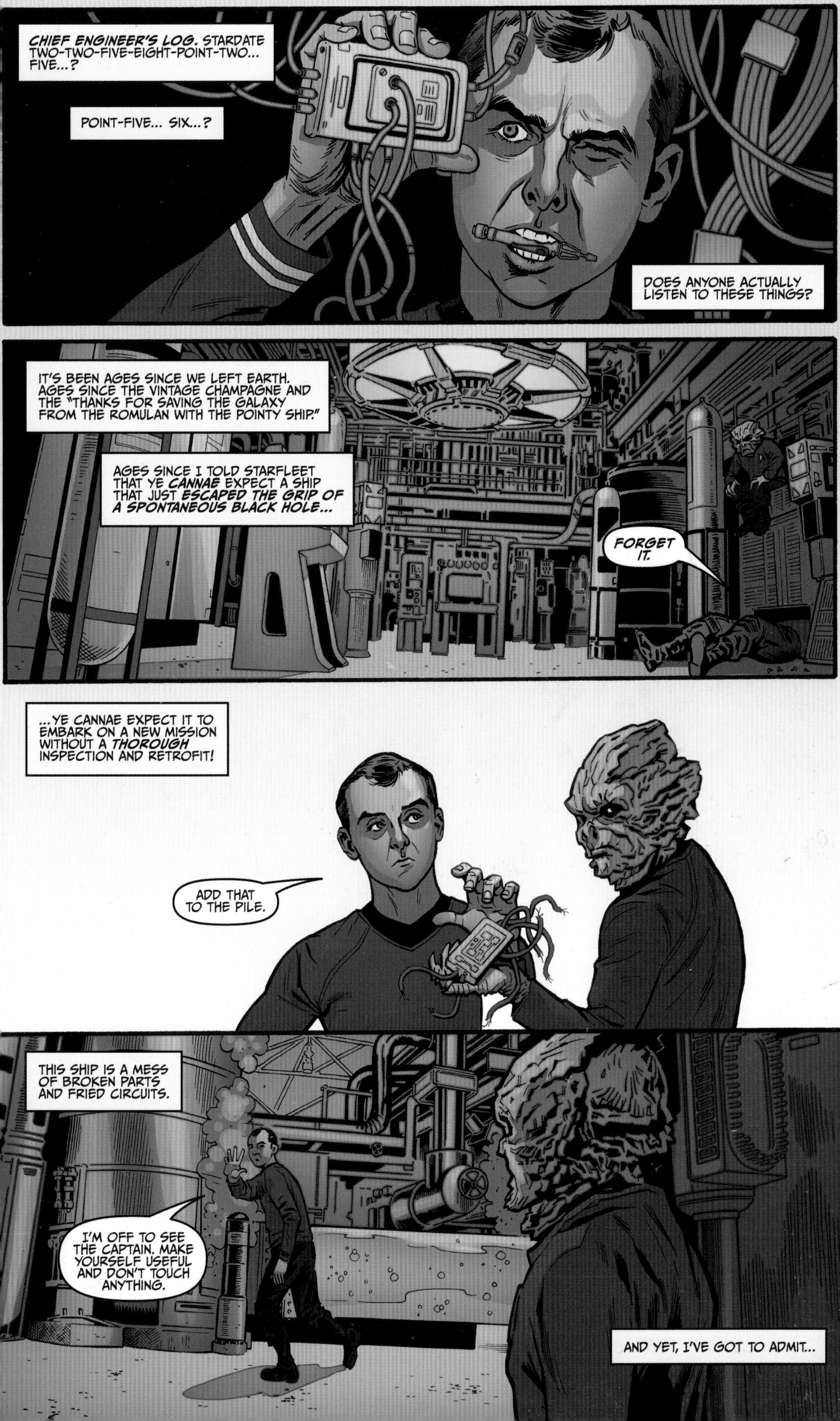
CHIEF ENGINEER'S LOG. STARDATE TWO-TWO-FIVE-EIGHT-POINT-TWO... FIVE...?
POINT-FIVE... SIX...?
DOES ANYONE ACTUALLY LISTEN TO THESE THINGS?
IT'S BEEN AGES SINCE WE LEFT EARTH. AGES SINCE THE VINTAGE CHAMPAGNE AND THE "THANKS FOR SAVING THE GALAXY FROM THE ROMULAN WITH THE POINTY SHIP."
AGES SINCE I TOLD STARFLEET THAT YE CANNAE EXPECT A SHIP THAT JUST ESCAPED THE GRIP OF A SPONTANEOUS BLACK HOLE...
FORGET IT.
...YE CANNAE EXPECT IT TO EMBARK ON A NEW MISSION WITHOUT A THOROUGH INSPECTION AND RETROFIT!
ADD THAT TO THE PILE.
THIS SHIP IS A MESS OF BROKEN PARTS AND FRIED CIRCUITS.
I'M OFF TO SEE THE CAPTAIN. MAKE YOURSELF USEFUL AND DON'T TOUCH ANYTHING.
AND YET, I'VE GOT TO ADMIT...

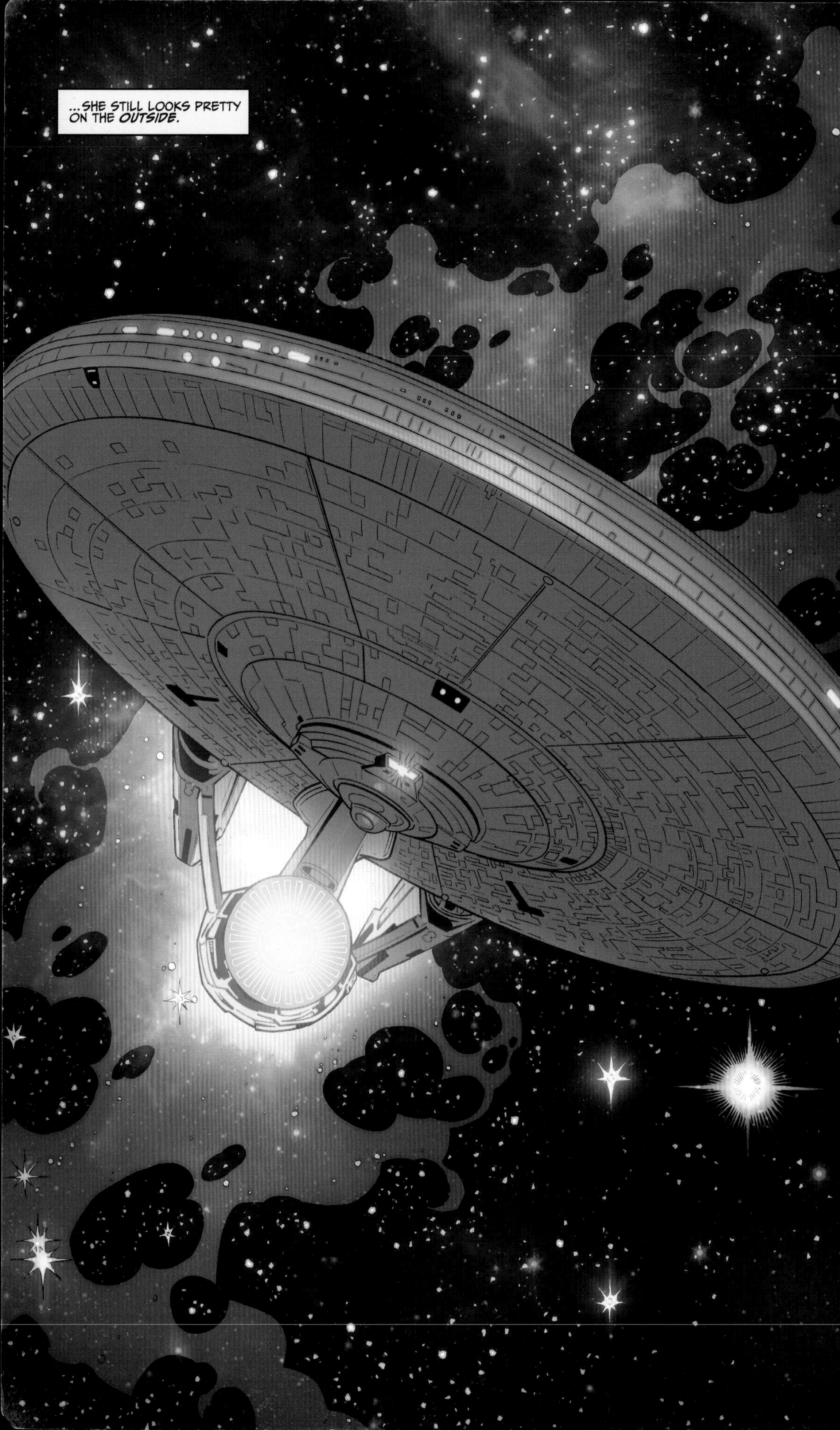
...SHE STILL LOOKS PRETTY ON THE *OUTSIDE*.

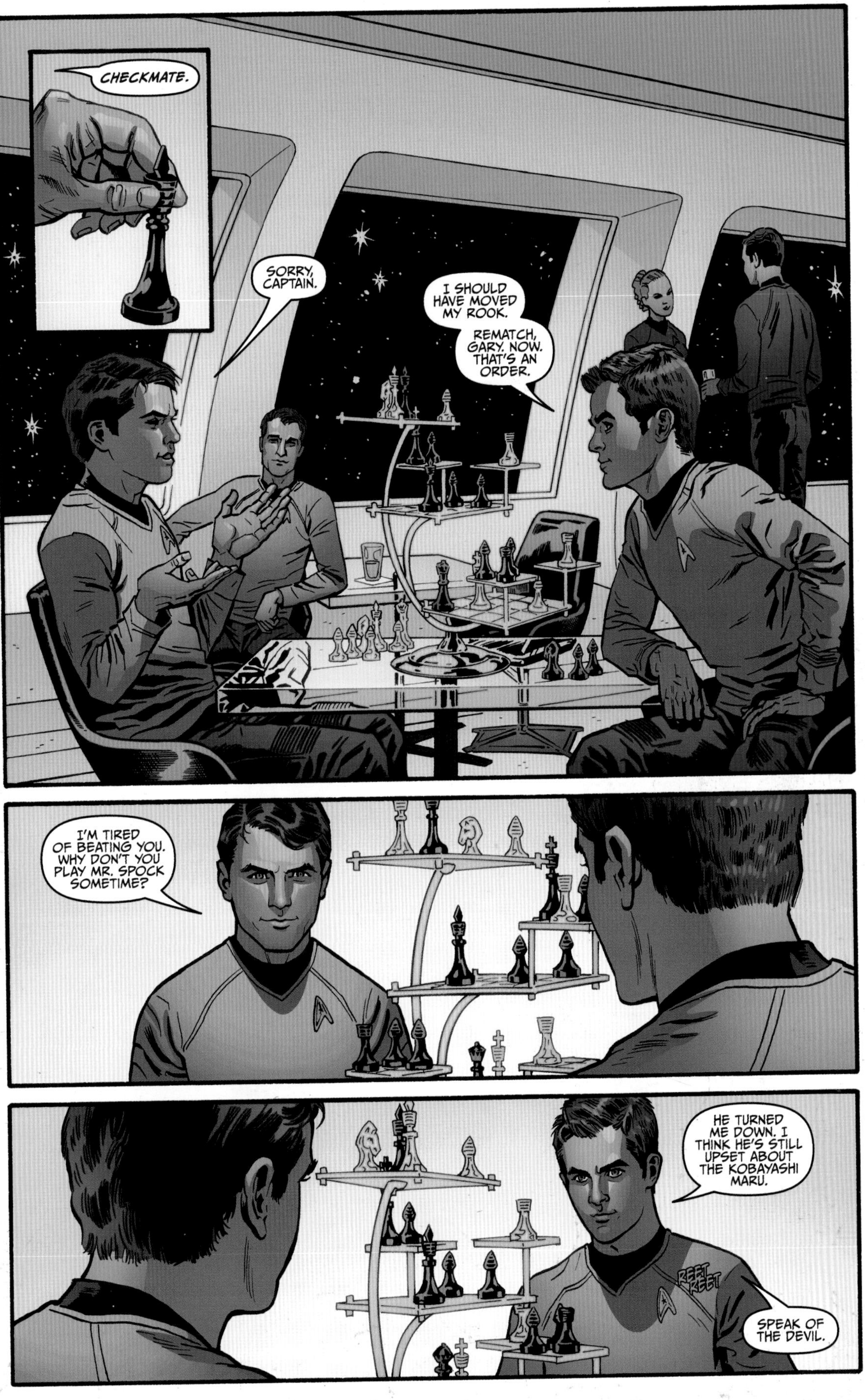
CHECKMATE.
SORRY, CAPTAIN.
I SHOULD HAVE MOVED MY ROOK.
REMATCH, GARY. NOW. THAT'S AN ORDER.
I'M TIRED OF BEATING YOU. WHY DON'T YOU PLAY MR. SPOCK SOMETIME?
HE TURNED ME DOWN. I THINK HE'S STILL UPSET ABOUT THE KOBAYASHI MARU.
REET REET
SPEAK OF THE DEVIL.

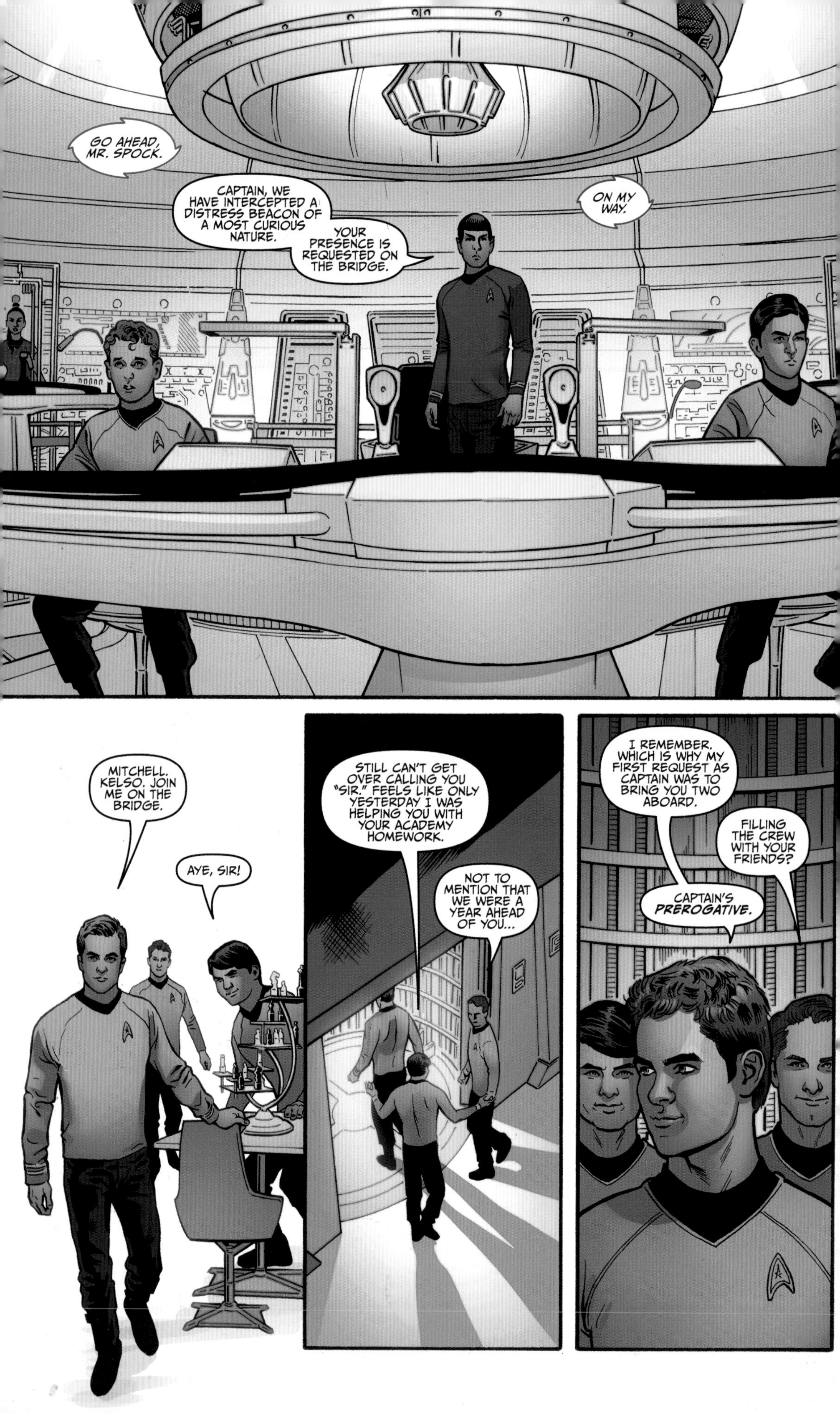
GO AHEAD, MR. SPOCK.
CAPTAIN, WE HAVE INTERCEPTED A DISTRESS BEACON OF A MOST CURIOUS NATURE.
YOUR PRESENCE IS REQUESTED ON THE BRIDGE.
ON MY WAY.
MITCHELL. KELSO. JOIN ME ON THE BRIDGE.
AYE, SIR!
STILL CAN'T GET OVER CALLING YOU "SIR." FEELS LIKE ONLY YESTERDAY I WAS HELPING YOU WITH YOUR ACADEMY HOMEWORK.
NOT TO MENTION THAT WE WERE A YEAR AHEAD OF YOU...
I REMEMBER. WHICH IS WHY MY FIRST REQUEST AS CAPTAIN WAS TO BRING YOU TWO ABOARD.
FILLING THE CREW WITH YOUR FRIENDS?
CAPTAIN'S *PREROGATIVE.*

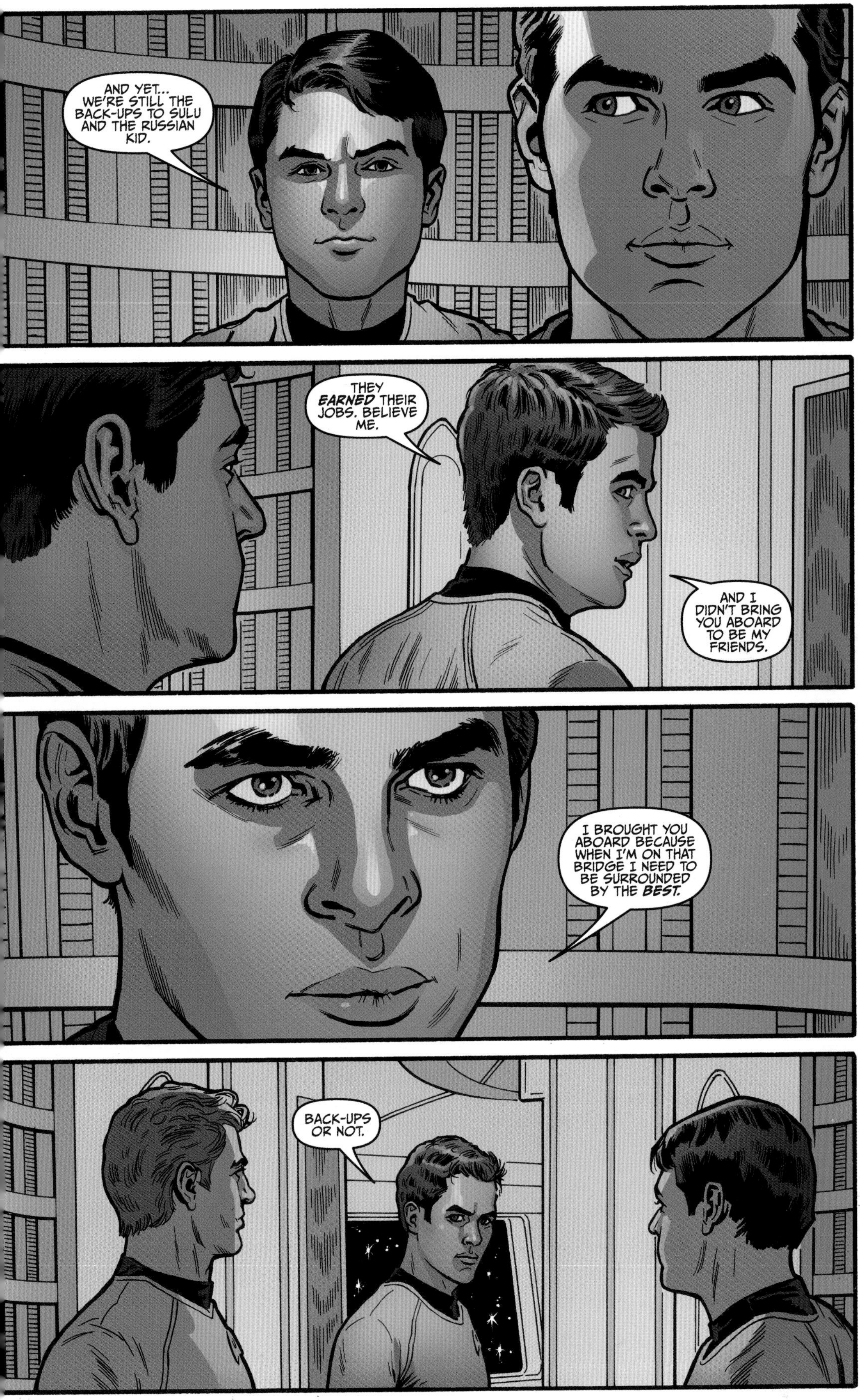
AND YET... WE'RE STILL THE BACK-UPS TO SULU AND THE RUSSIAN KID.
THEY *EARNED* THEIR JOBS. BELIEVE ME.
AND I DIDN'T BRING YOU ABOARD TO BE MY FRIENDS.
I BROUGHT YOU ABOARD BECAUSE WHEN I'M ON THAT BRIDGE I NEED TO BE SURROUNDED BY THE *BEST.*
BACK-UPS OR NOT.

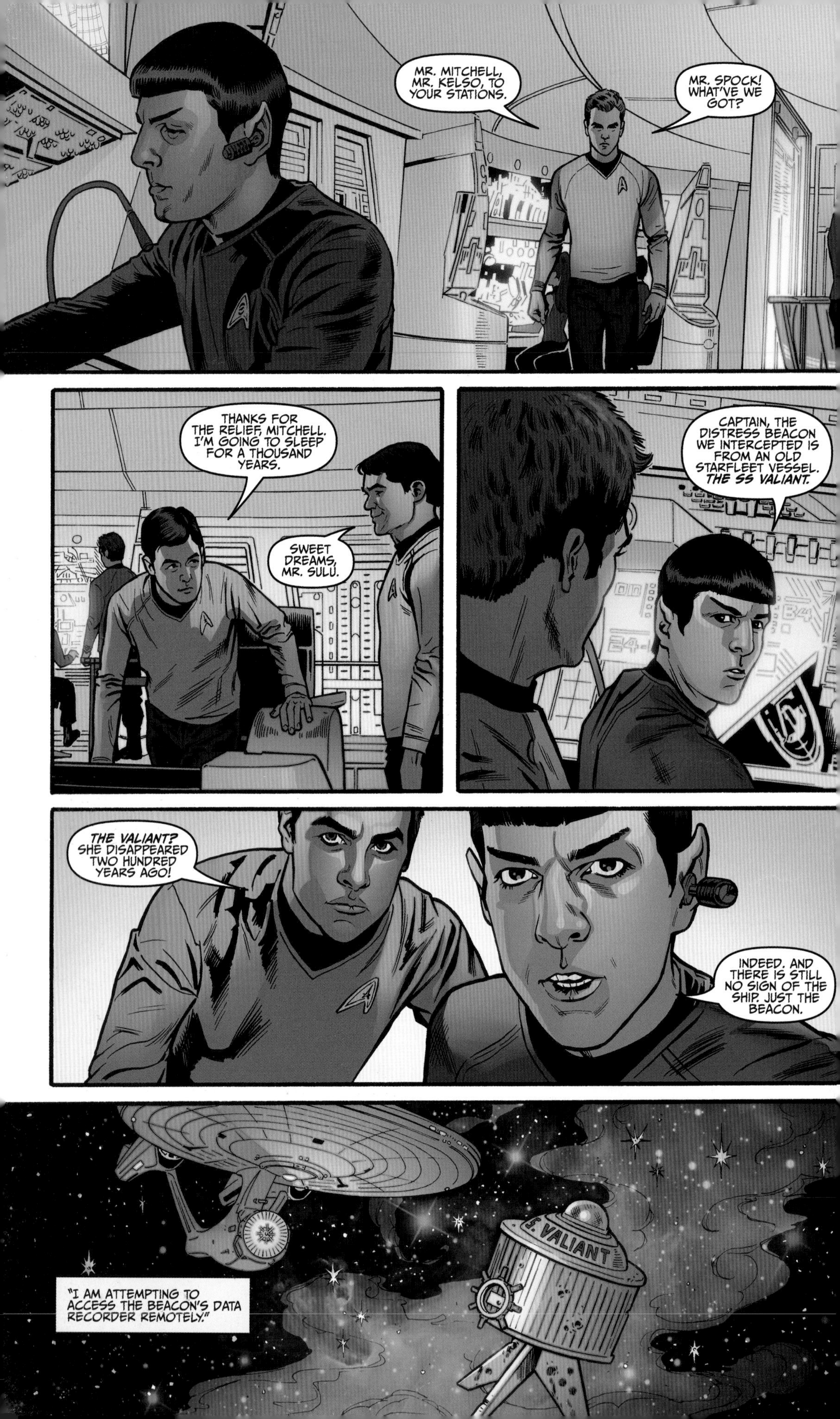
MR. MITCHELL, MR. KELSO, TO YOUR STATIONS.
MR. SPOCK! WHAT'VE WE GOT?
THANKS FOR THE RELIEF, MITCHELL. I'M GOING TO SLEEP FOR A THOUSAND YEARS.
SWEET DREAMS, MR. SULU.
CAPTAIN, THE DISTRESS BEACON WE INTERCEPTED IS FROM AN OLD STARFLEET VESSEL. *THE SS VALIANT.*
THE VALIANT? SHE DISAPPEARED TWO HUNDRED YEARS AGO!
INDEED. AND THERE IS STILL NO SIGN OF THE SHIP. JUST THE BEACON.
S. VALIANT
"I AM ATTEMPTING TO ACCESS THE BEACON'S DATA RECORDER REMOTELY."

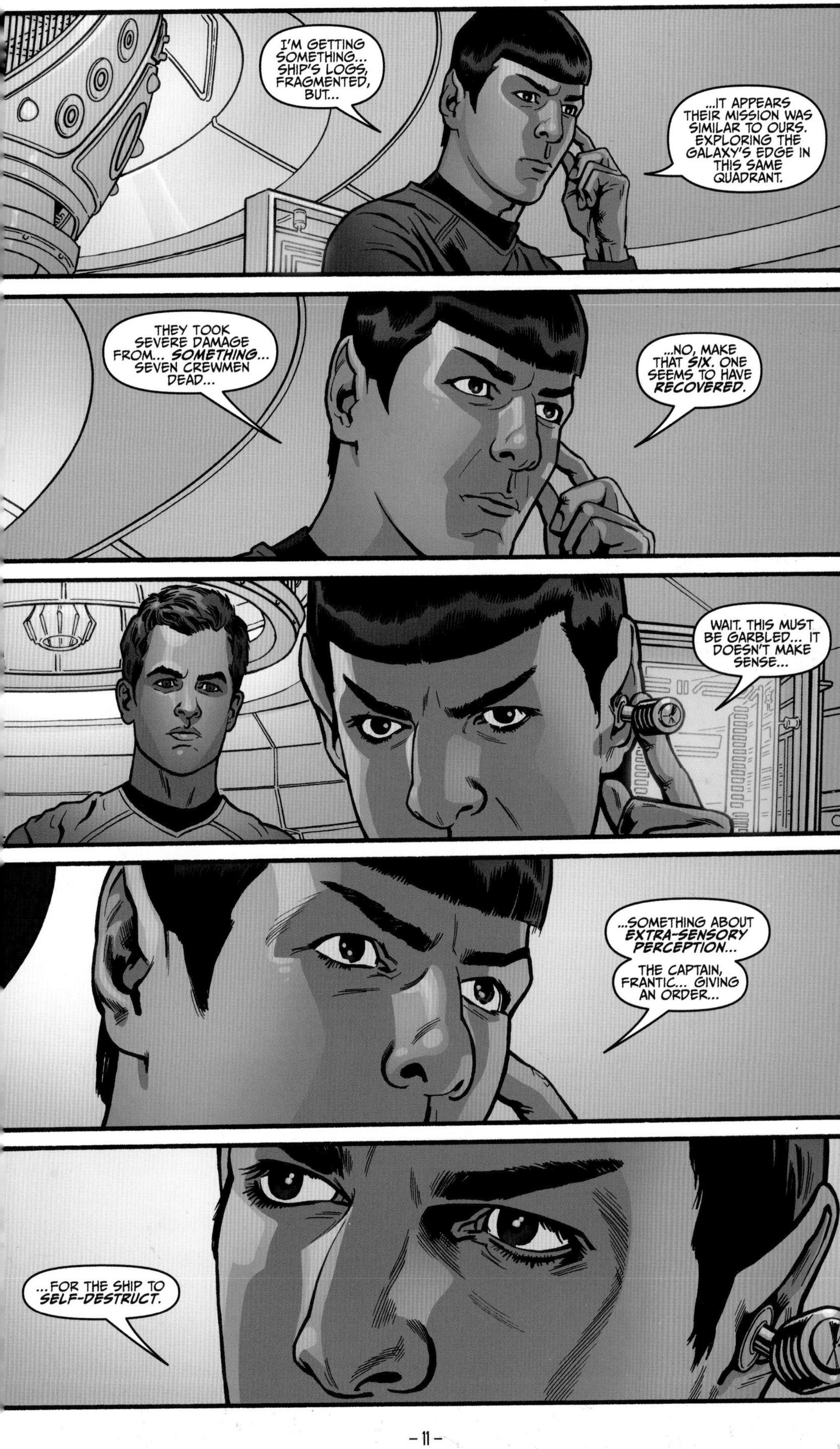
I'M GETTING SOMETHING... SHIP'S LOGS, FRAGMENTED, BUT...
...IT APPEARS THEIR MISSION WAS SIMILAR TO OURS. EXPLORING THE GALAXY'S EDGE IN THIS SAME QUADRANT.
THEY TOOK SEVERE DAMAGE FROM... SOMETHING... SEVEN CREWMEN DEAD...
...NO, MAKE THAT SIX. ONE SEEMS TO HAVE RECOVERED.
WAIT. THIS MUST BE GARBLED... IT DOESN'T MAKE SENSE...
...SOMETHING ABOUT EXTRA-SENSORY PERCEPTION...
THE CAPTAIN, FRANTIC... GIVING AN ORDER...
...FOR THE SHIP TO SELF-DESTRUCT.

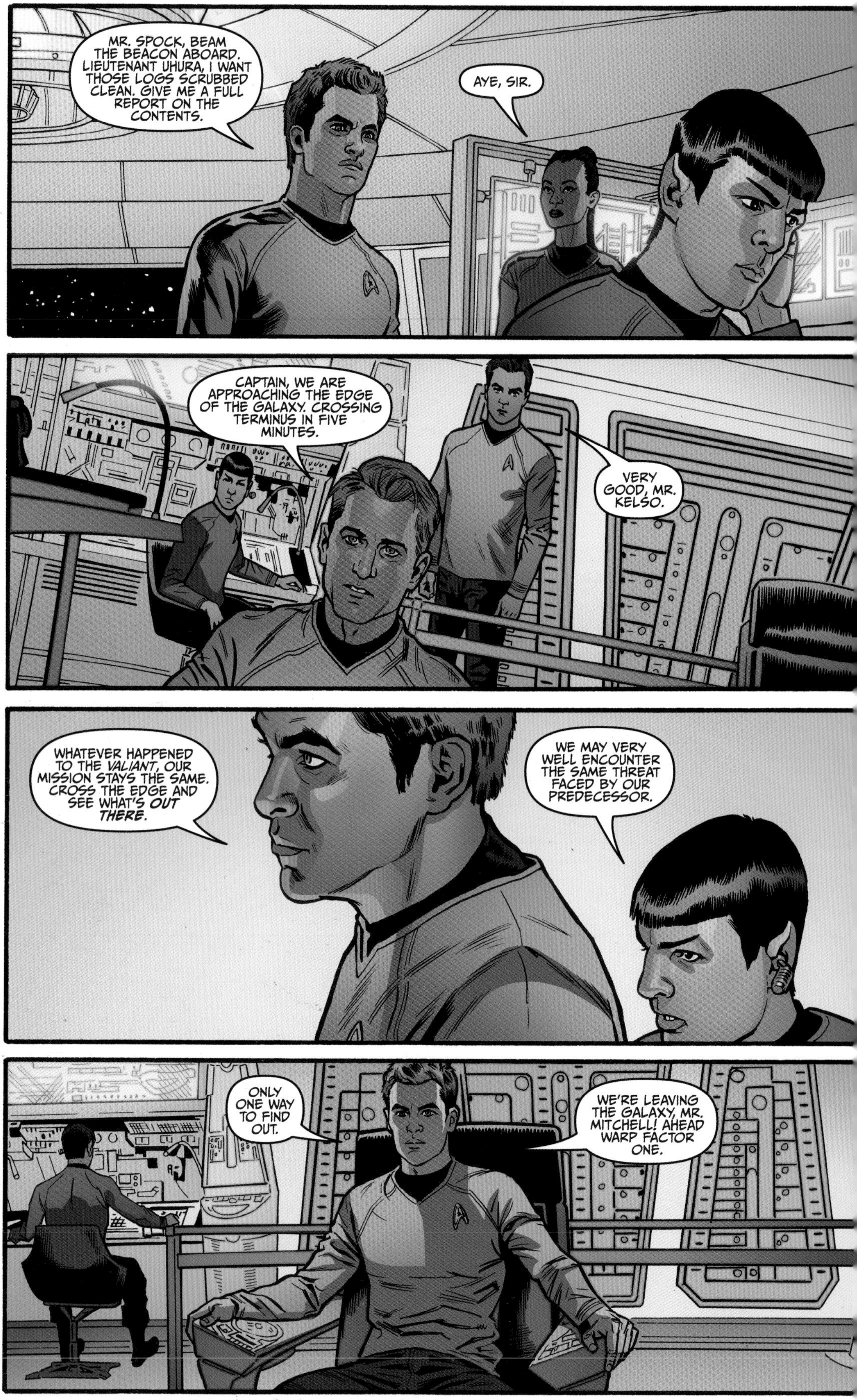
MR. SPOCK, BEAM THE BEACON ABOARD. LIEUTENANT UHURA, I WANT THOSE LOGS SCRUBBED CLEAN. GIVE ME A FULL REPORT ON THE CONTENTS.
AYE, SIR.
CAPTAIN, WE ARE APPROACHING THE EDGE OF THE GALAXY. CROSSING TERMINUS IN FIVE MINUTES.
VERY GOOD, MR. KELSO.
WHATEVER HAPPENED TO THE *VALIANT*, OUR MISSION STAYS THE SAME. CROSS THE EDGE AND SEE WHAT'S ***OUT THERE***.
WE MAY VERY WELL ENCOUNTER THE SAME THREAT FACED BY OUR PREDECESSOR.
ONLY ONE WAY TO FIND OUT.
WE'RE LEAVING THE GALAXY, MR. MITCHELL! AHEAD WARP FACTOR ONE.

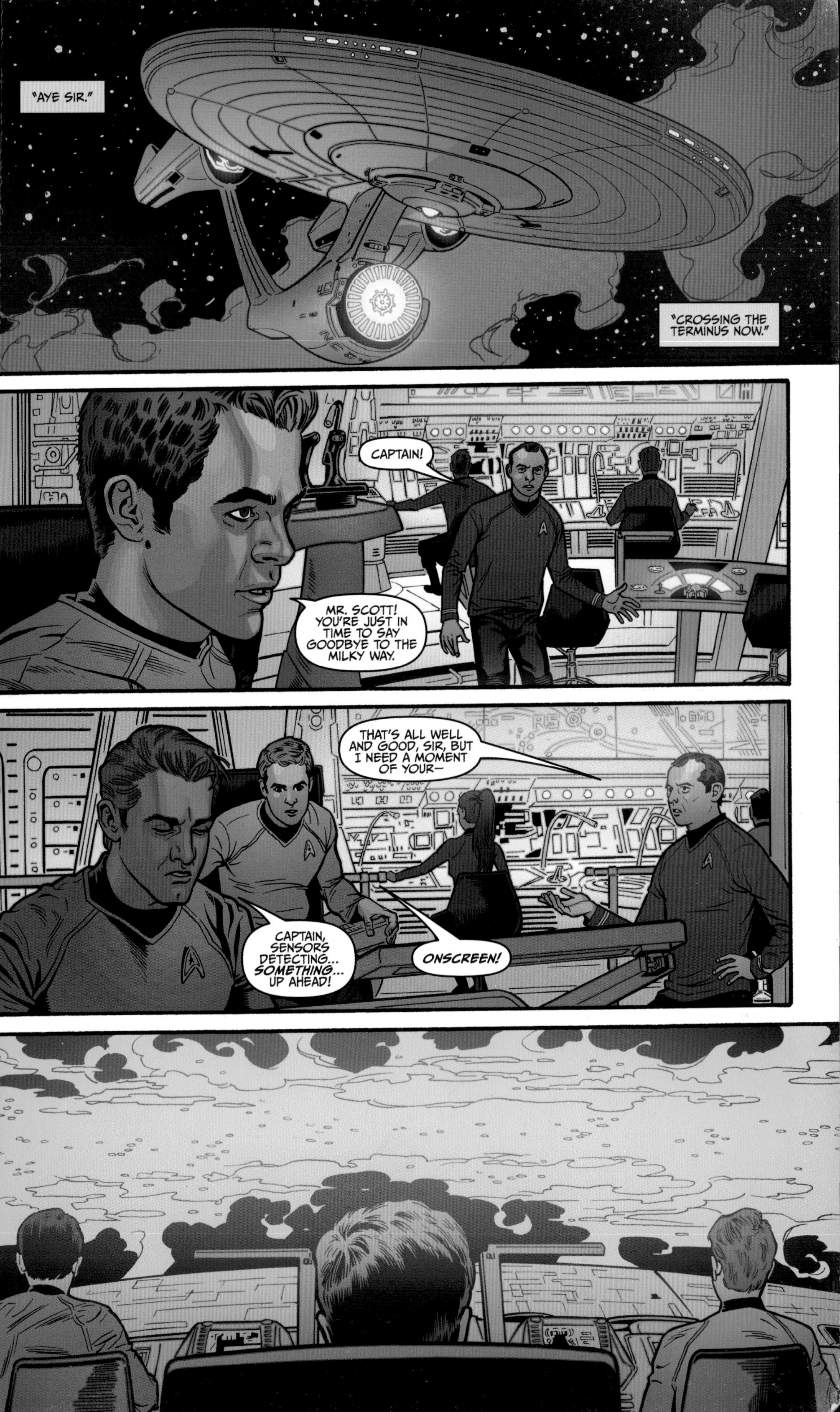
"AYE SIR."
"CROSSING THE TERMINUS NOW."
CAPTAIN!
MR. SCOTT! YOU'RE JUST IN TIME TO SAY GOODBYE TO THE MILKY WAY.
THAT'S ALL WELL AND GOOD, SIR, BUT I NEED A MOMENT OF YOUR—
CAPTAIN, SENSORS DETECTING... SOMETHING... UP AHEAD!
ONSCREEN!

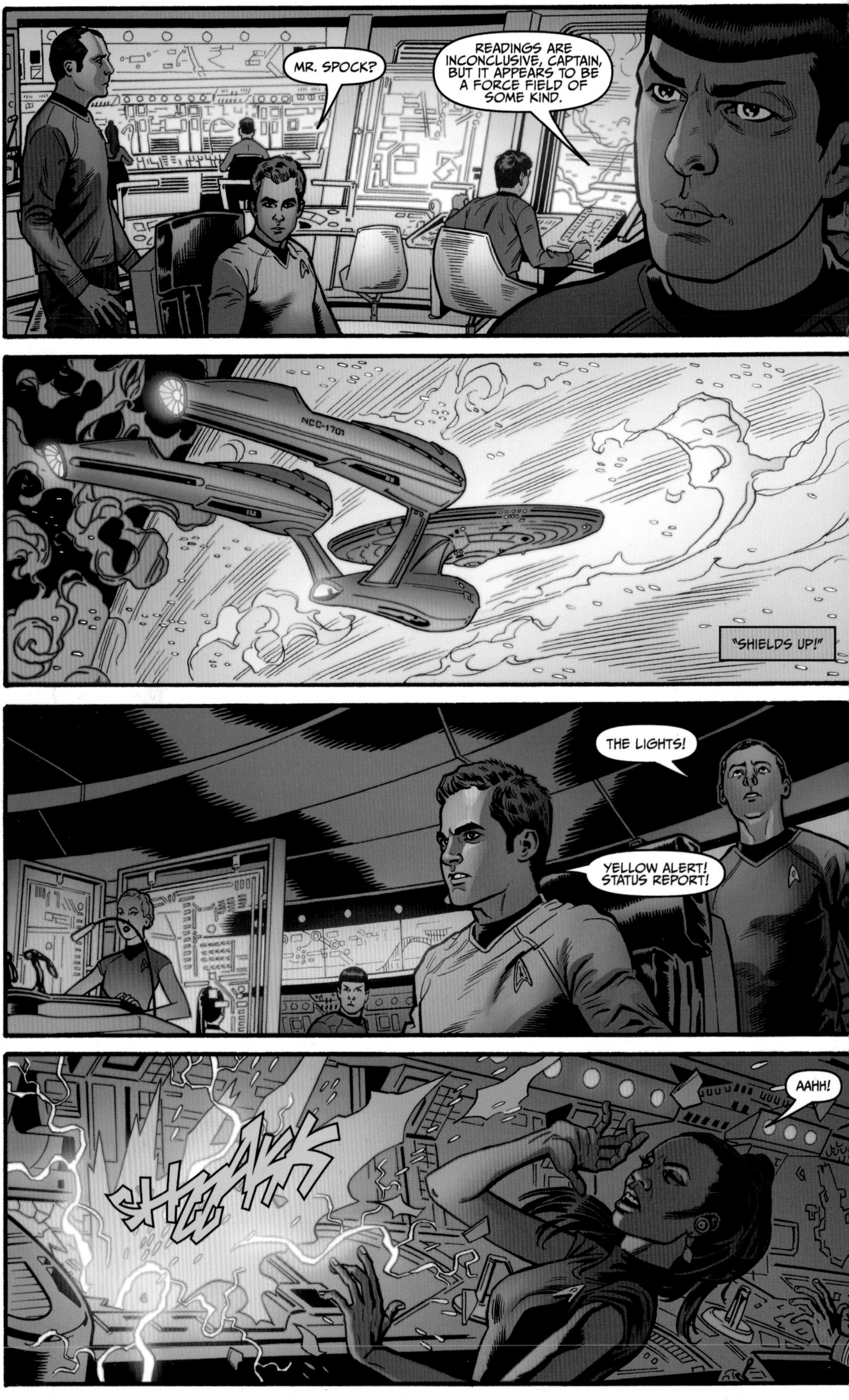
MR. SPOCK?
READINGS ARE INCONCLUSIVE, CAPTAIN, BUT IT APPEARS TO BE A FORCE FIELD OF SOME KIND.
NCC-1701
"SHIELDS UP!"
THE LIGHTS!
YELLOW ALERT! STATUS REPORT!
AAHH!

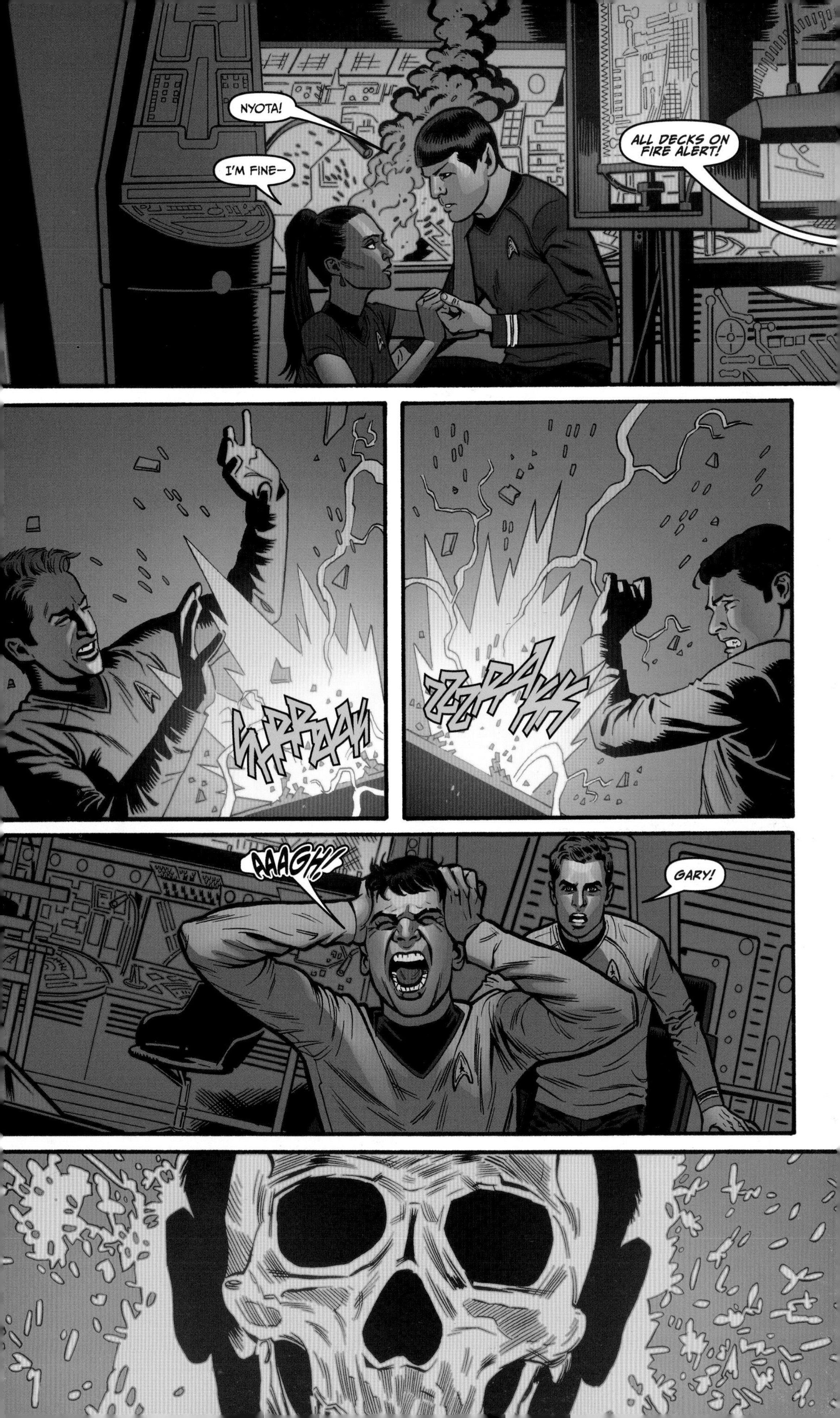
NYOTA!
I'M FINE—
ALL DECKS ON FIRE ALERT!
AAAGH!
GARY!

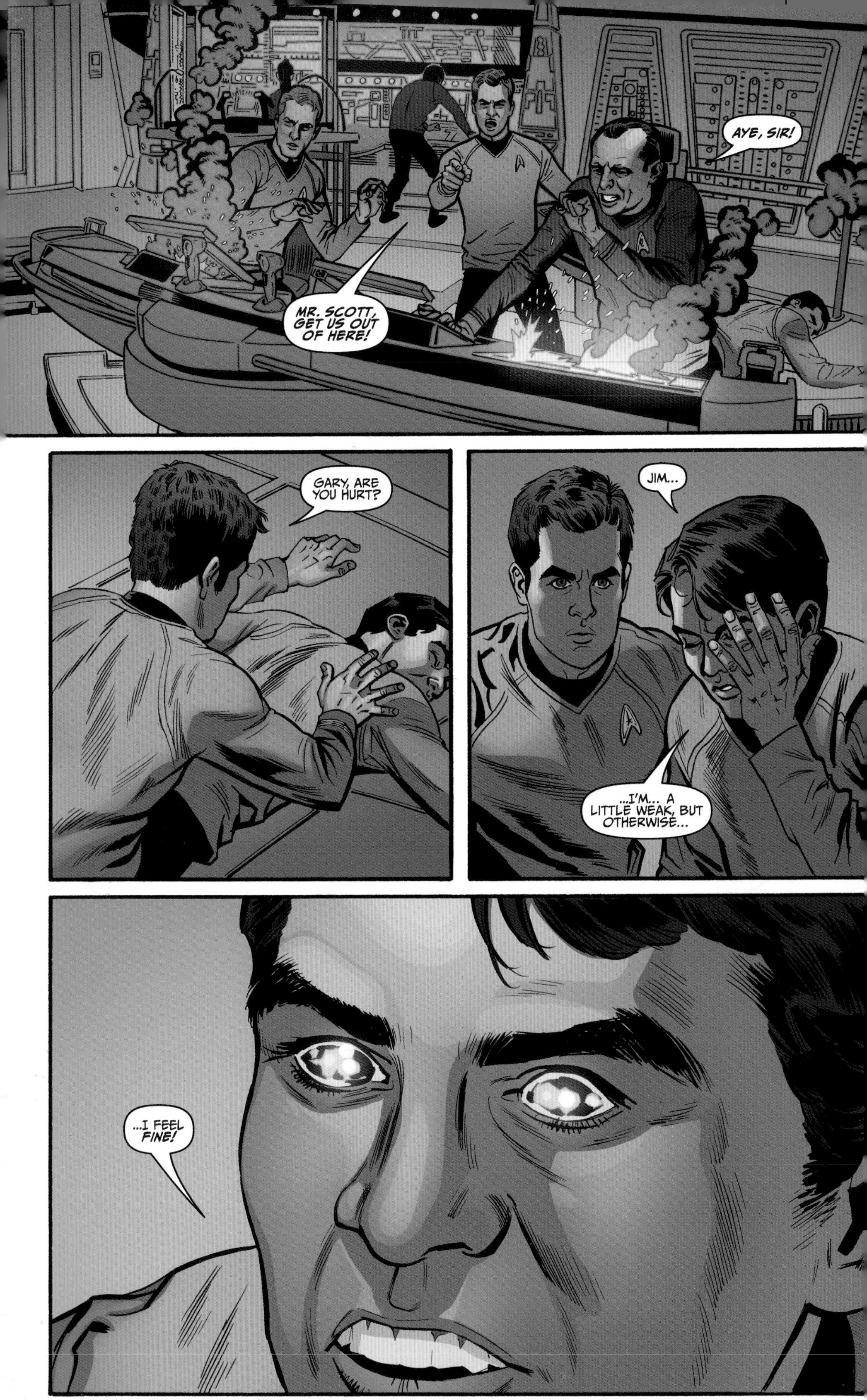
AYE, SIR!
MR. SCOTT, GET US OUT OF HERE!
GARY, ARE YOU HURT?
JIM...
...I'M... A LITTLE WEAK, BUT OTHERWISE...
...I FEEL FINE!

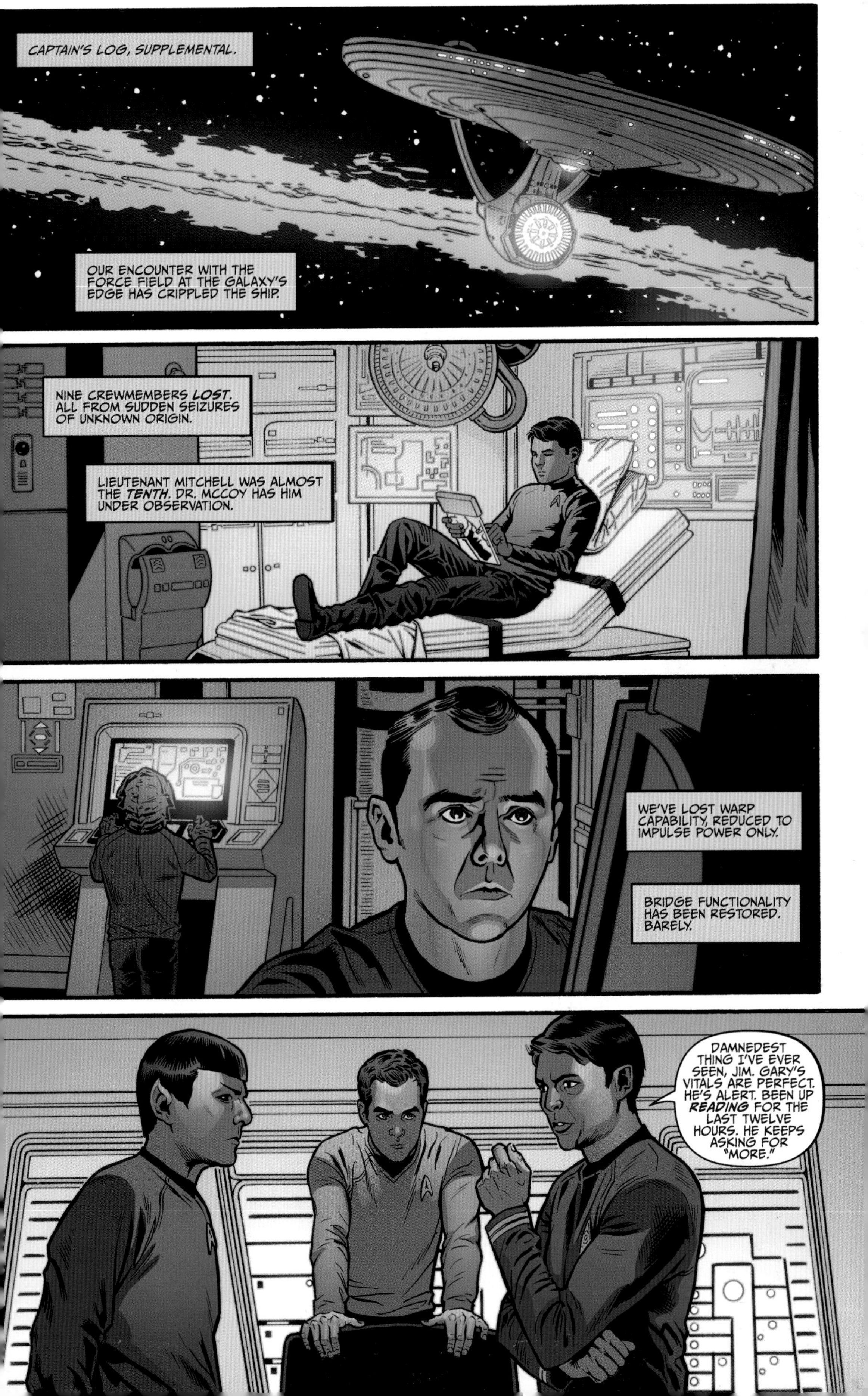
CAPTAIN'S LOG, SUPPLEMENTAL.
OUR ENCOUNTER WITH THE FORCE FIELD AT THE GALAXY'S EDGE HAS CRIPPLED THE SHIP.
NINE CREWMEMBERS **LOST**. ALL FROM SUDDEN SEIZURES OF UNKNOWN ORIGIN.
LIEUTENANT MITCHELL WAS ALMOST THE **TENTH**. DR. MCCOY HAS HIM UNDER OBSERVATION.
WE'VE LOST WARP CAPABILITY, REDUCED TO IMPULSE POWER ONLY.
BRIDGE FUNCTIONALITY HAS BEEN RESTORED. BARELY.
DAMNEDEST THING I'VE EVER SEEN, JIM. GARY'S VITALS ARE PERFECT. HE'S ALERT. BEEN UP **READING** FOR THE LAST TWELVE HOURS. HE KEEPS ASKING FOR "MORE."

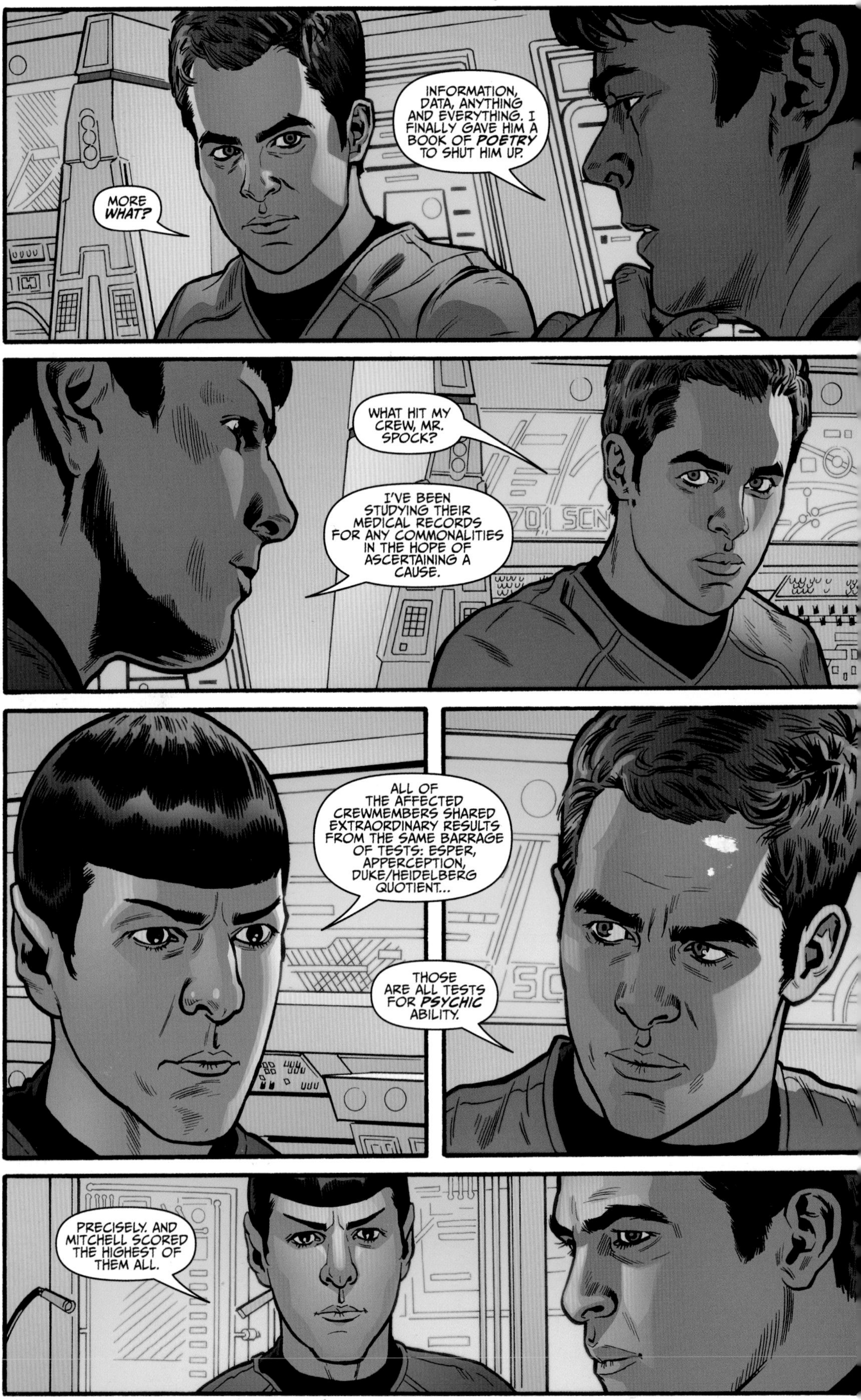

INFORMATION, DATA, ANYTHING AND EVERYTHING. I FINALLY GAVE HIM A BOOK OF *POETRY* TO SHUT HIM UP.
MORE *WHAT?*
WHAT HIT MY CREW, MR. SPOCK?
I'VE BEEN STUDYING THEIR MEDICAL RECORDS FOR ANY COMMONALITIES IN THE HOPE OF ASCERTAINING A CAUSE.
ALL OF THE AFFECTED CREWMEMBERS SHARED EXTRAORDINARY RESULTS FROM THE SAME BARRAGE OF TESTS: ESPER, APPERCEPTION, DUKE/HEIDELBERG QUOTIENT...
THOSE ARE ALL TESTS FOR *PSYCHIC* ABILITY.
PRECISELY. AND MITCHELL SCORED THE HIGHEST OF THEM ALL.

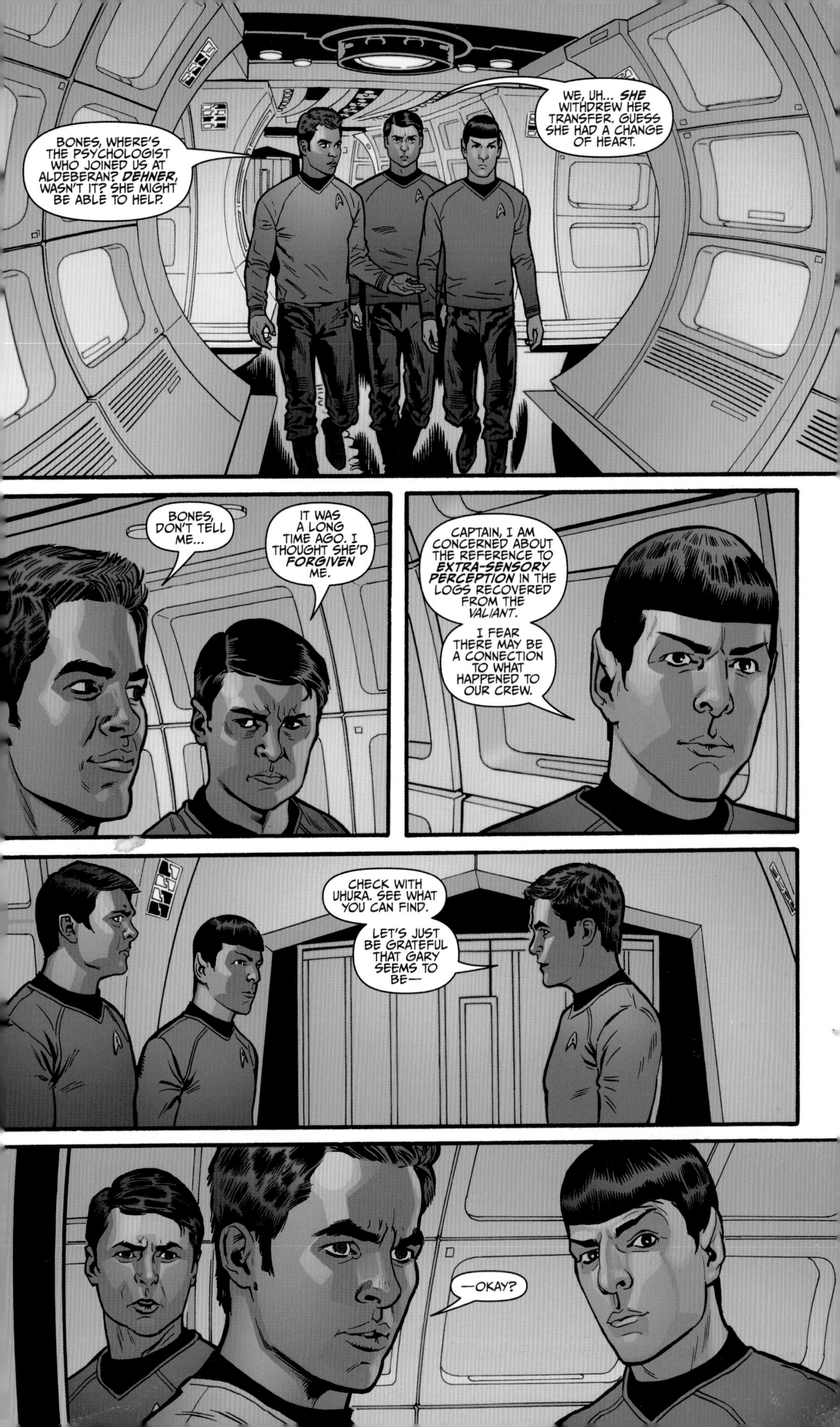
BONES, WHERE'S THE PSYCHOLOGIST WHO JOINED US AT ALDEBERAN? DEHNER, WASN'T IT? SHE MIGHT BE ABLE TO HELP.
WE, UH... SHE WITHDREW HER TRANSFER. GUESS SHE HAD A CHANGE OF HEART.
BONES, DON'T TELL ME...
IT WAS A LONG TIME AGO. I THOUGHT SHE'D FORGIVEN ME.
CAPTAIN, I AM CONCERNED ABOUT THE REFERENCE TO EXTRA-SENSORY PERCEPTION IN THE LOGS RECOVERED FROM THE VALIANT.
I FEAR THERE MAY BE A CONNECTION TO WHAT HAPPENED TO OUR CREW.
CHECK WITH UHURA. SEE WHAT YOU CAN FIND.
LET'S JUST BE GRATEFUL THAT GARY SEEMS TO BE—
—OKAY?

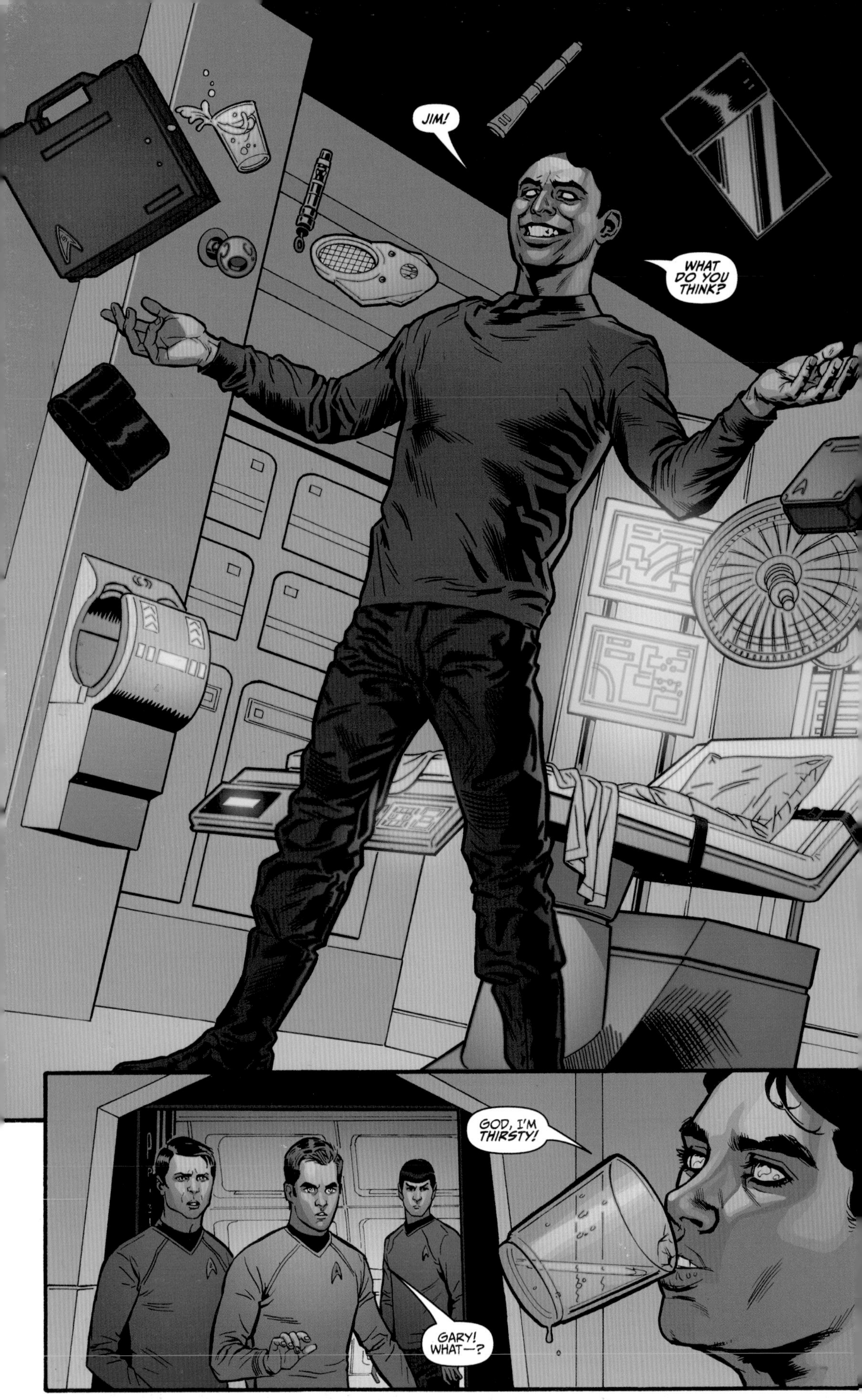
JIM!
WHAT DO YOU THINK?
GOD, I'M THIRSTY!
GARY! WHAT—?

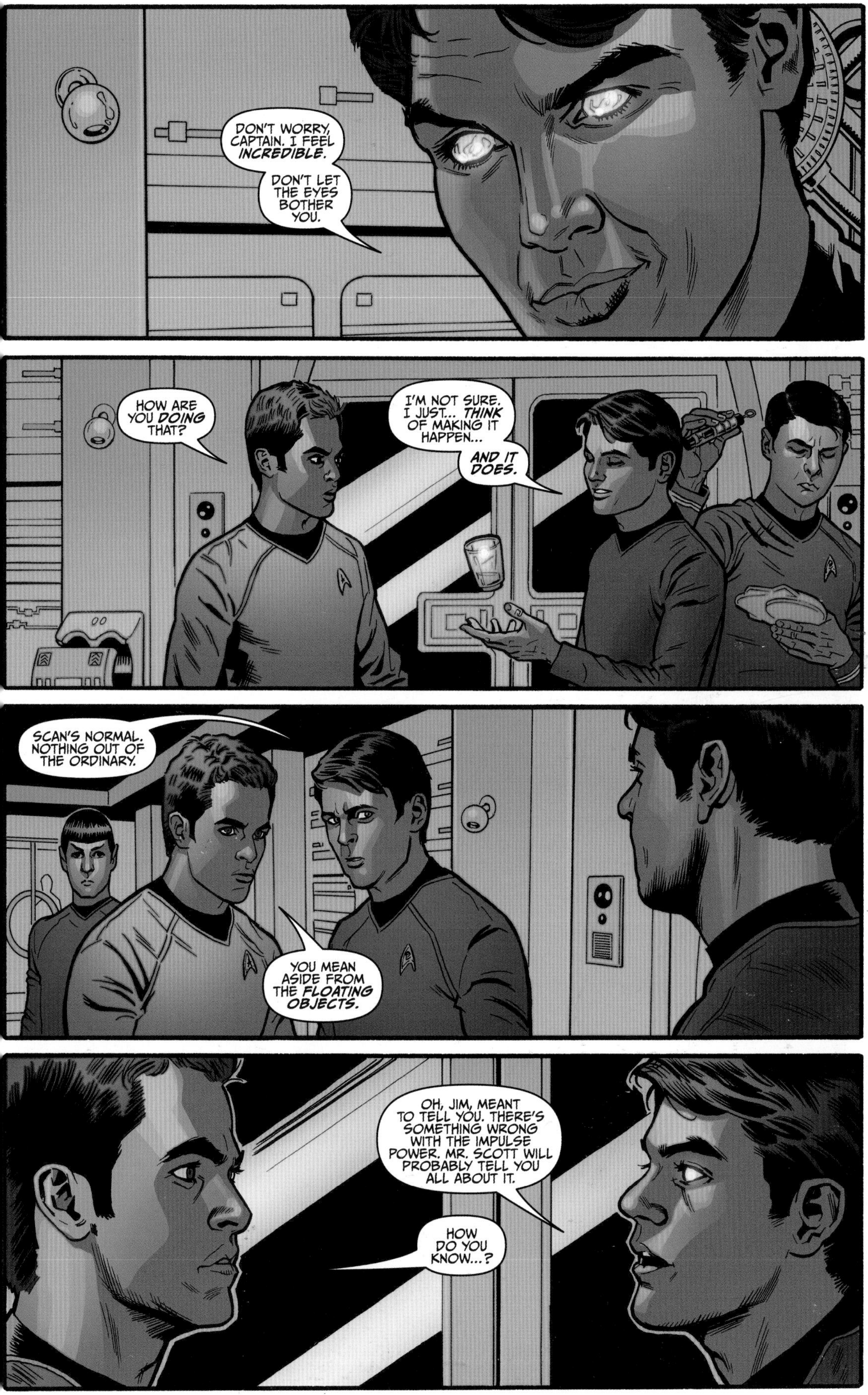

DON'T WORRY, CAPTAIN. I FEEL INCREDIBLE.
DON'T LET THE EYES BOTHER YOU.
HOW ARE YOU DOING THAT?
I'M NOT SURE. I JUST... THINK OF MAKING IT HAPPEN...
AND IT DOES.
SCAN'S NORMAL. NOTHING OUT OF THE ORDINARY.
YOU MEAN ASIDE FROM THE FLOATING OBJECTS.
OH, JIM, MEANT TO TELL YOU. THERE'S SOMETHING WRONG WITH THE IMPULSE POWER. MR. SCOTT WILL PROBABLY TELL YOU ALL ABOUT IT.
HOW DO YOU KNOW...?

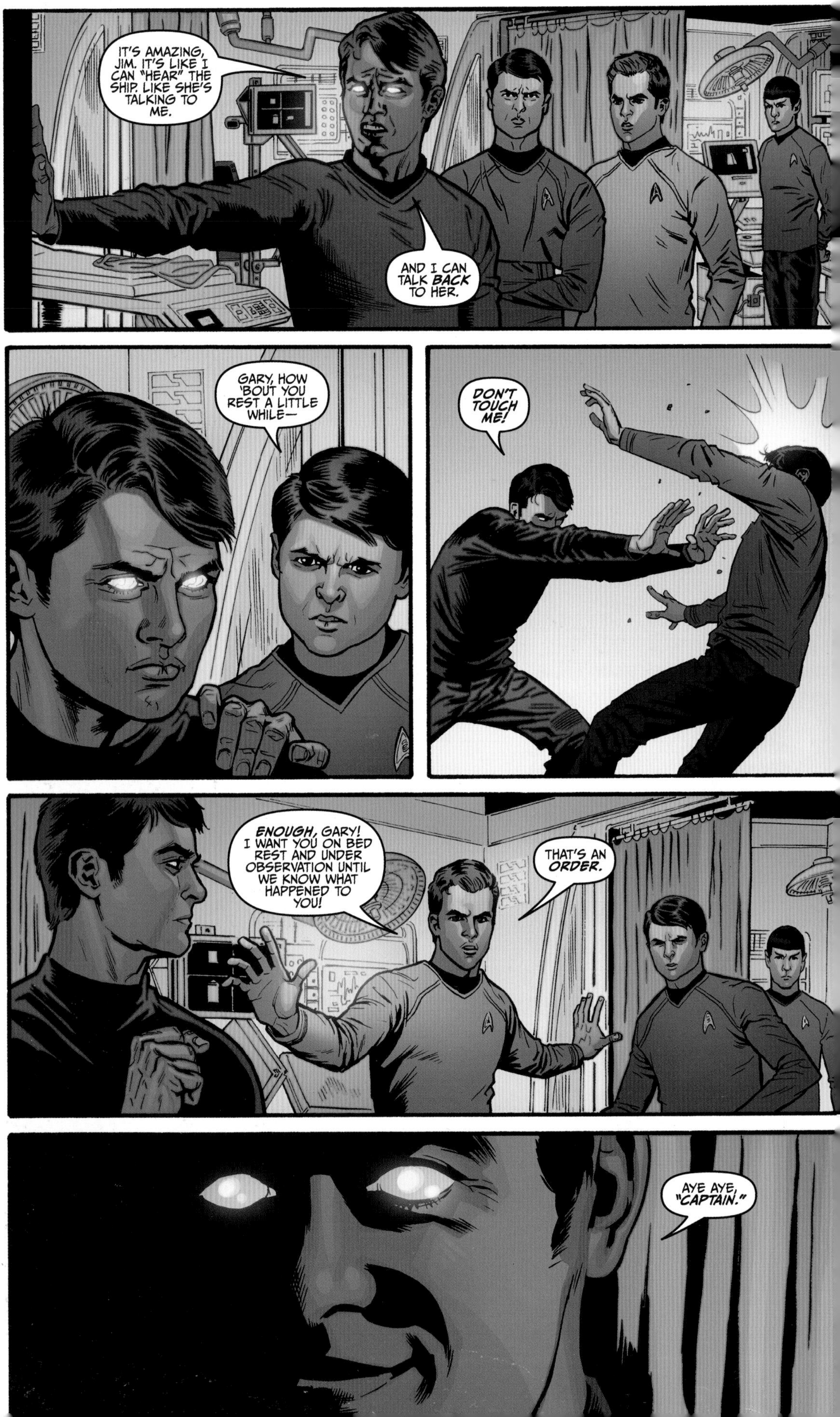
IT'S AMAZING, JIM. IT'S LIKE I CAN "HEAR" THE SHIP, LIKE SHE'S TALKING TO ME.
AND I CAN TALK *BACK* TO HER.
GARY, HOW 'BOUT YOU REST A LITTLE WHILE—
DON'T TOUCH ME!
ENOUGH, GARY! I WANT YOU ON BED REST AND UNDER OBSERVATION UNTIL WE KNOW WHAT HAPPENED TO YOU!
THAT'S AN *ORDER.*
AYE AYE, *"CAPTAIN."*

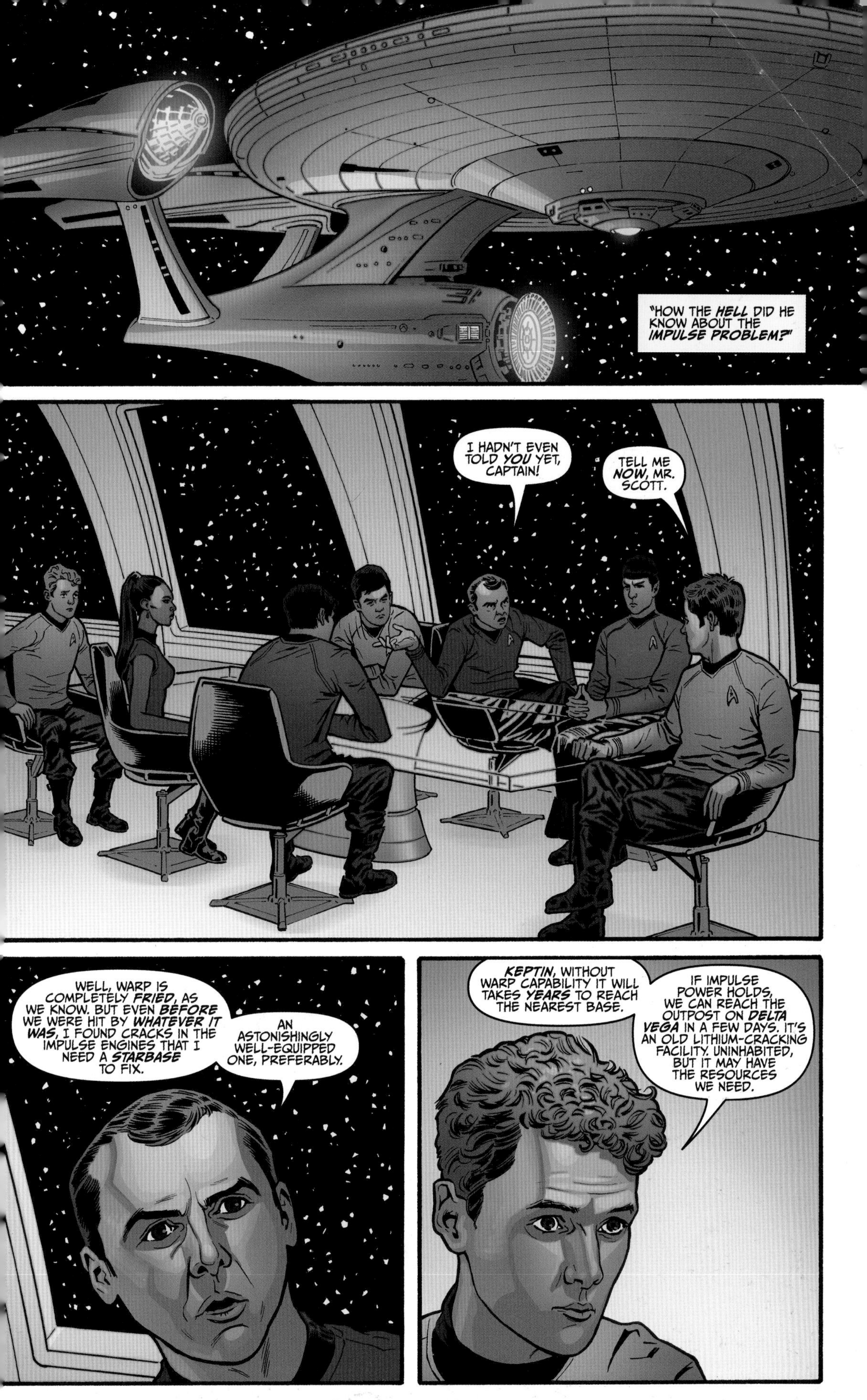
"HOW THE HELL DID HE KNOW ABOUT THE IMPULSE PROBLEM?"
I HADN'T EVEN TOLD YOU YET, CAPTAIN!
TELL ME NOW, MR. SCOTT.
WELL, WARP IS COMPLETELY FRIED, AS WE KNOW. BUT EVEN BEFORE WE WERE HIT BY WHATEVER IT WAS, I FOUND CRACKS IN THE IMPULSE ENGINES THAT I NEED A STARBASE TO FIX.
AN ASTONISHINGLY WELL-EQUIPPED ONE, PREFERABLY.
KEPTIN, WITHOUT WARP CAPABILITY IT WILL TAKES YEARS TO REACH THE NEAREST BASE.
IF IMPULSE POWER HOLDS, WE CAN REACH THE OUTPOST ON DELTA VEGA IN A FEW DAYS. IT'S AN OLD LITHIUM-CRACKING FACILITY. UNINHABITED, BUT IT MAY HAVE THE RESOURCES WE NEED.

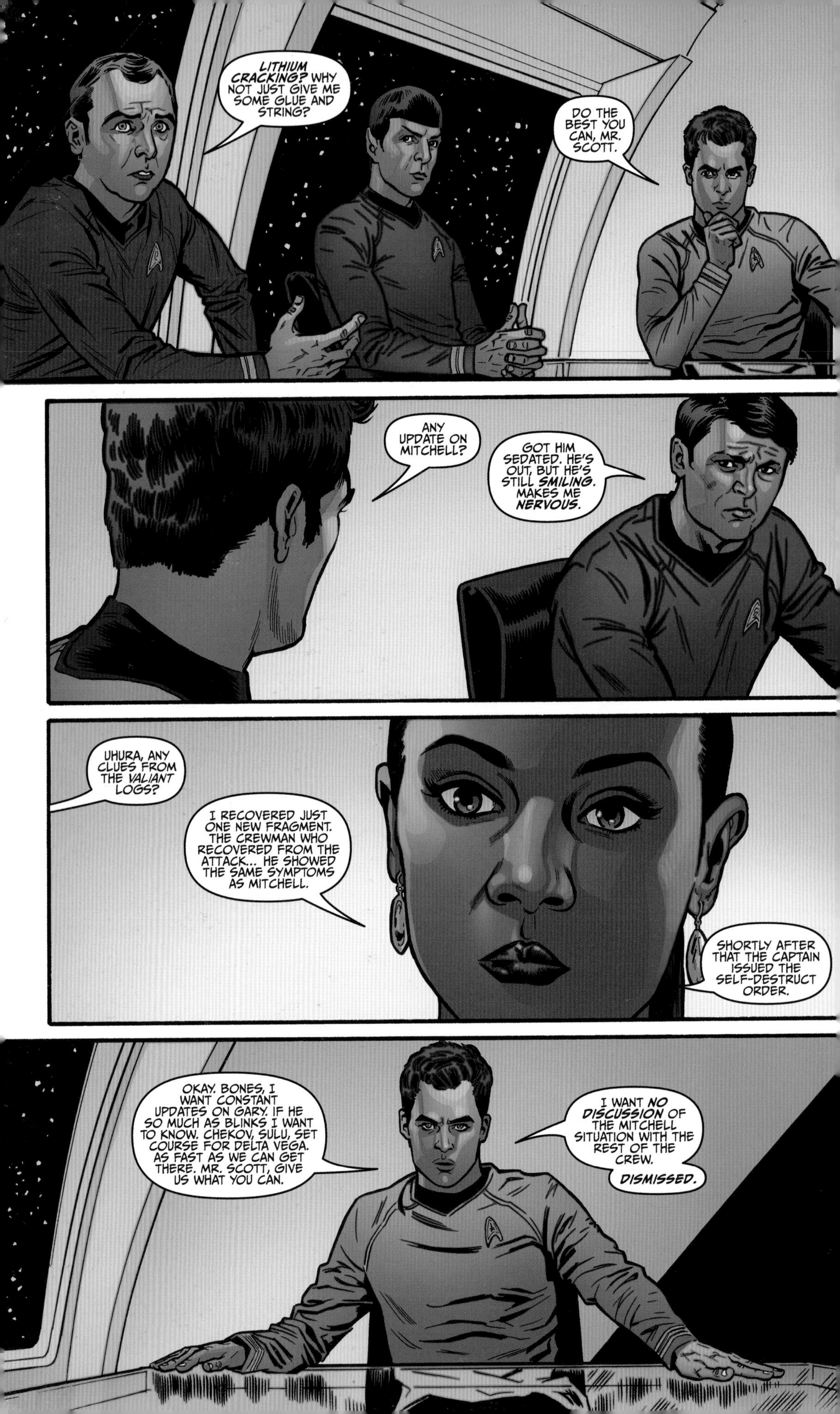
LITHIUM CRACKING? WHY NOT JUST GIVE ME SOME GLUE AND STRING?
DO THE BEST YOU CAN, MR. SCOTT.
ANY UPDATE ON MITCHELL?
GOT HIM SEDATED. HE'S OUT, BUT HE'S STILL SMILING. MAKES ME NERVOUS.
UHURA, ANY CLUES FROM THE VALIANT LOGS?
I RECOVERED JUST ONE NEW FRAGMENT. THE CREWMAN WHO RECOVERED FROM THE ATTACK... HE SHOWED THE SAME SYMPTOMS AS MITCHELL.
SHORTLY AFTER THAT THE CAPTAIN ISSUED THE SELF-DESTRUCT ORDER.
OKAY. BONES, I WANT CONSTANT UPDATES ON GARY. IF HE SO MUCH AS BLINKS I WANT TO KNOW. CHEKOV, SULU, SET COURSE FOR DELTA VEGA. AS FAST AS WE CAN GET THERE. MR. SCOTT, GIVE US WHAT YOU CAN.
I WANT NO DISCUSSION OF THE MITCHELL SITUATION WITH THE REST OF THE CREW.
DISMISSED.

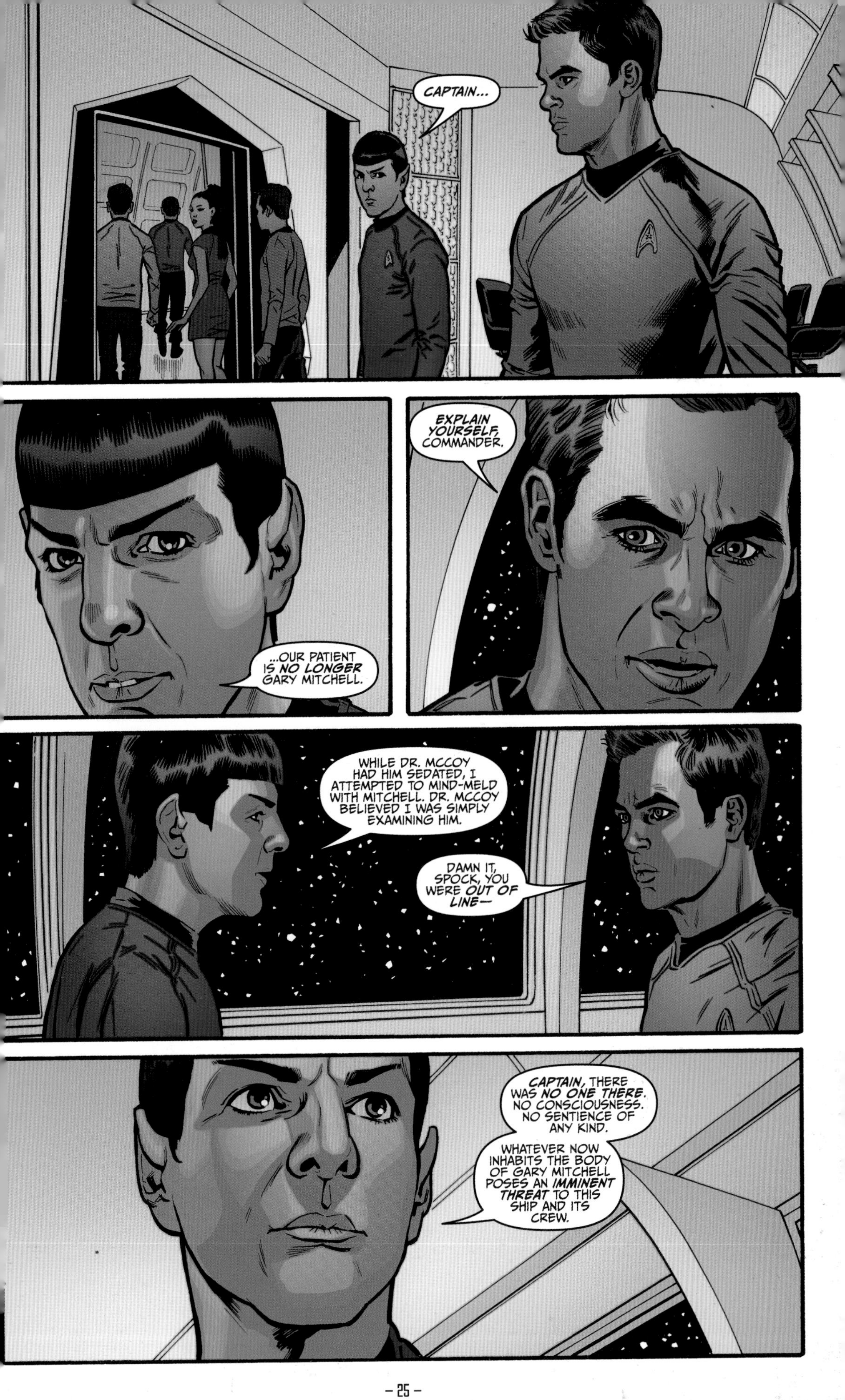
CAPTAIN...
EXPLAIN YOURSELF, COMMANDER.
...OUR PATIENT IS NO LONGER GARY MITCHELL.
WHILE DR. MCCOY HAD HIM SEDATED, I ATTEMPTED TO MIND-MELD WITH MITCHELL. DR. MCCOY BELIEVED I WAS SIMPLY EXAMINING HIM.
DAMN IT, SPOCK, YOU WERE OUT OF LINE—
CAPTAIN, THERE WAS NO ONE THERE. NO CONSCIOUSNESS. NO SENTIENCE OF ANY KIND.
WHATEVER NOW INHABITS THE BODY OF GARY MITCHELL POSES AN IMMINENT THREAT TO THIS SHIP AND ITS CREW.

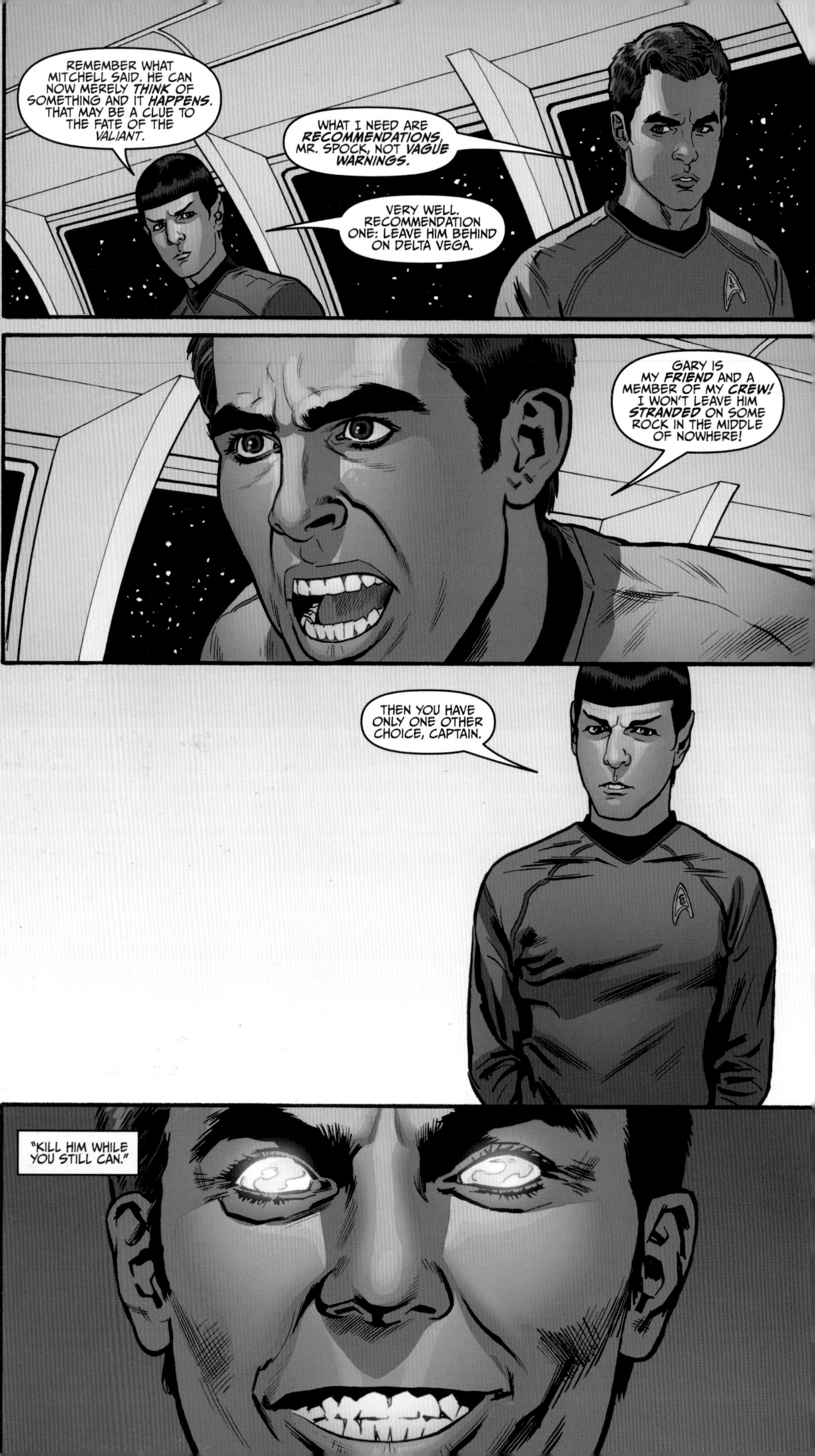
REMEMBER WHAT MITCHELL SAID. HE CAN NOW MERELY *THINK* OF SOMETHING AND IT *HAPPENS*. THAT MAY BE A CLUE TO THE FATE OF THE *VALIANT*.
WHAT I NEED ARE **RECOMMENDATIONS**, MR. SPOCK, NOT **VAGUE WARNINGS**.
VERY WELL. RECOMMENDATION ONE: LEAVE HIM BEHIND ON DELTA VEGA.
GARY IS MY **FRIEND** AND A MEMBER OF MY **CREW!** I WON'T LEAVE HIM **STRANDED** ON SOME ROCK IN THE MIDDLE OF NOWHERE!
THEN YOU HAVE ONLY ONE OTHER CHOICE, CAPTAIN.
"KILL HIM WHILE YOU STILL CAN."

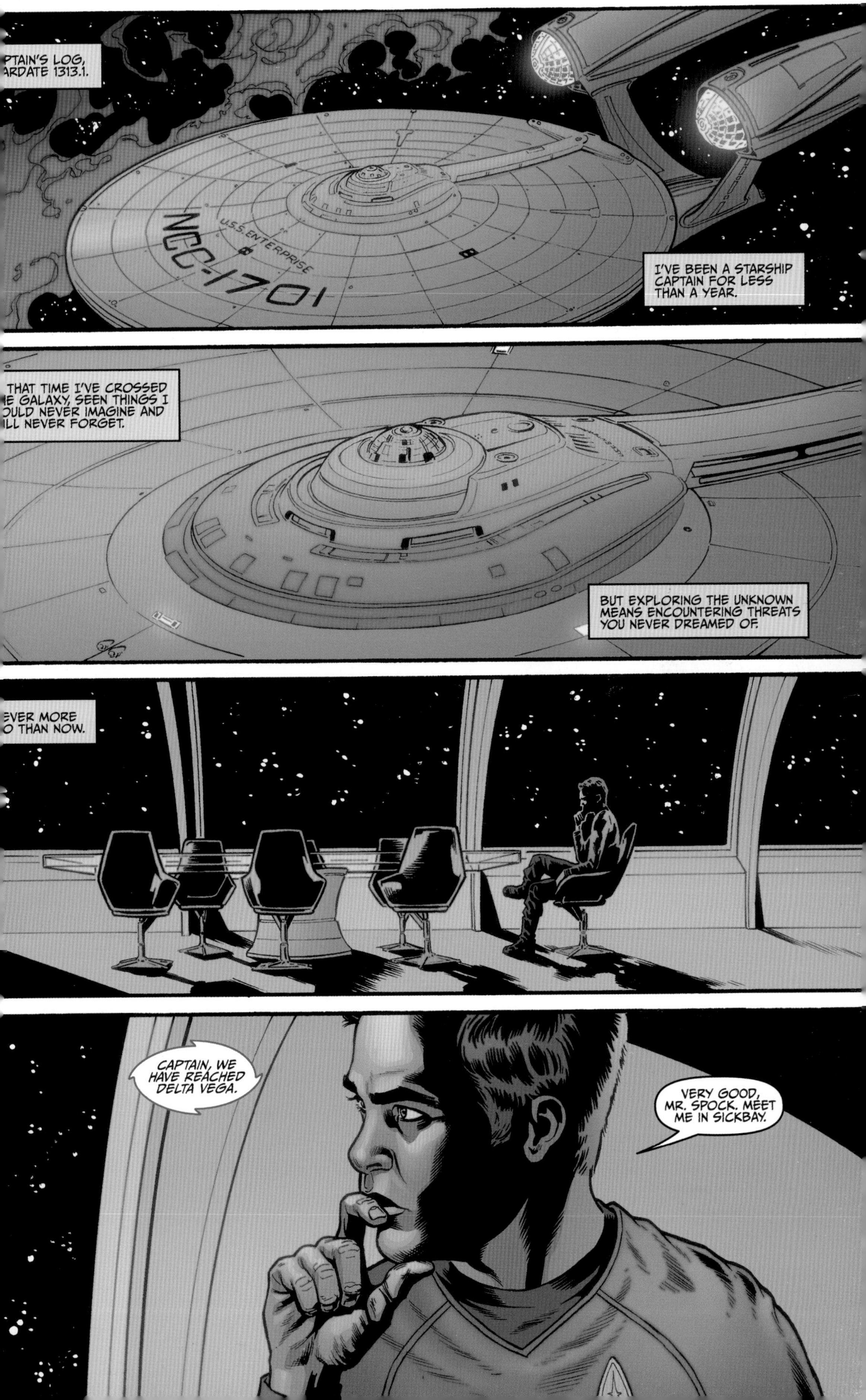
PTAIN'S LOG,
ARDATE 1313.1.
U.S.S. ENTERPRISE
NCC-1701
I'VE BEEN A STARSHIP CAPTAIN FOR LESS THAN A YEAR.
THAT TIME I'VE CROSSED
E GALAXY, SEEN THINGS I
OULD NEVER IMAGINE AND
ILL NEVER FORGET.
BUT EXPLORING THE UNKNOWN MEANS ENCOUNTERING THREATS YOU NEVER DREAMED OF.
EVER MORE
O THAN NOW.
CAPTAIN, WE HAVE REACHED DELTA VEGA.
VERY GOOD, MR. SPOCK. MEET ME IN SICKBAY.

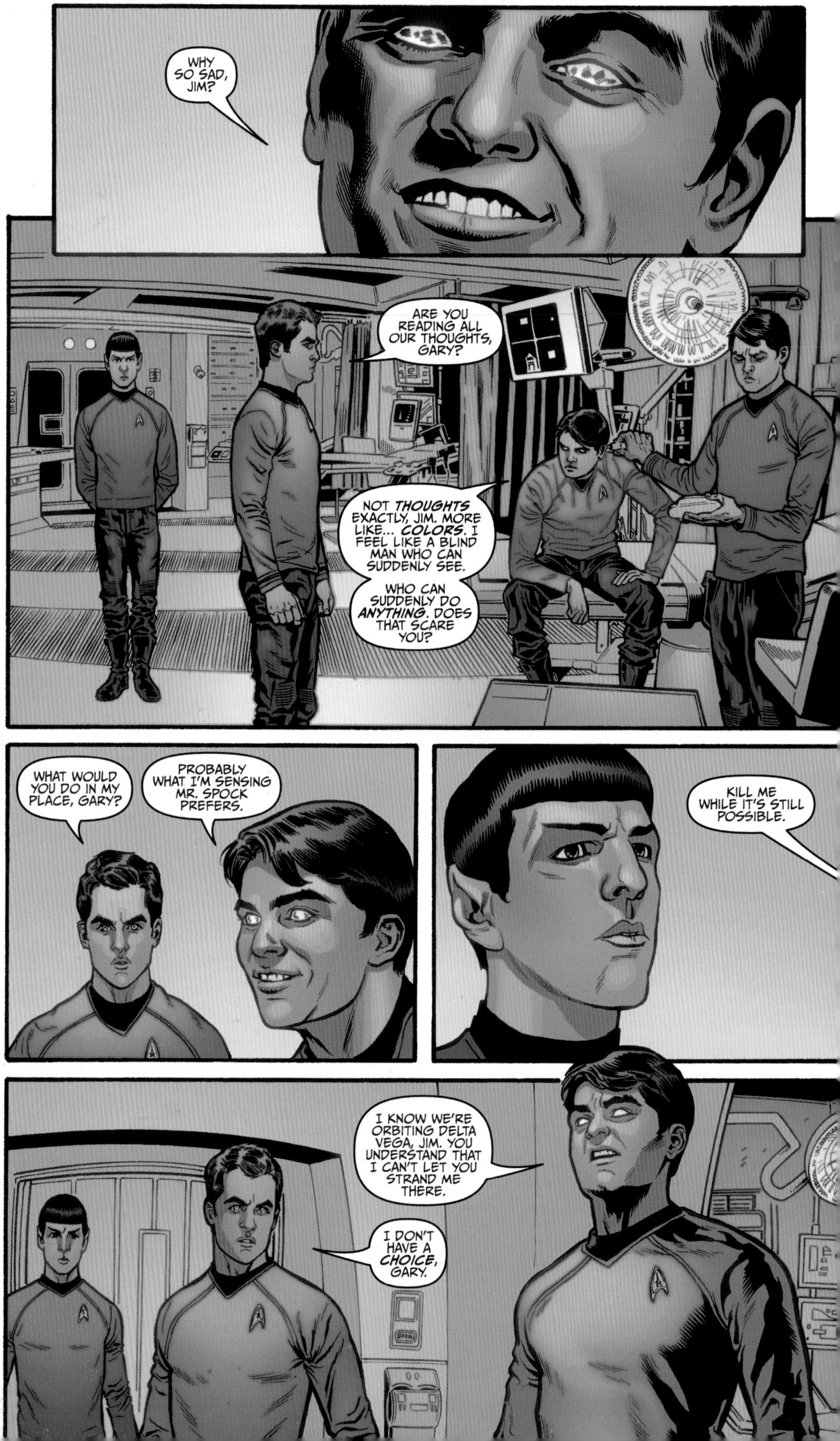
WHY SO SAD, JIM?
ARE YOU READING ALL OUR THOUGHTS, GARY?
NOT THOUGHTS EXACTLY, JIM. MORE LIKE... COLORS. I FEEL LIKE A BLIND MAN WHO CAN SUDDENLY SEE.
WHO CAN SUDDENLY DO ANYTHING. DOES THAT SCARE YOU?
WHAT WOULD YOU DO IN MY PLACE, GARY?
PROBABLY WHAT I'M SENSING MR. SPOCK PREFERS.
KILL ME WHILE IT'S STILL POSSIBLE.
I KNOW WE'RE ORBITING DELTA VEGA, JIM. YOU UNDERSTAND THAT I CAN'T LET YOU STRAND ME THERE.
I DON'T HAVE A CHOICE, GARY.

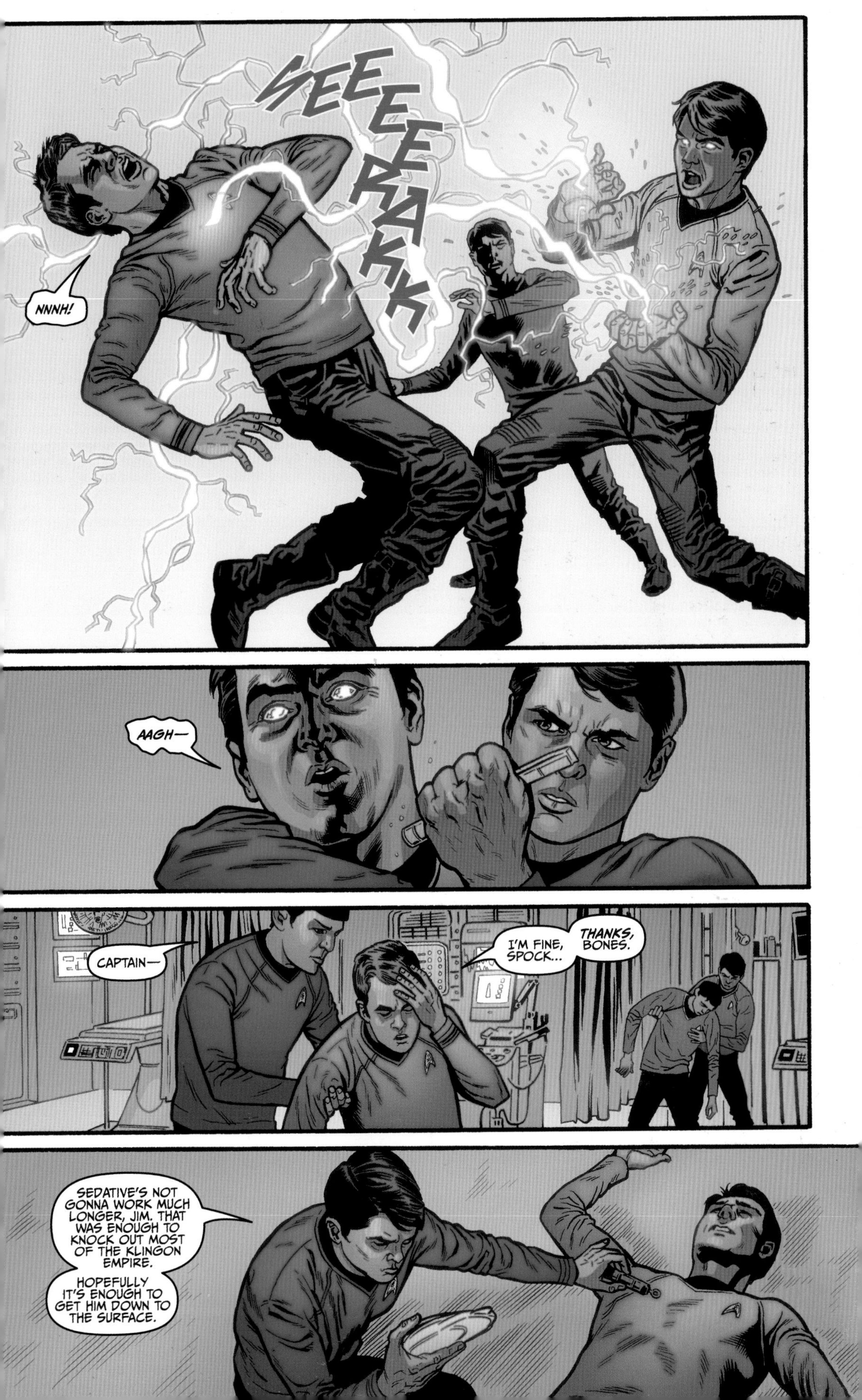
SEEEEERAKK
NNNH!
AAGH—
CAPTAIN—
I'M FINE, SPOCK...
THANKS, BONES.
SEDATIVE'S NOT GONNA WORK MUCH LONGER, JIM. THAT WAS ENOUGH TO KNOCK OUT MOST OF THE KLINGON EMPIRE.
HOPEFULLY IT'S ENOUGH TO GET HIM DOWN TO THE SURFACE.

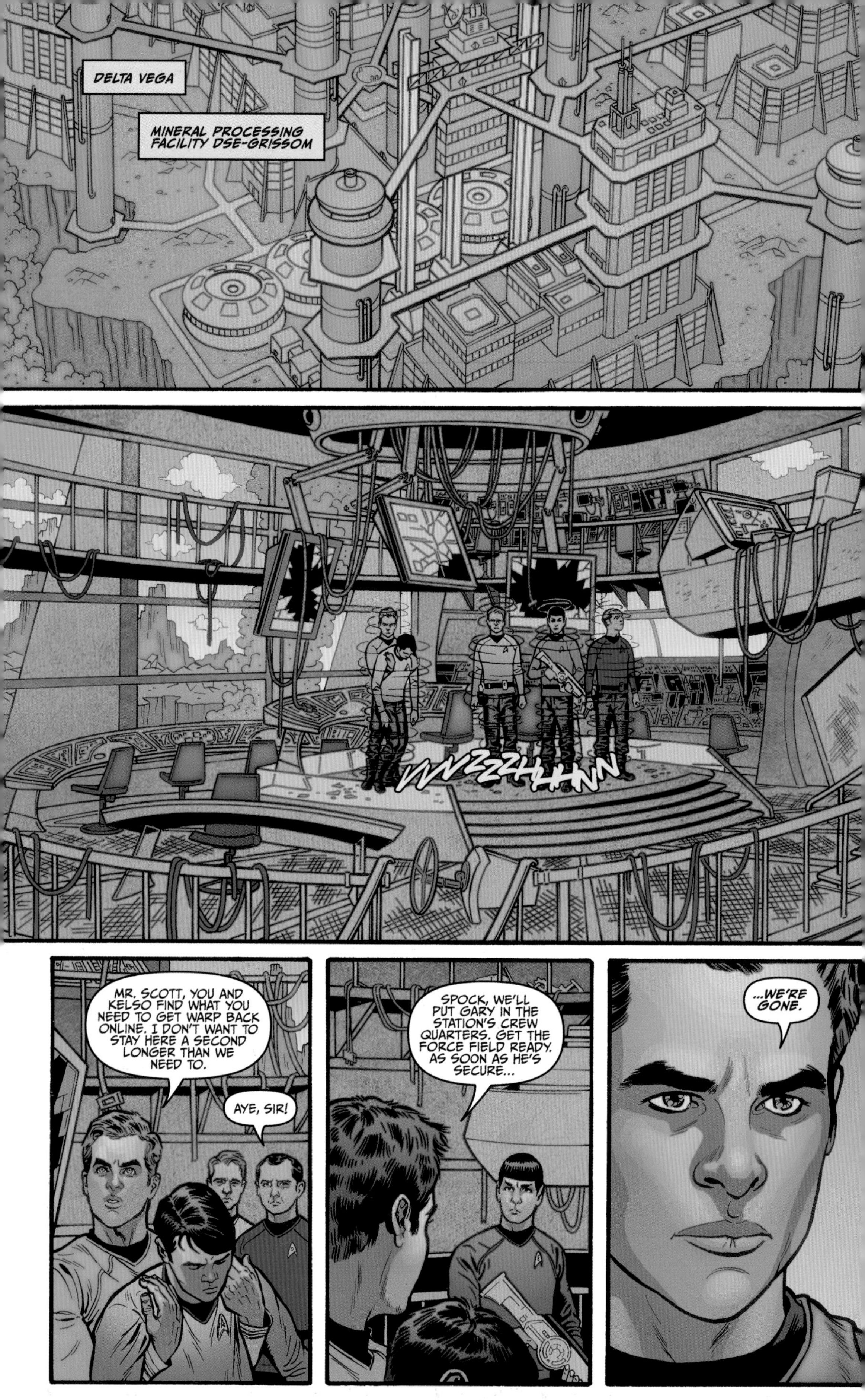
DELTA VEGA
MINERAL PROCESSING FACILITY DSE-GRISSOM
VVVVZZZHHHNN
MR. SCOTT, YOU AND KELSO FIND WHAT YOU NEED TO GET WARP BACK ONLINE. I DON'T WANT TO STAY HERE A SECOND LONGER THAN WE NEED TO.
AYE, SIR!
SPOCK, WE'LL PUT GARY IN THE STATION'S CREW QUARTERS. GET THE FORCE FIELD READY. AS SOON AS HE'S SECURE...
...WE'RE GONE.

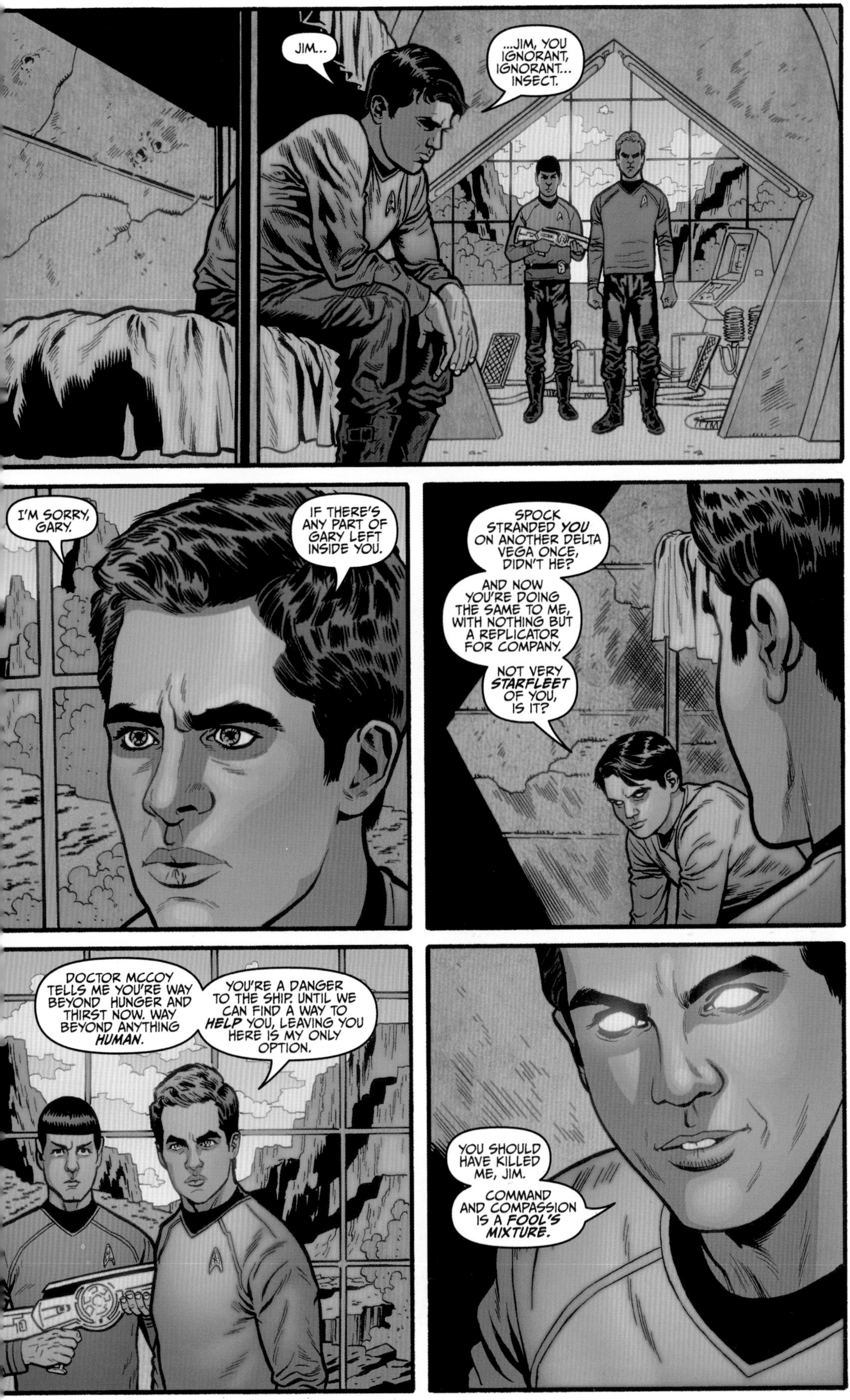
JIM...
...JIM, YOU IGNORANT, IGNORANT... INSECT.
I'M SORRY, GARY.
IF THERE'S ANY PART OF GARY LEFT INSIDE YOU.
SPOCK STRANDED YOU ON ANOTHER DELTA VEGA ONCE, DIDN'T HE?
AND NOW YOU'RE DOING THE SAME TO ME, WITH NOTHING BUT A REPLICATOR FOR COMPANY.
NOT VERY STARFLEET OF YOU, IS IT?
DOCTOR MCCOY TELLS ME YOU'RE WAY BEYOND HUNGER AND THIRST NOW. WAY BEYOND ANYTHING HUMAN.
YOU'RE A DANGER TO THE SHIP. UNTIL WE CAN FIND A WAY TO HELP YOU, LEAVING YOU HERE IS MY ONLY OPTION.
YOU SHOULD HAVE KILLED ME, JIM.
COMMAND AND COMPASSION IS A FOOL'S MIXTURE.

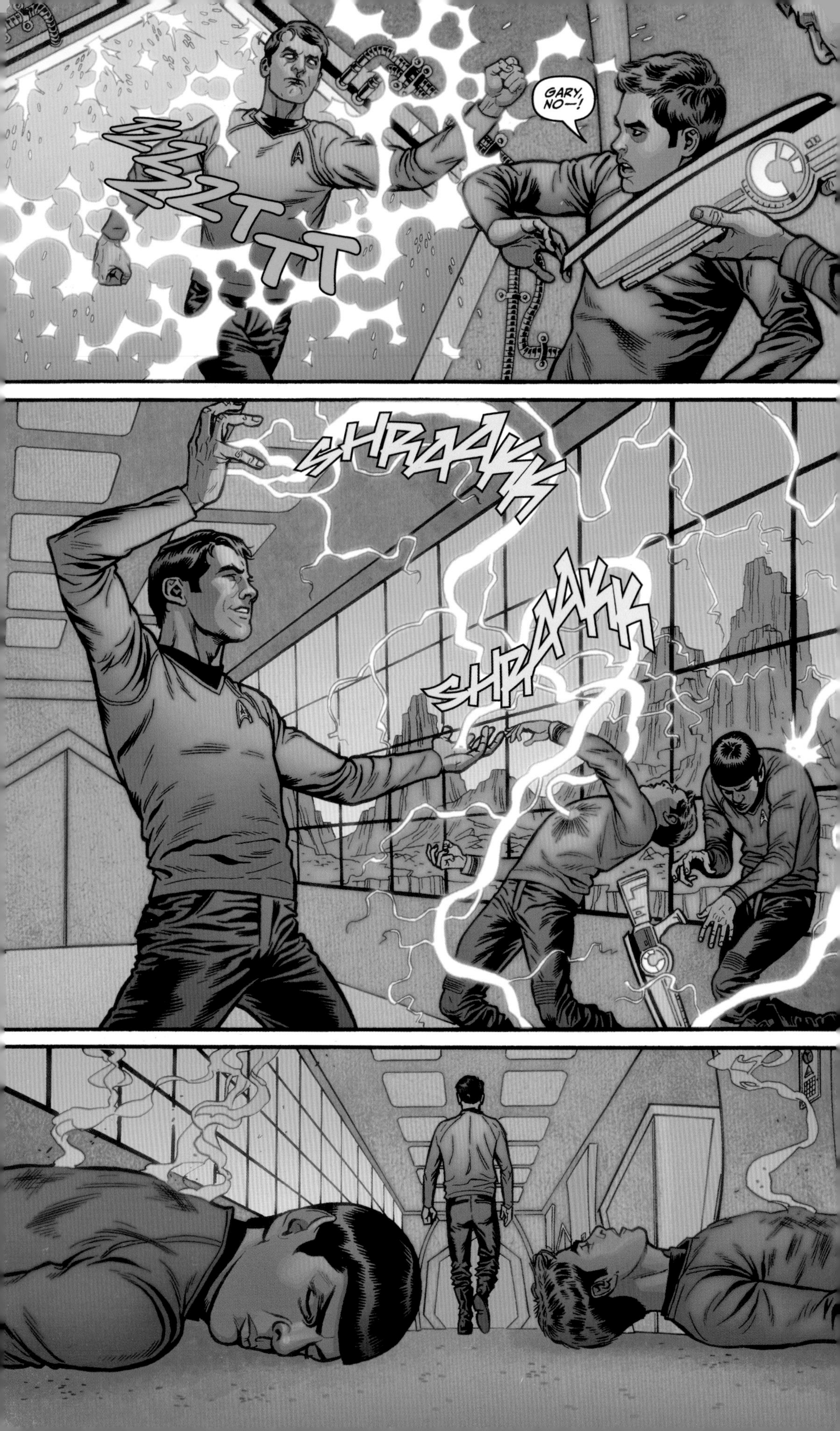
ZZZZTTT
GARY, NO—!
SHRAAKK
SHRAAKK

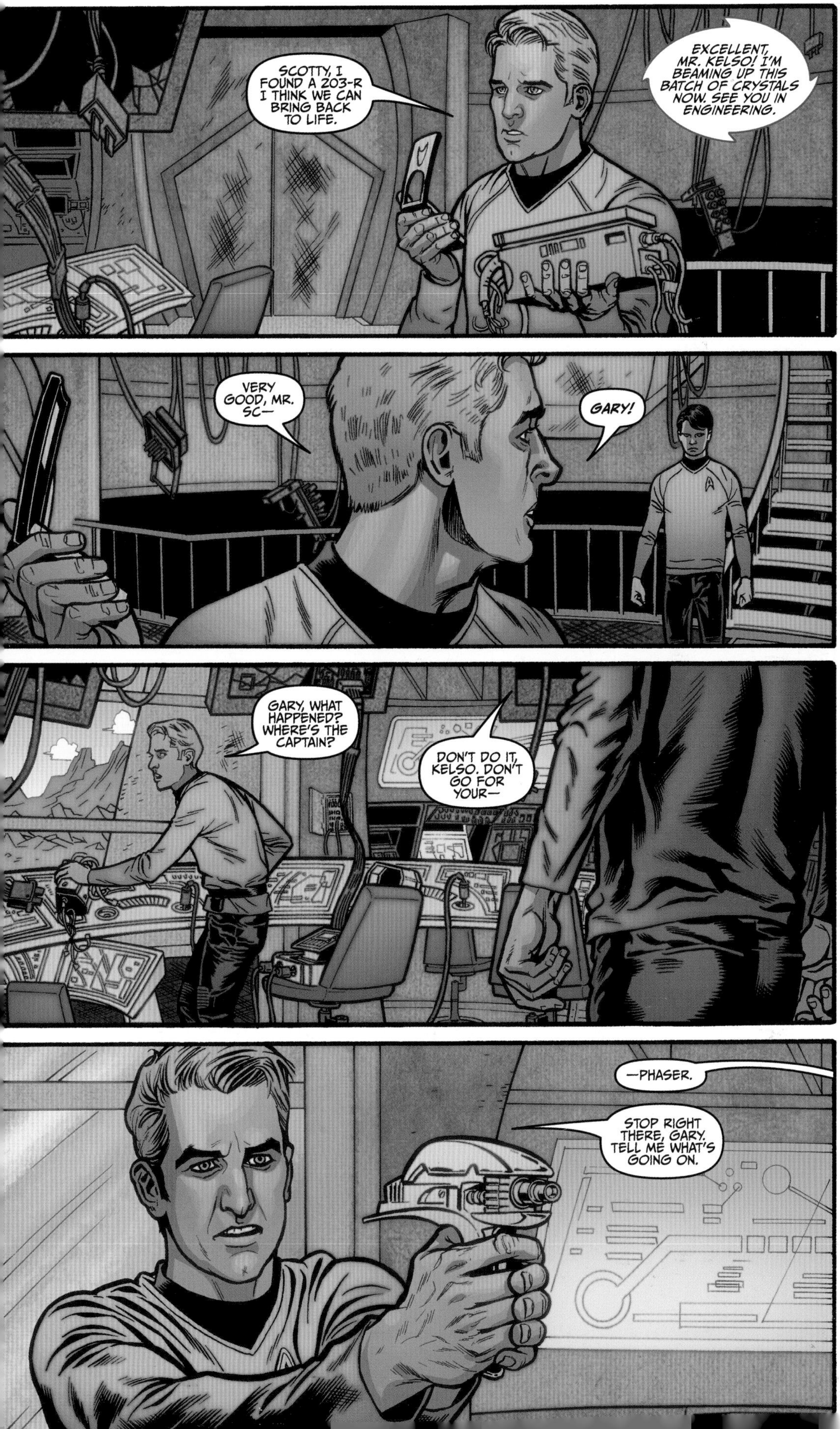

SCOTTY, I FOUND A 203-R I THINK WE CAN BRING BACK TO LIFE.
EXCELLENT, MR. KELSO! I'M BEAMING UP THIS BATCH OF CRYSTALS NOW. SEE YOU IN ENGINEERING.
VERY GOOD, MR. SC—
GARY!
GARY, WHAT HAPPENED? WHERE'S THE CAPTAIN?
DON'T DO IT, KELSO. DON'T GO FOR YOUR—
—PHASER.
STOP RIGHT THERE, GARY. TELL ME WHAT'S GOING ON.

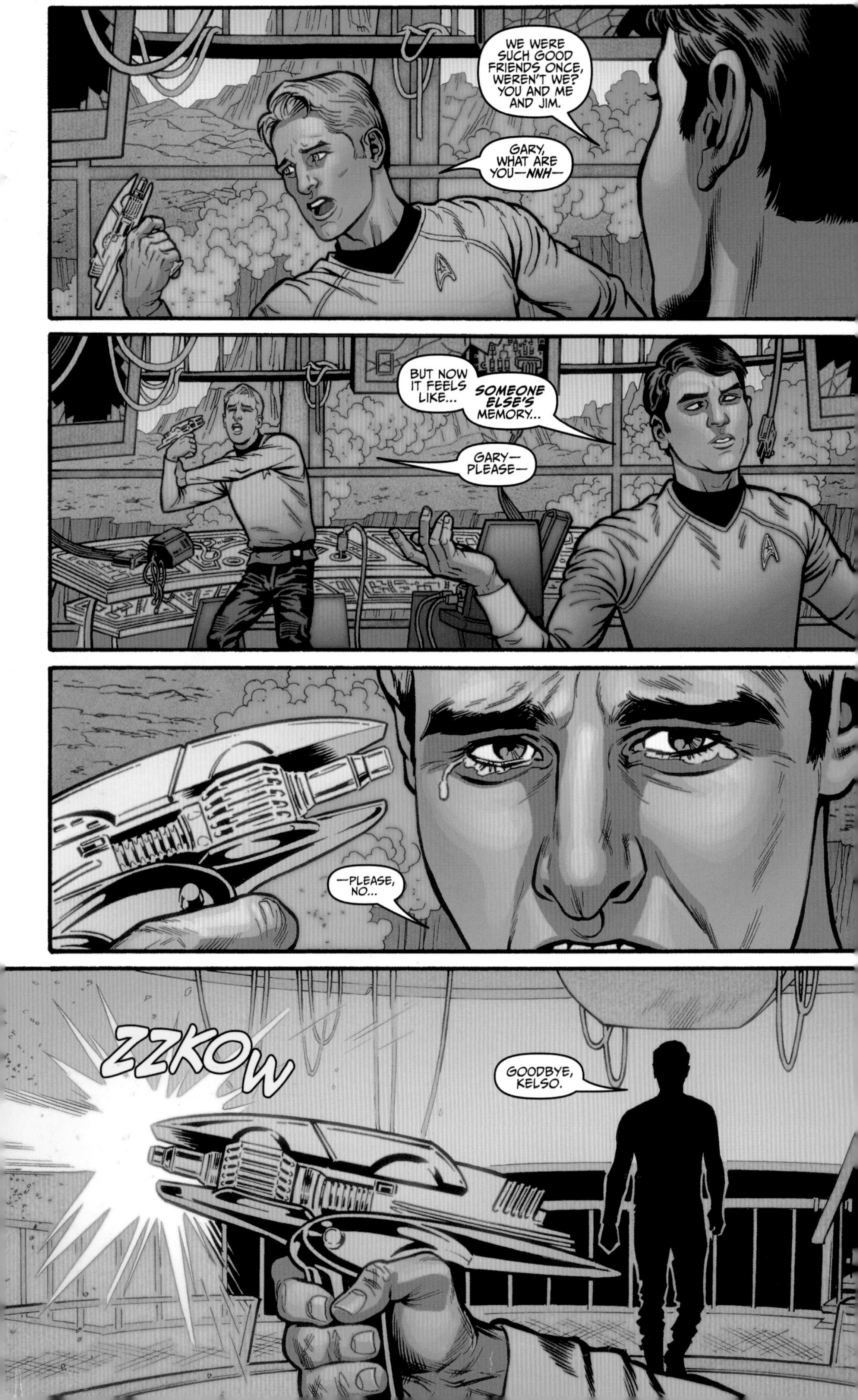
WE WERE SUCH GOOD FRIENDS ONCE, WEREN'T WE? YOU AND ME AND JIM.
GARY, WHAT ARE YOU—NNH—
BUT NOW IT FEELS LIKE... SOMEONE ELSE'S MEMORY...
GARY—PLEASE—
—PLEASE, NO...
ZZKOW
GOODBYE, KELSO.

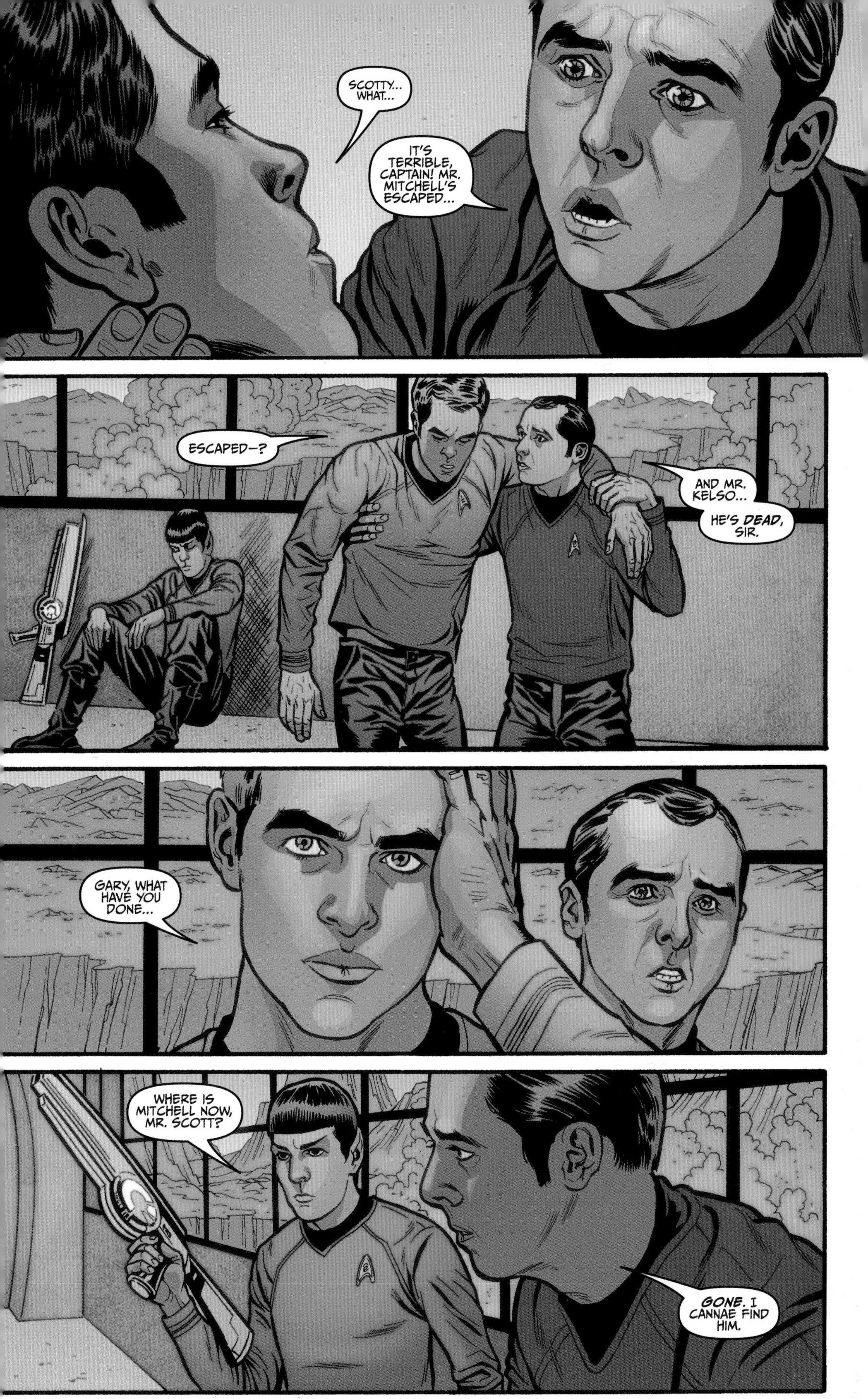
SCOTTY... WHAT...
IT'S TERRIBLE, CAPTAIN! MR. MITCHELL'S ESCAPED...
ESCAPED--?
AND MR. KELSO...
HE'S DEAD, SIR.
GARY, WHAT HAVE YOU DONE...
WHERE IS MITCHELL NOW, MR. SCOTT?
GONE. I CANNAE FIND HIM.

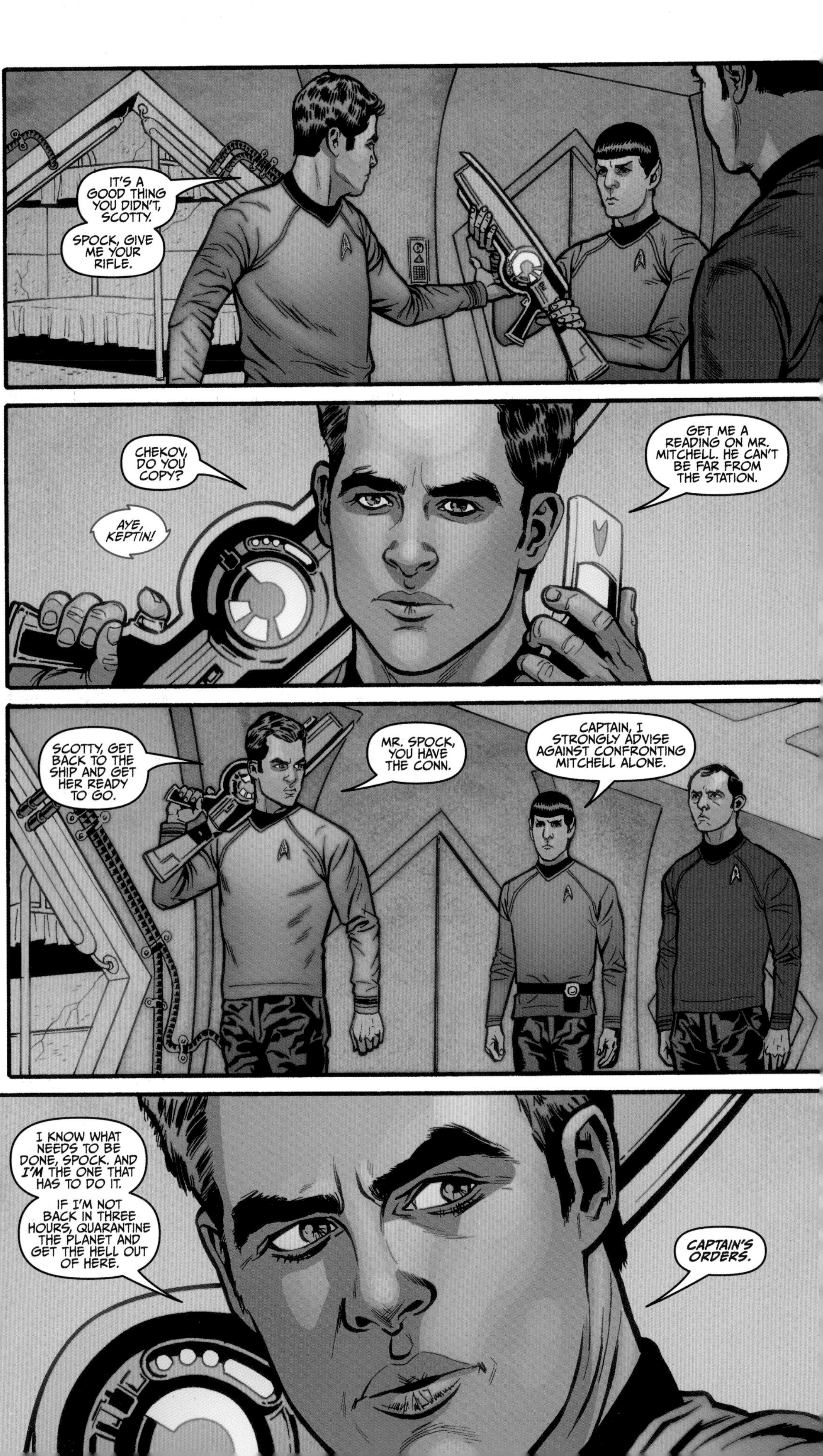
IT'S A GOOD THING YOU DIDN'T, SCOTTY.
SPOCK, GIVE ME YOUR RIFLE.
CHEKOV, DO YOU COPY?
AYE, KEPTIN!
GET ME A READING ON MR. MITCHELL. HE CAN'T BE FAR FROM THE STATION.
SCOTTY, GET BACK TO THE SHIP AND GET HER READY TO GO.
MR. SPOCK, YOU HAVE THE CONN.
CAPTAIN, I STRONGLY ADVISE AGAINST CONFRONTING MITCHELL ALONE.
I KNOW WHAT NEEDS TO BE DONE, SPOCK. AND I'M THE ONE THAT HAS TO DO IT.
IF I'M NOT BACK IN THREE HOURS, QUARANTINE THE PLANET AND GET THE HELL OUT OF HERE.
CAPTAIN'S ORDERS.

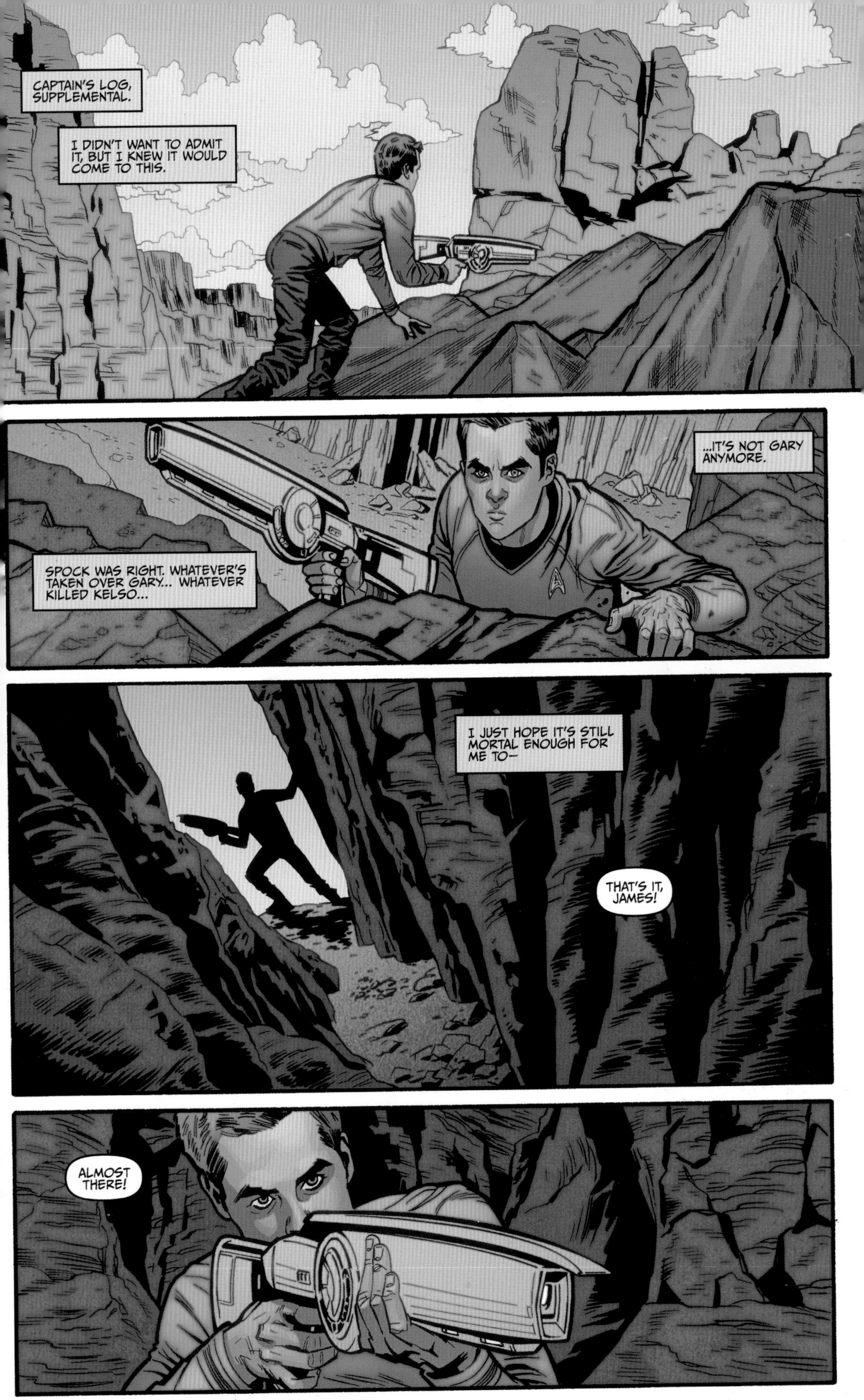

CAPTAIN'S LOG, SUPPLEMENTAL.
I DIDN'T WANT TO ADMIT IT, BUT I KNEW IT WOULD COME TO THIS.
SPOCK WAS RIGHT. WHATEVER'S TAKEN OVER GARY... WHATEVER KILLED KELSO...
...IT'S NOT GARY ANYMORE.
I JUST HOPE IT'S STILL MORTAL ENOUGH FOR ME TO–
THAT'S IT, JAMES!
ALMOST THERE!

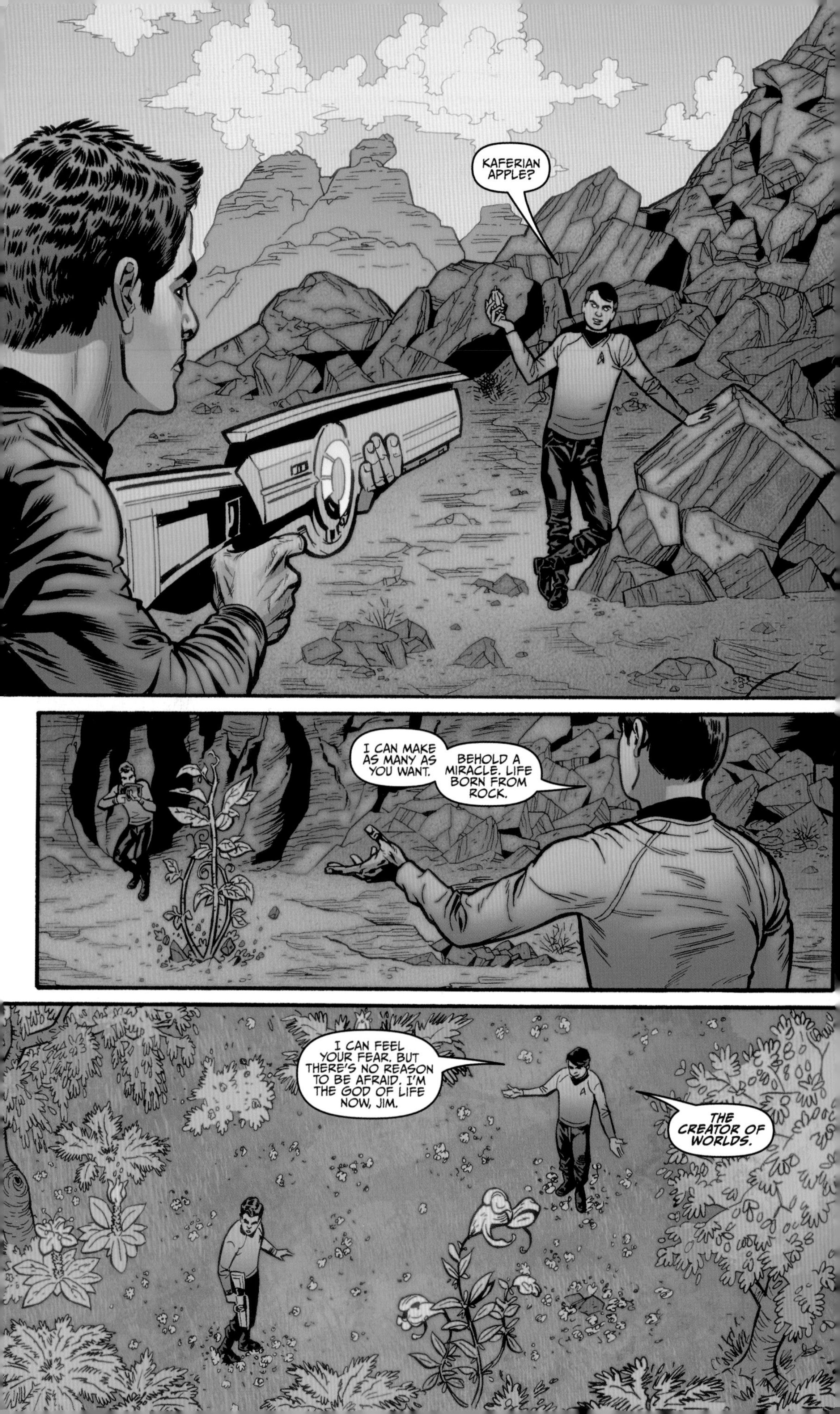
KAFERIAN APPLE?
I CAN MAKE AS MANY AS YOU WANT.
BEHOLD A MIRACLE. LIFE BORN FROM ROCK.
I CAN FEEL YOUR FEAR. BUT THERE'S NO REASON TO BE AFRAID. I'M THE GOD OF LIFE NOW, JIM.
THE CREATOR OF WORLDS.

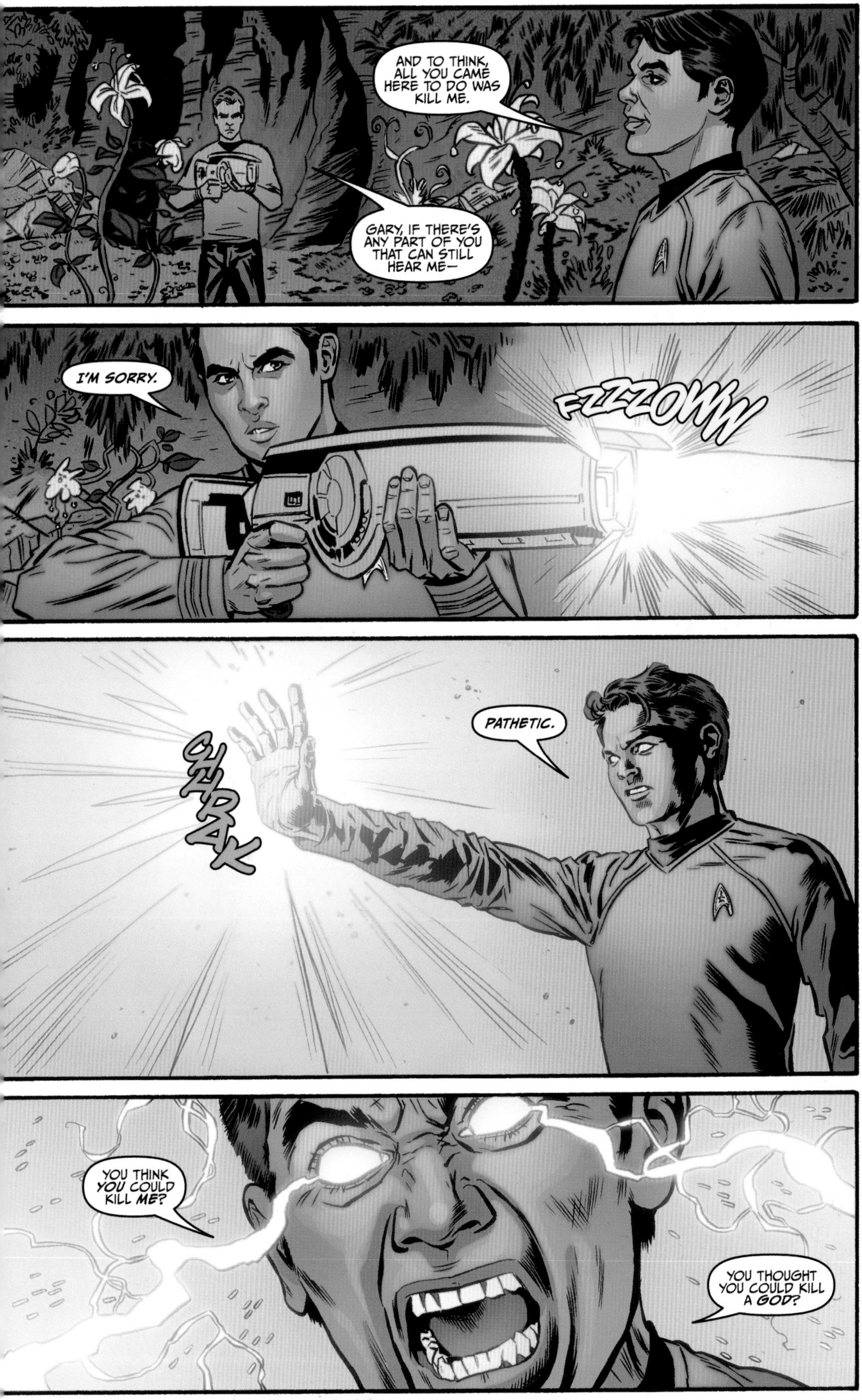
AND TO THINK, ALL YOU CAME HERE TO DO WAS KILL ME.
GARY, IF THERE'S ANY PART OF YOU THAT CAN STILL HEAR ME—
I'M SORRY.
FZZZOWW
PATHETIC.
CHRAK
YOU THINK *YOU* COULD KILL *ME*?
YOU THOUGHT YOU COULD KILL A *GOD*?

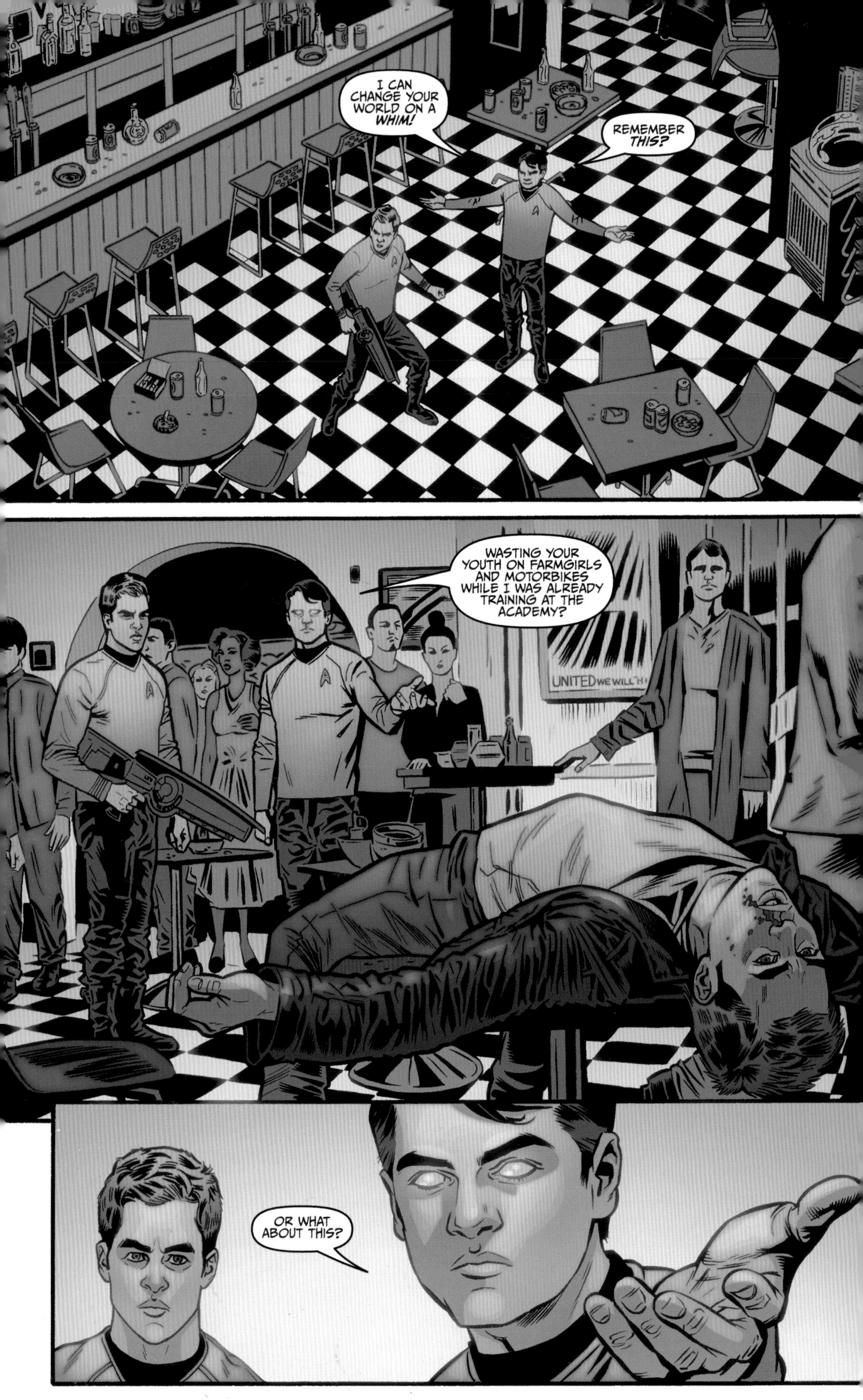
I CAN CHANGE YOUR WORLD ON A WHIM!
REMEMBER THIS?
WASTING YOUR YOUTH ON FARMGIRLS AND MOTORBIKES WHILE I WAS ALREADY TRAINING AT THE ACADEMY?
UNITED WE WILL
OR WHAT ABOUT THIS?

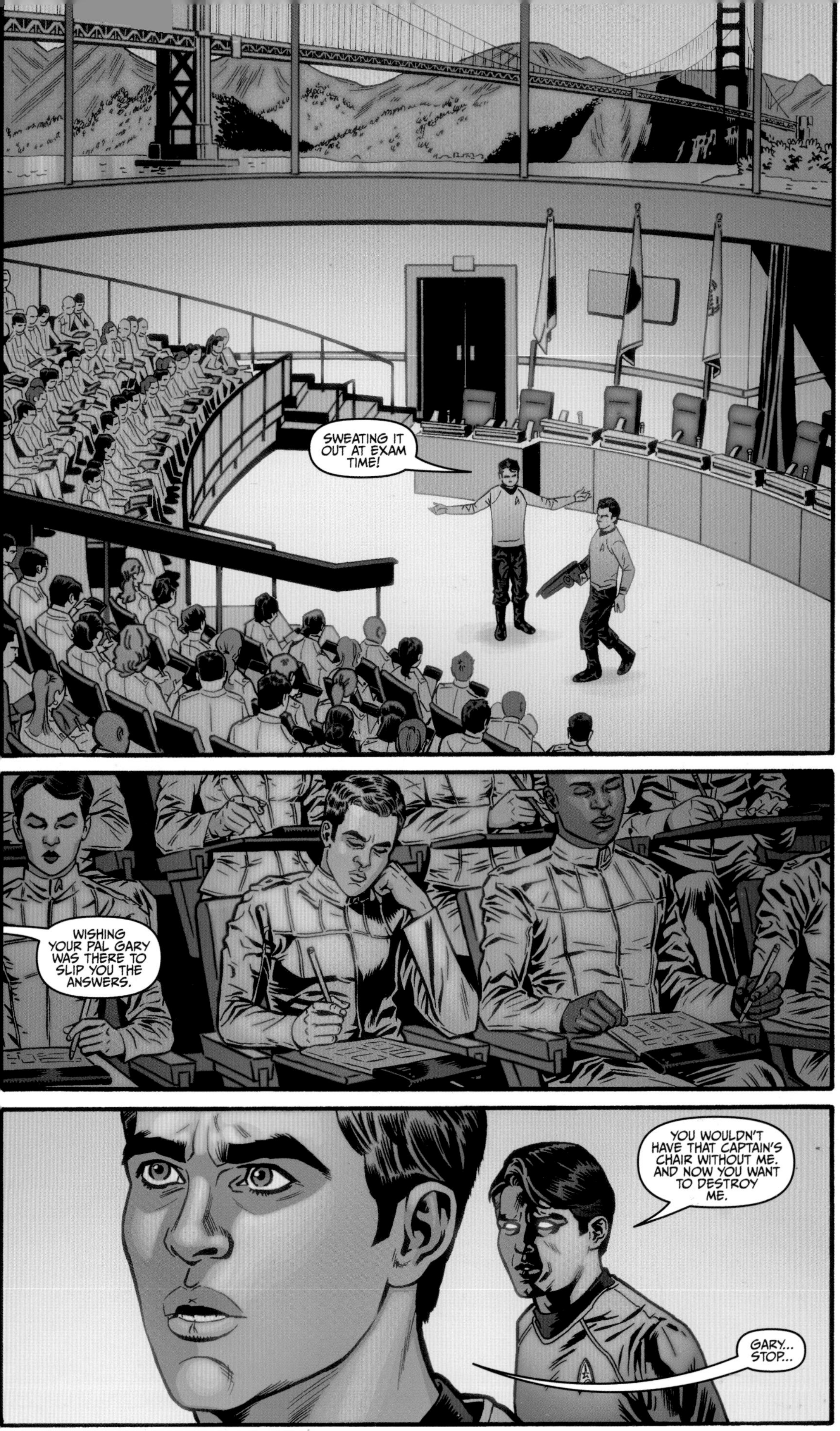
SWEATING IT OUT AT EXAM TIME!
WISHING YOUR PAL GARY WAS THERE TO SLIP YOU THE ANSWERS.
YOU WOULDN'T HAVE THAT CAPTAIN'S CHAIR WITHOUT ME. AND NOW YOU WANT TO DESTROY ME.
GARY... STOP...

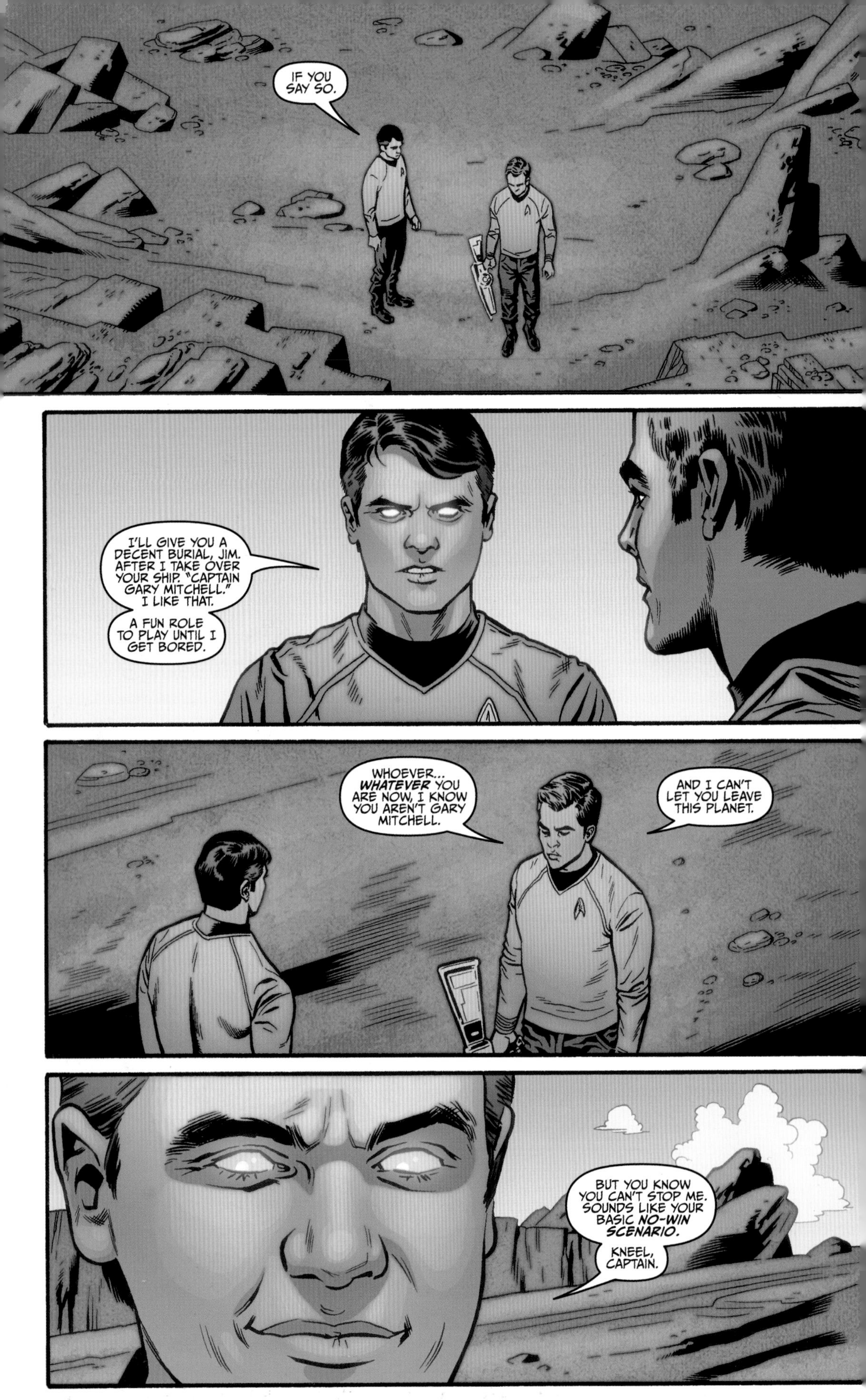
IF YOU SAY SO.
I'LL GIVE YOU A DECENT BURIAL, JIM. AFTER I TAKE OVER YOUR SHIP. "CAPTAIN GARY MITCHELL." I LIKE THAT.
A FUN ROLE TO PLAY UNTIL I GET BORED.
WHOEVER... *WHATEVER* YOU ARE NOW, I KNOW YOU AREN'T GARY MITCHELL.
AND I CAN'T LET YOU LEAVE THIS PLANET.
BUT YOU KNOW YOU CAN'T STOP ME. SOUNDS LIKE YOUR BASIC *NO-WIN SCENARIO.*
KNEEL, CAPTAIN.

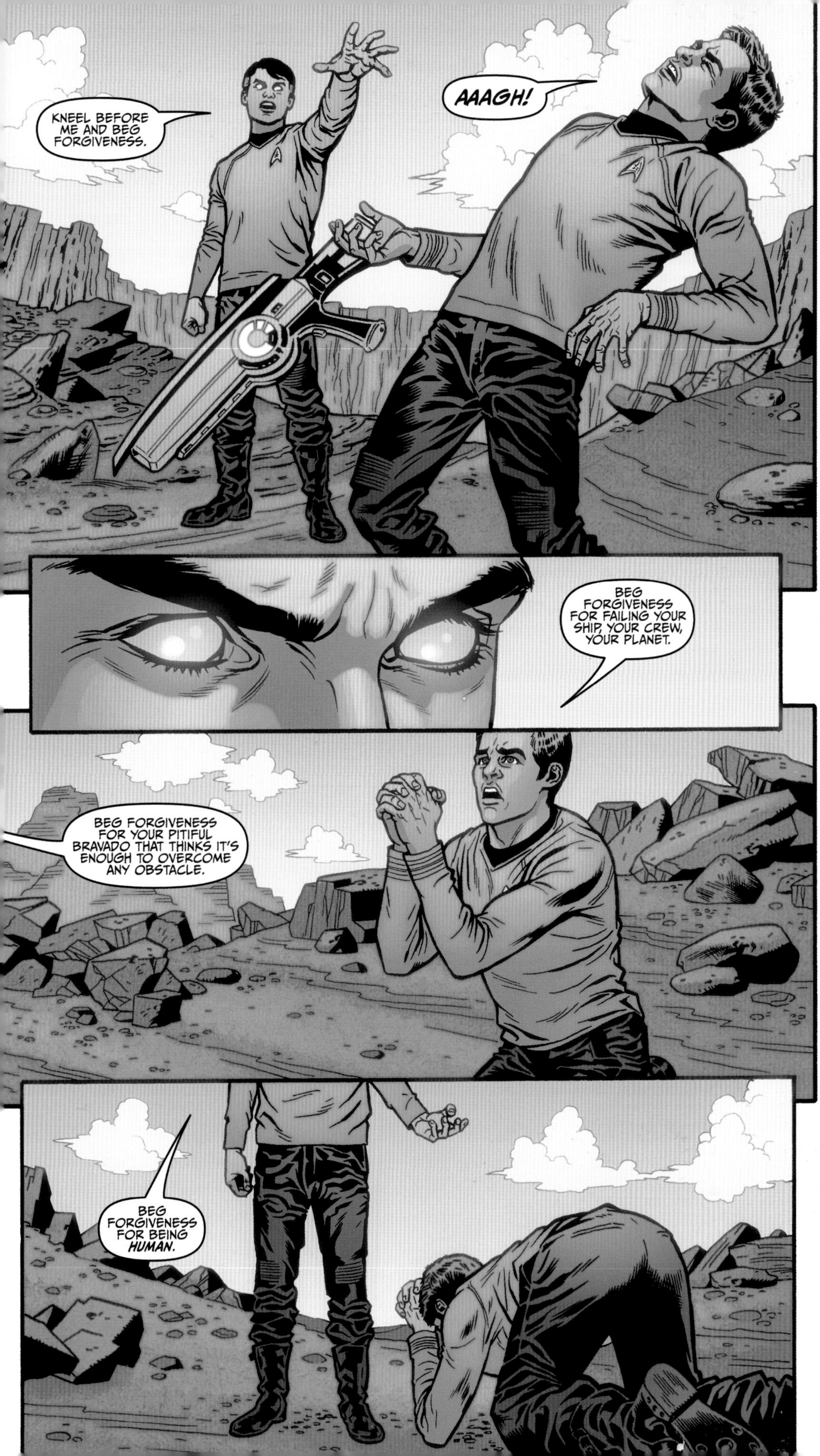
KNEEL BEFORE ME AND BEG FORGIVENESS.
AAAGH!
BEG FORGIVENESS FOR FAILING YOUR SHIP, YOUR CREW, YOUR PLANET.
BEG FORGIVENESS FOR YOUR PITIFUL BRAVADO THAT THINKS IT'S ENOUGH TO OVERCOME ANY OBSTACLE.
BEG FORGIVENESS FOR BEING *HUMAN*.

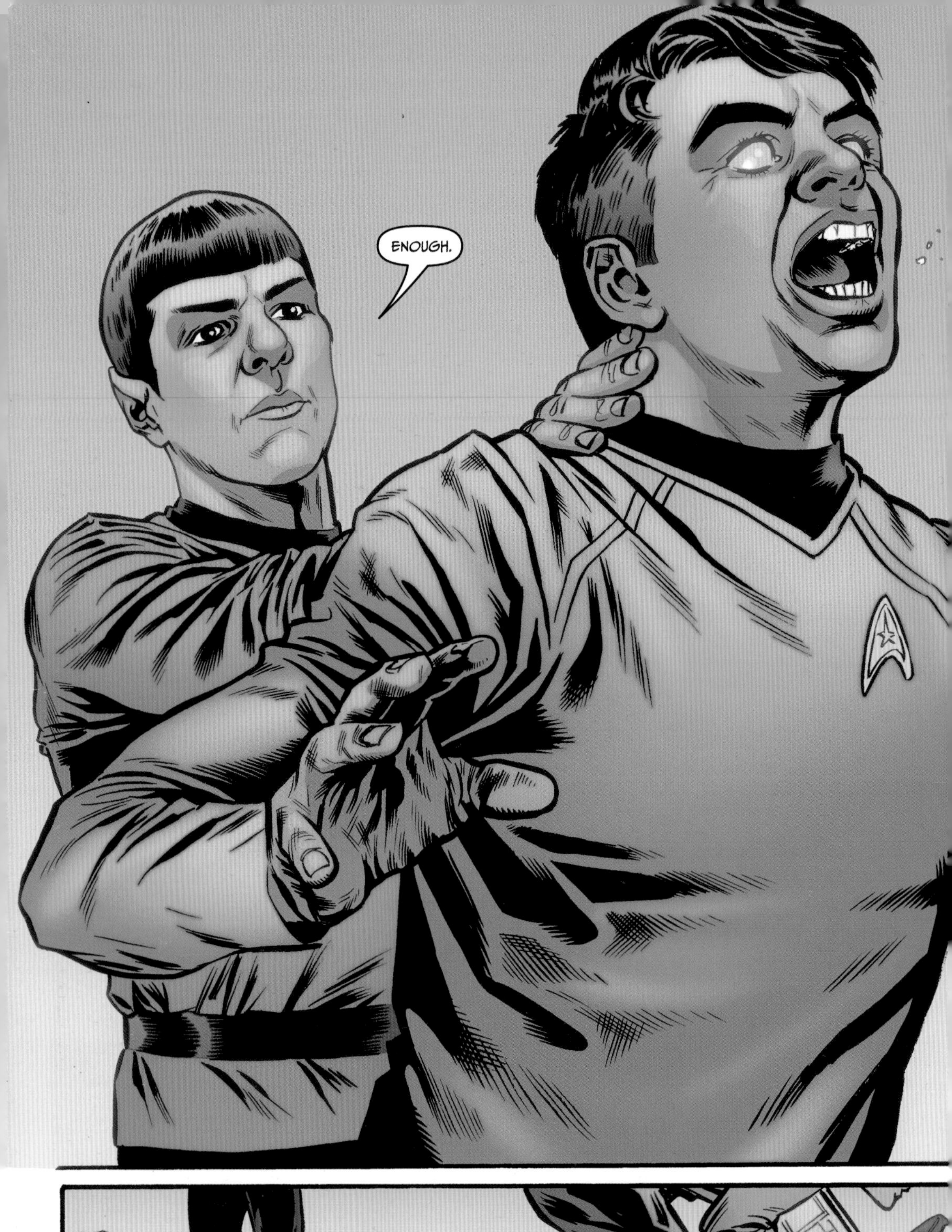
ENOUGH.

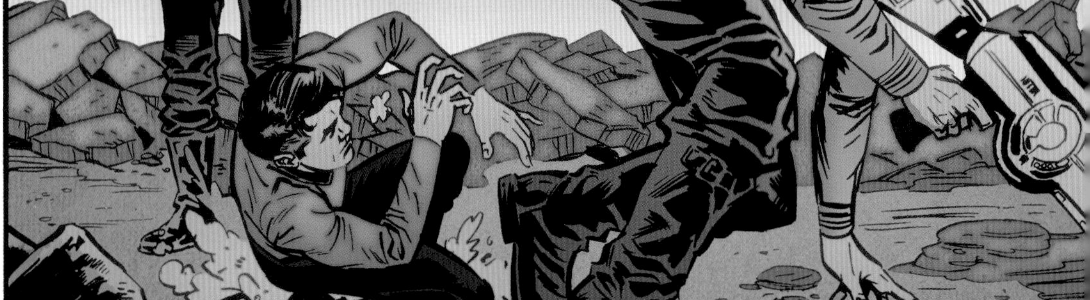

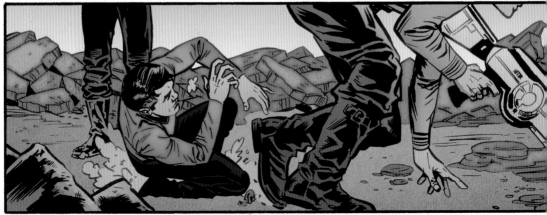

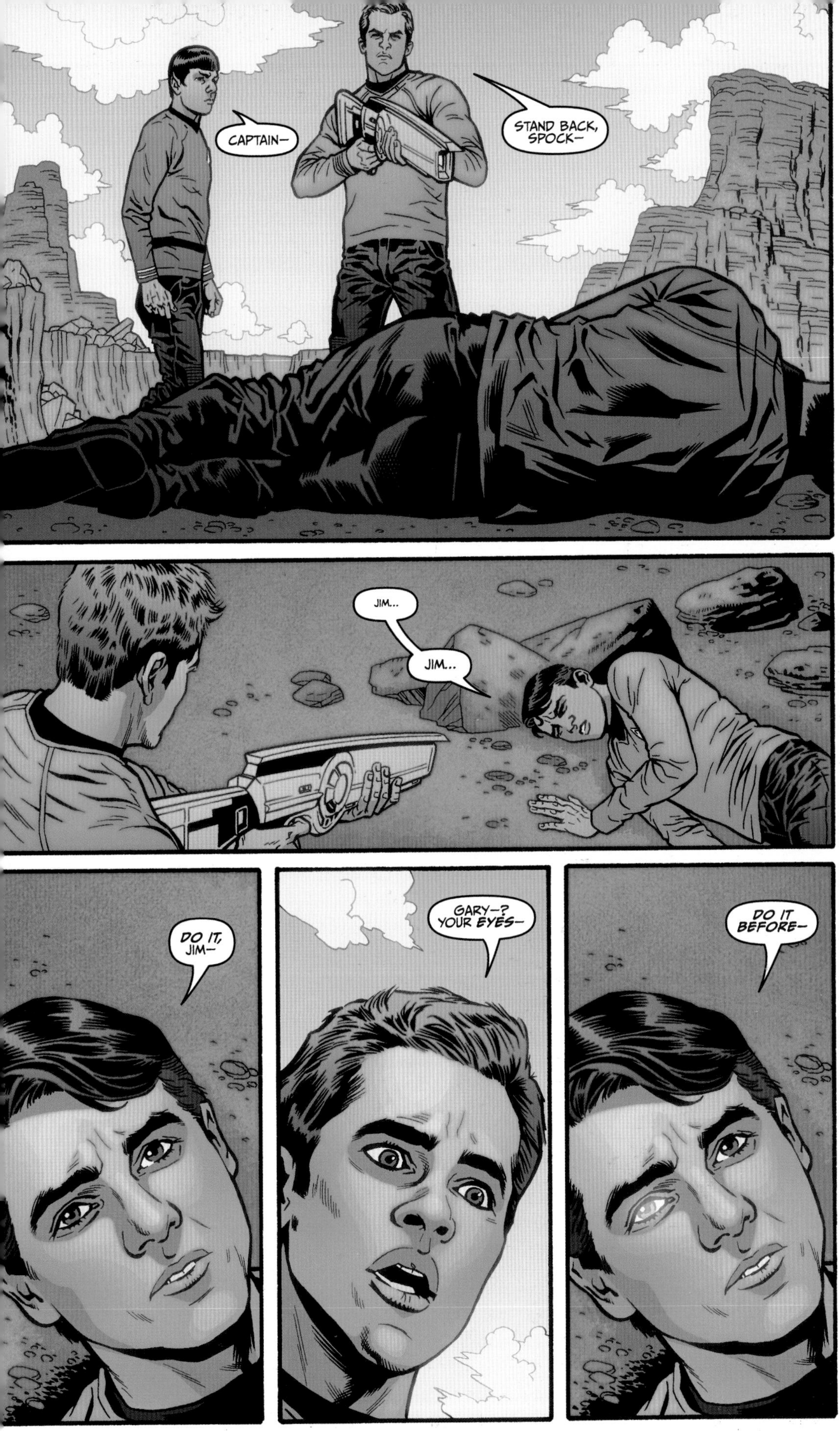
CAPTAIN—
STAND BACK, SPOCK—
JIM...
JIM...
DO IT, JIM—
GARY—? YOUR EYES—
DO IT BEFORE—

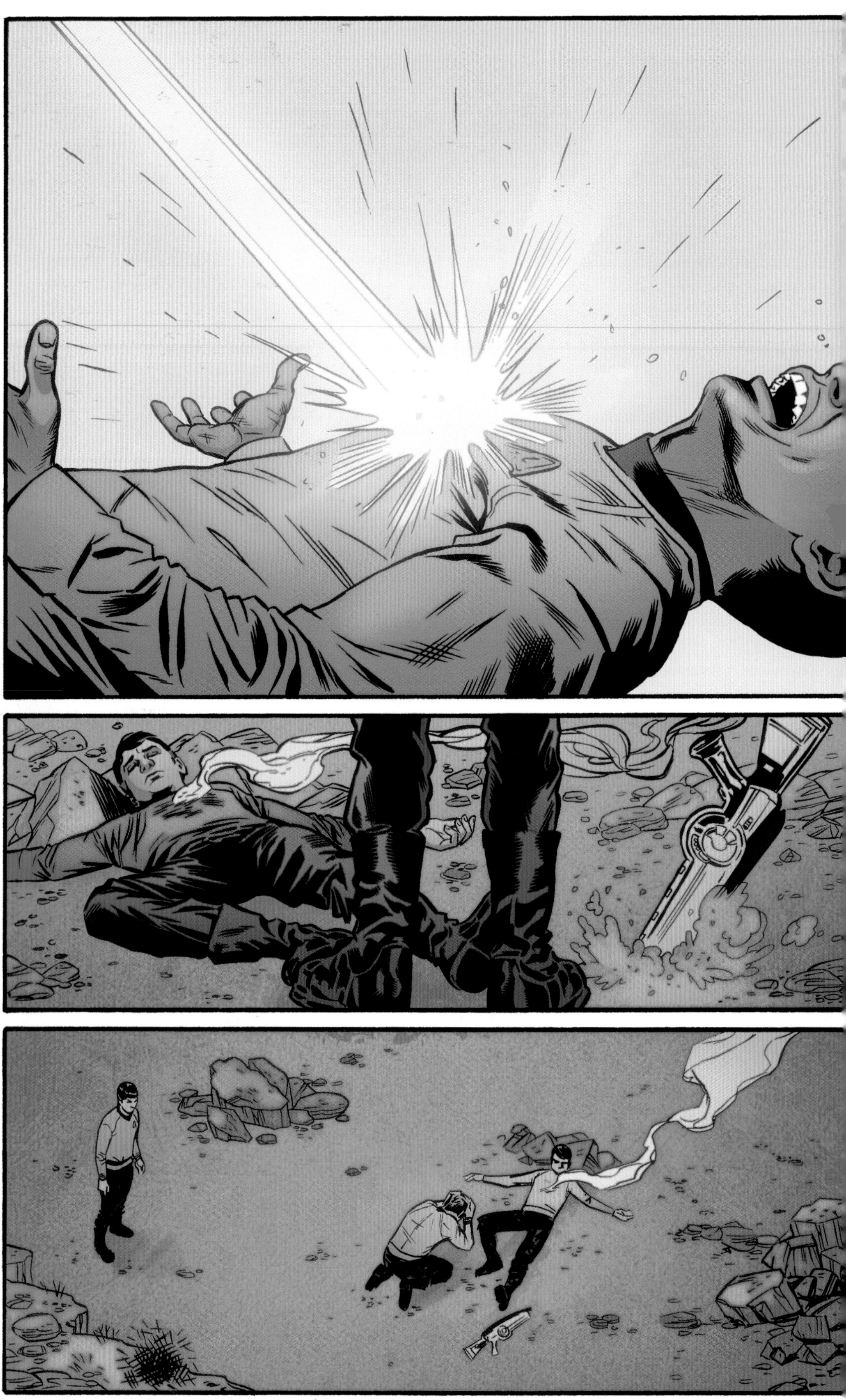

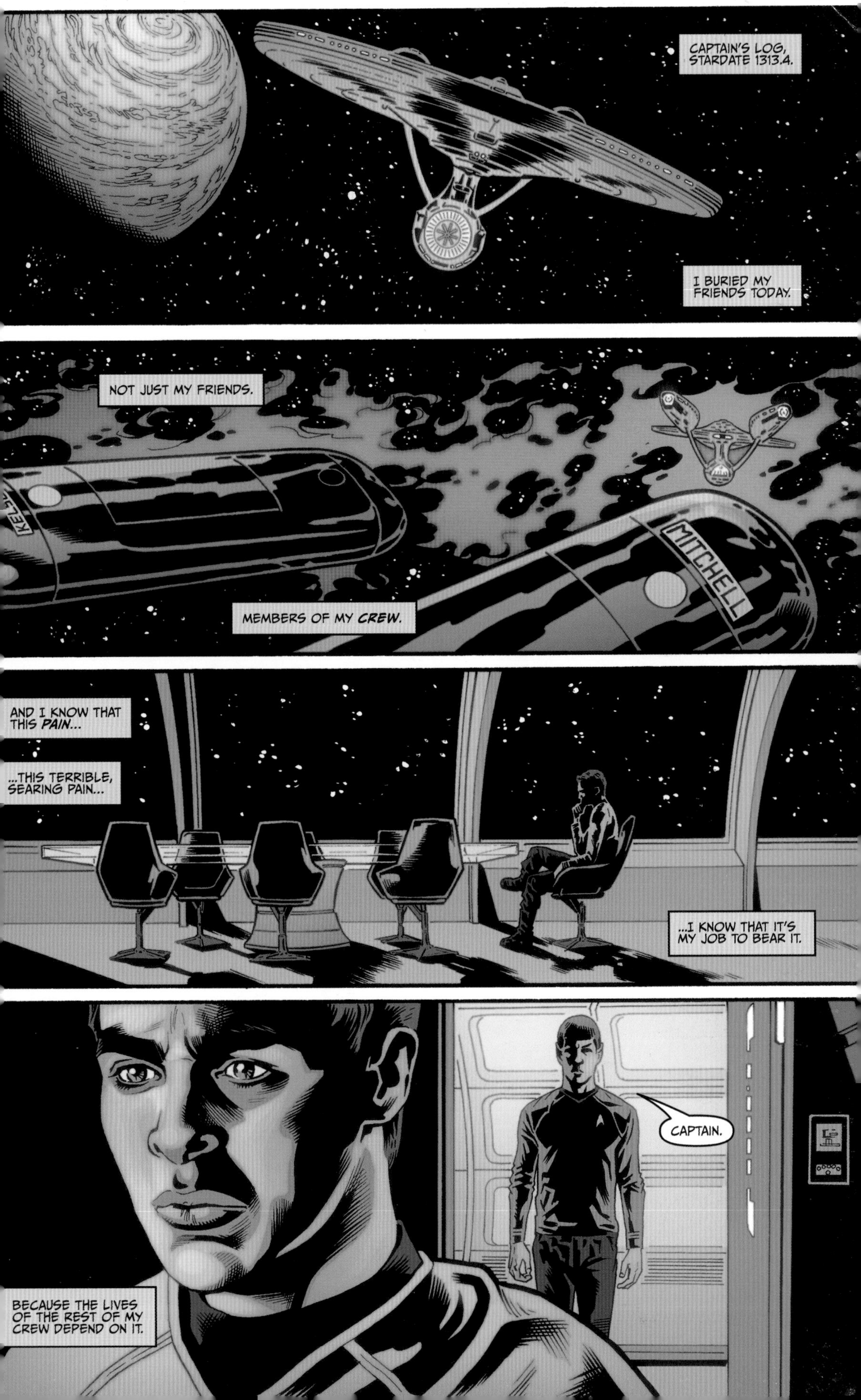
CAPTAIN'S LOG, STARDATE 1313.4.
I BURIED MY FRIENDS TODAY.
NOT JUST MY FRIENDS.
MITCHELL
MEMBERS OF MY *CREW*.
AND I KNOW THAT THIS *PAIN*...
...THIS TERRIBLE, SEARING PAIN...
...I KNOW THAT IT'S MY JOB TO BEAR IT.
CAPTAIN.
BECAUSE THE LIVES OF THE REST OF MY CREW DEPEND ON IT.

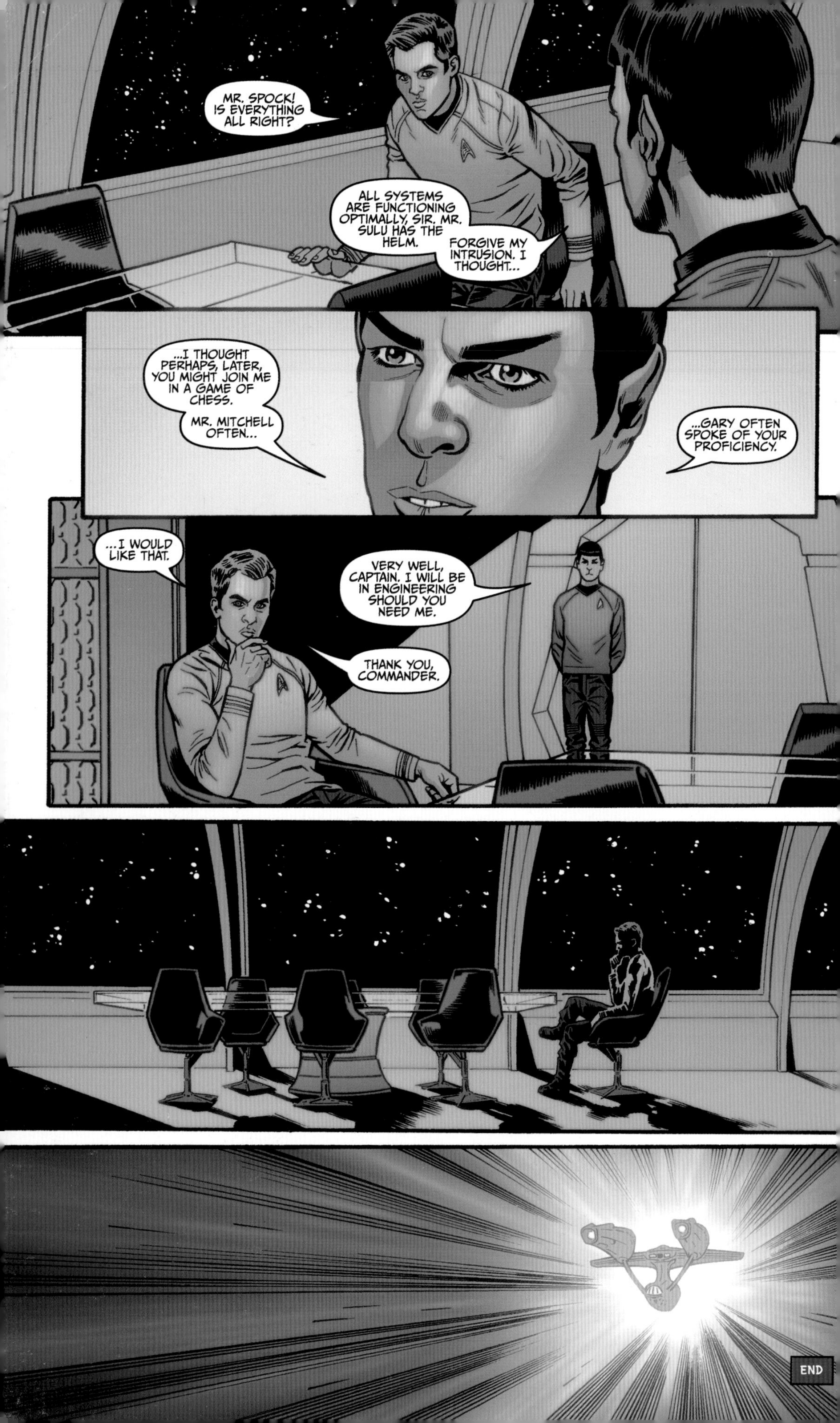
MR. SPOCK! IS EVERYTHING ALL RIGHT?
ALL SYSTEMS ARE FUNCTIONING OPTIMALLY, SIR. MR. SULU HAS THE HELM.
FORGIVE MY INTRUSION. I THOUGHT...
...I THOUGHT PERHAPS, LATER, YOU MIGHT JOIN ME IN A GAME OF CHESS.
MR. MITCHELL OFTEN...
...GARY OFTEN SPOKE OF YOUR PROFICIENCY.
...I WOULD LIKE THAT.
VERY WELL, CAPTAIN. I WILL BE IN ENGINEERING SHOULD YOU NEED ME.
THANK YOU, COMMANDER.
END

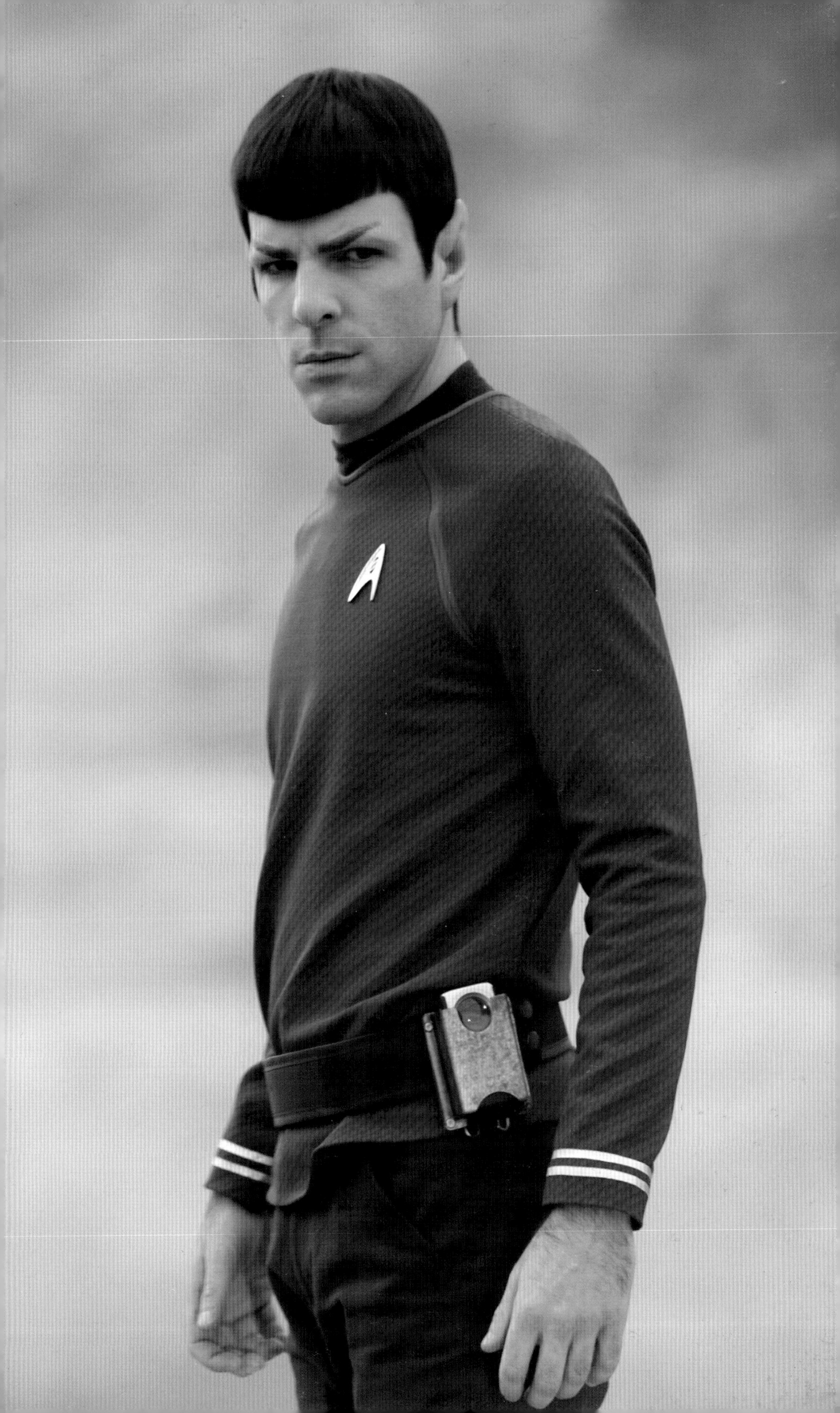

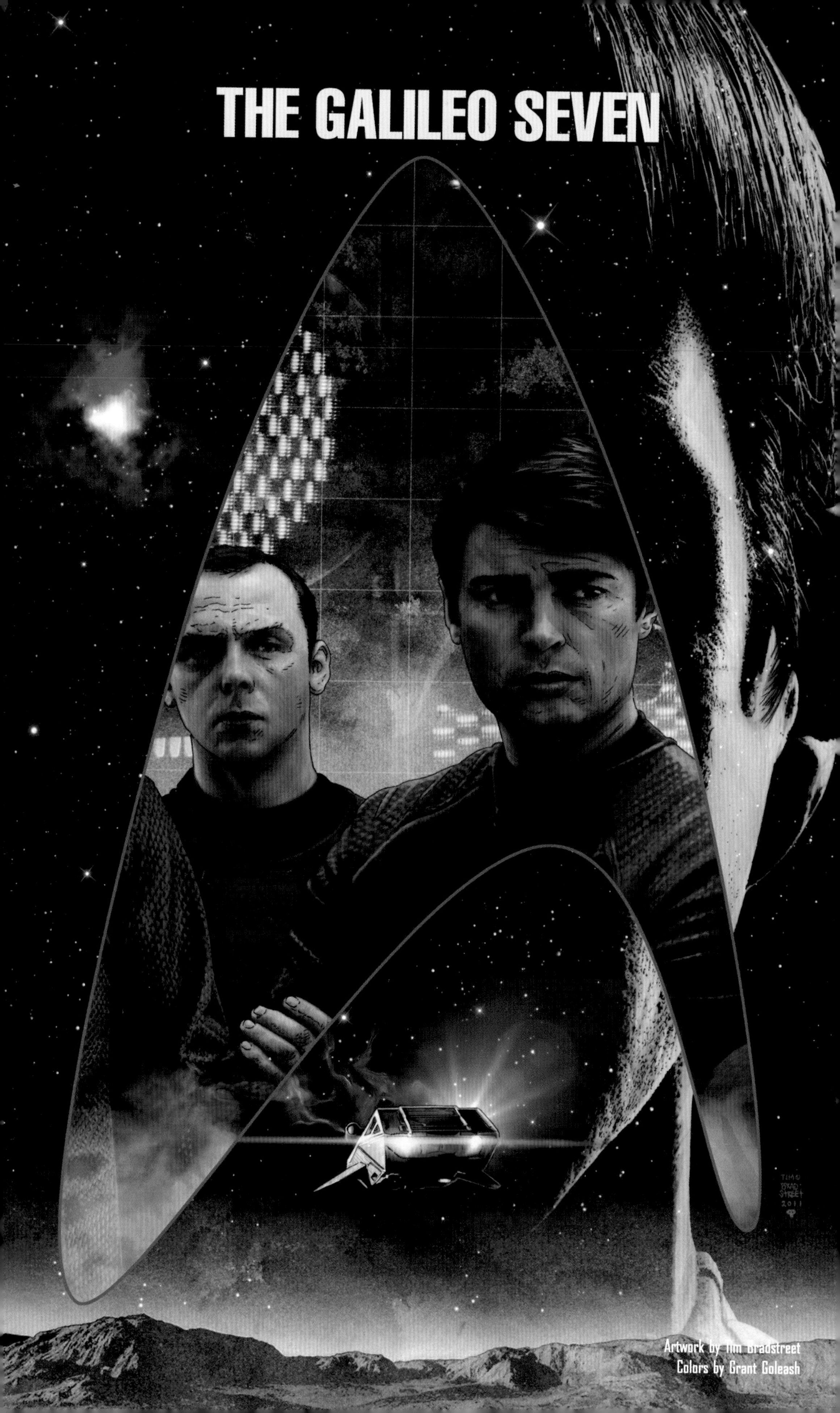
THE GALILEO SEVEN
Artwork by Tim Bradstreet
Colors by Grant Goleash

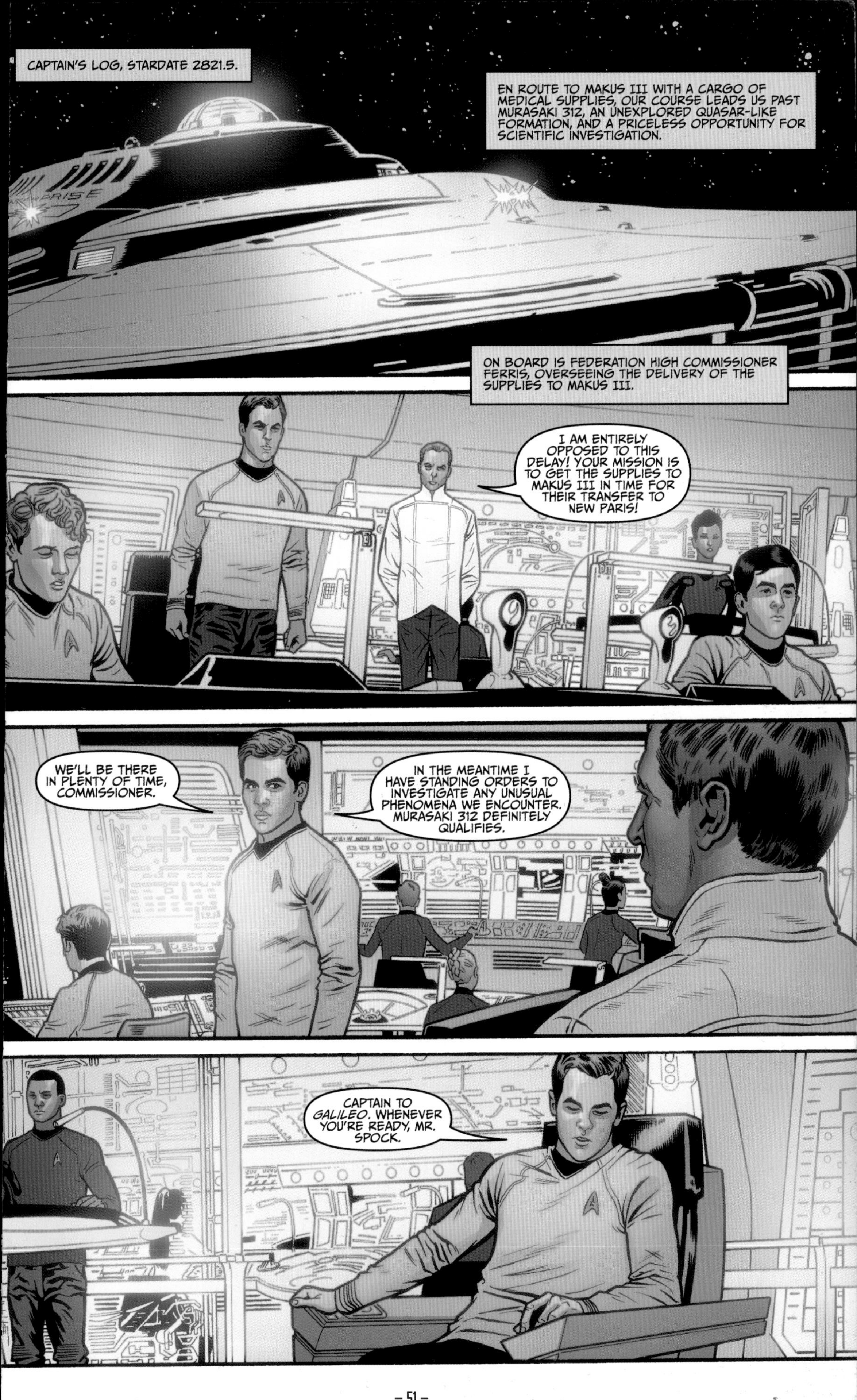

CAPTAIN'S LOG, STARDATE 2821.5.
EN ROUTE TO MAKUS III WITH A CARGO OF MEDICAL SUPPLIES, OUR COURSE LEADS US PAST MURASAKI 312, AN UNEXPLORED QUASAR-LIKE FORMATION, AND A PRICELESS OPPORTUNITY FOR SCIENTIFIC INVESTIGATION.
ON BOARD IS FEDERATION HIGH COMMISSIONER FERRIS, OVERSEEING THE DELIVERY OF THE SUPPLIES TO MAKUS III.
I AM ENTIRELY OPPOSED TO THIS DELAY! YOUR MISSION IS TO GET THE SUPPLIES TO MAKUS III IN TIME FOR THEIR TRANSFER TO NEW PARIS!
WE'LL BE THERE IN PLENTY OF TIME, COMMISSIONER.
IN THE MEANTIME I HAVE STANDING ORDERS TO INVESTIGATE ANY UNUSUAL PHENOMENA WE ENCOUNTER. MURASAKI 312 DEFINITELY QUALIFIES.
CAPTAIN TO GALILEO. WHENEVER YOU'RE READY, MR. SPOCK.

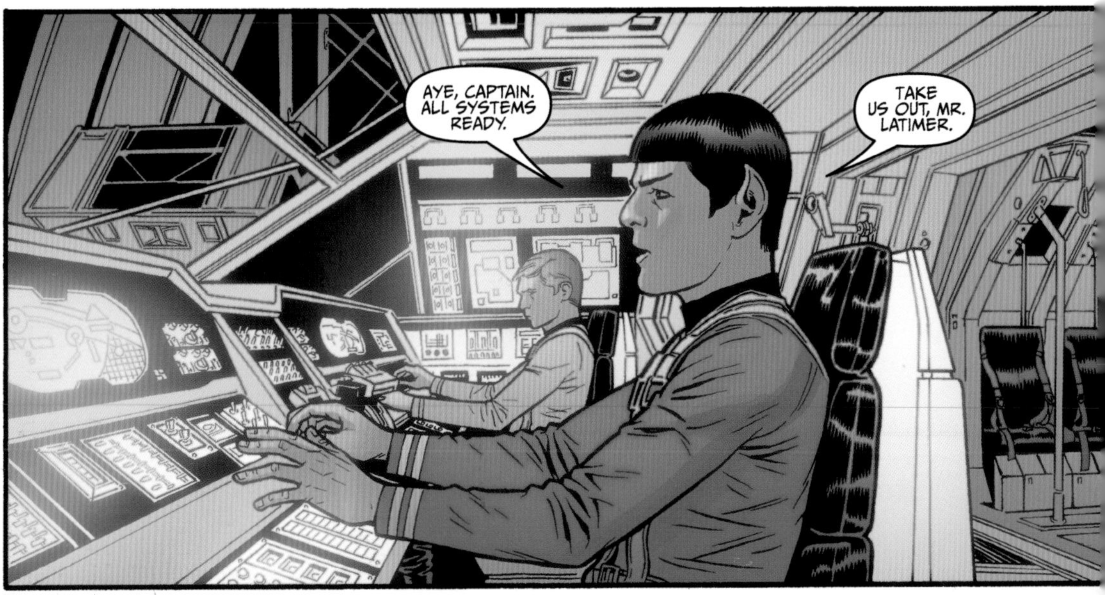
AYE, CAPTAIN. ALL SYSTEMS READY.
TAKE US OUT, MR. LATIMER.

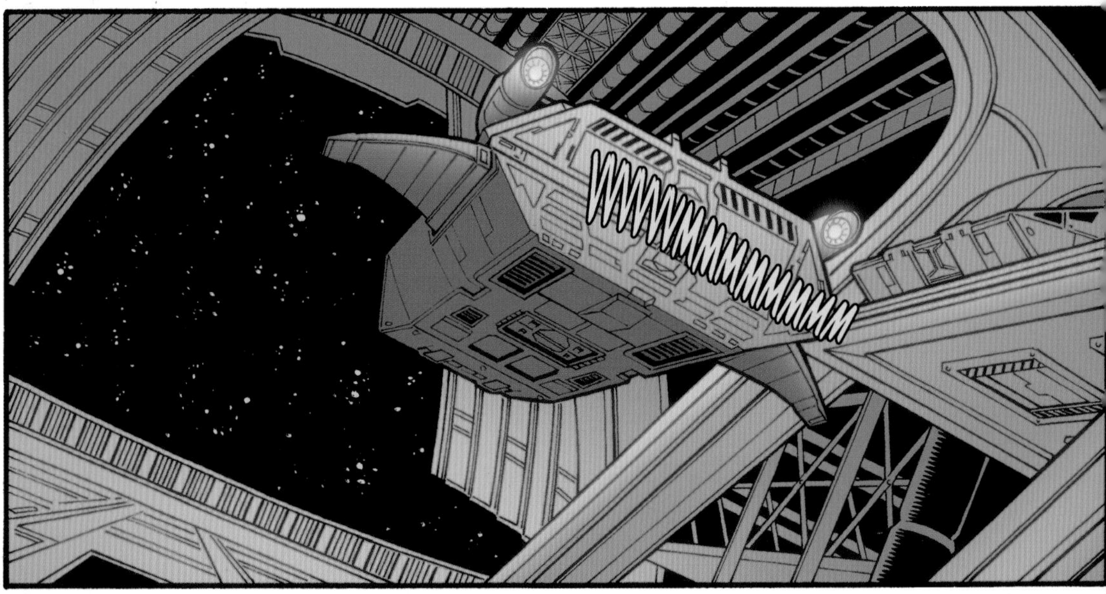
VVVVVVMMMMMMMMM

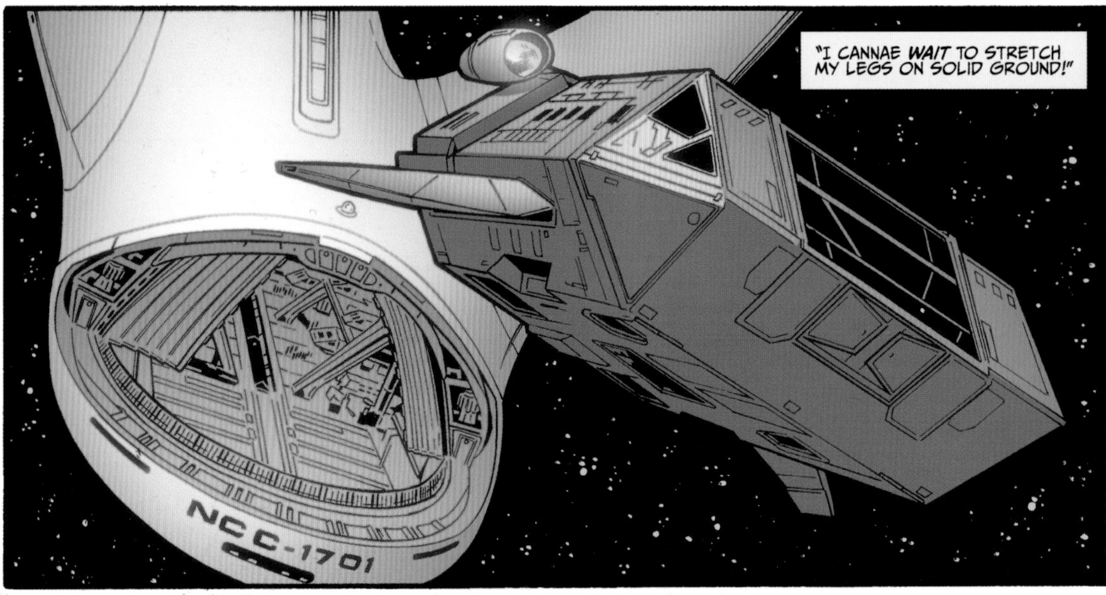
"I CANNAE WAIT TO STRETCH MY LEGS ON SOLID GROUND!"
NCC-1701

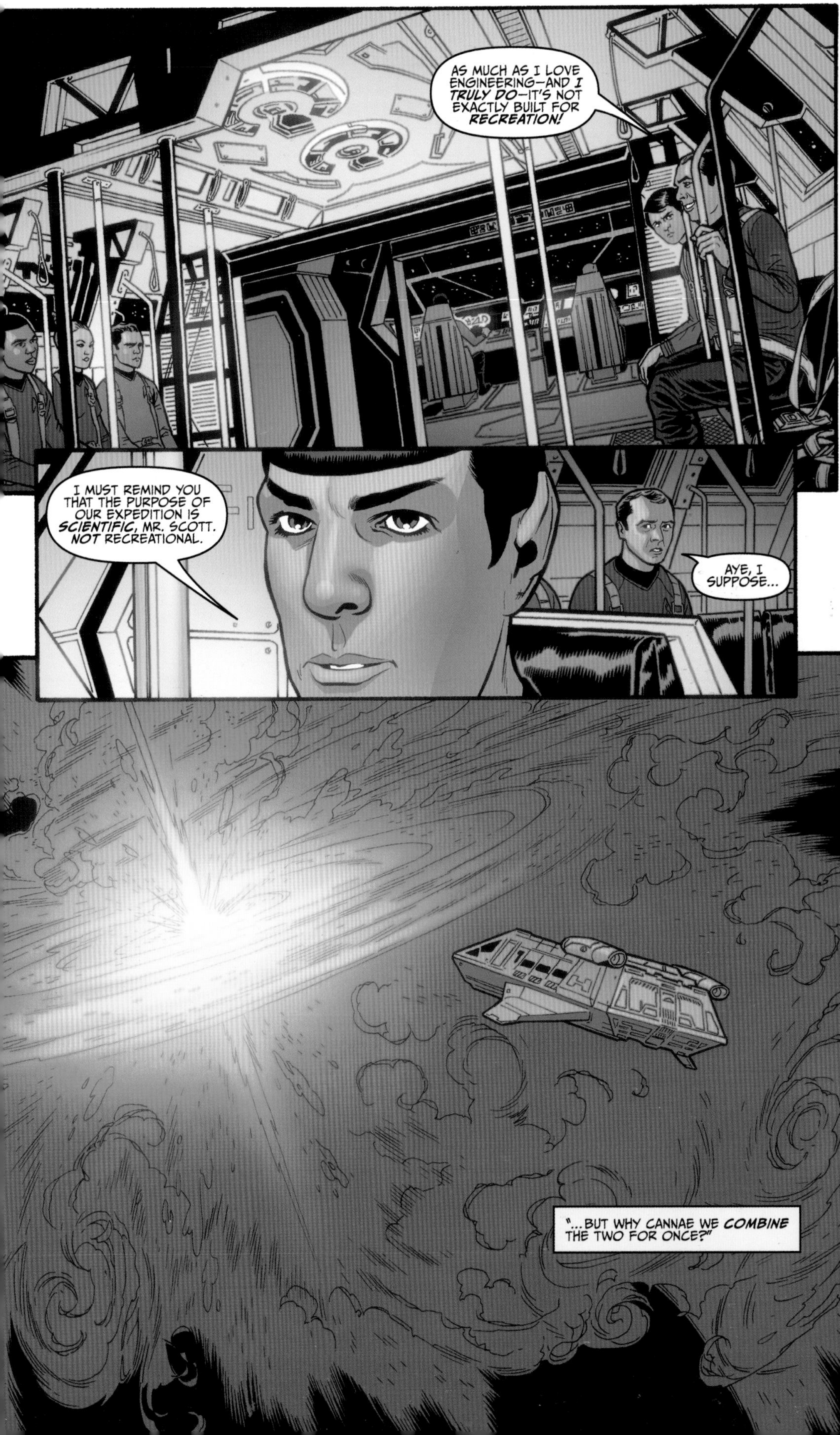
AS MUCH AS I LOVE ENGINEERING—AND I TRULY DO—IT'S NOT EXACTLY BUILT FOR RECREATION!
I MUST REMIND YOU THAT THE PURPOSE OF OUR EXPEDITION IS SCIENTIFIC, MR. SCOTT. NOT RECREATIONAL.
AYE, I SUPPOSE...
"...BUT WHY CANNAE WE COMBINE THE TWO FOR ONCE?"

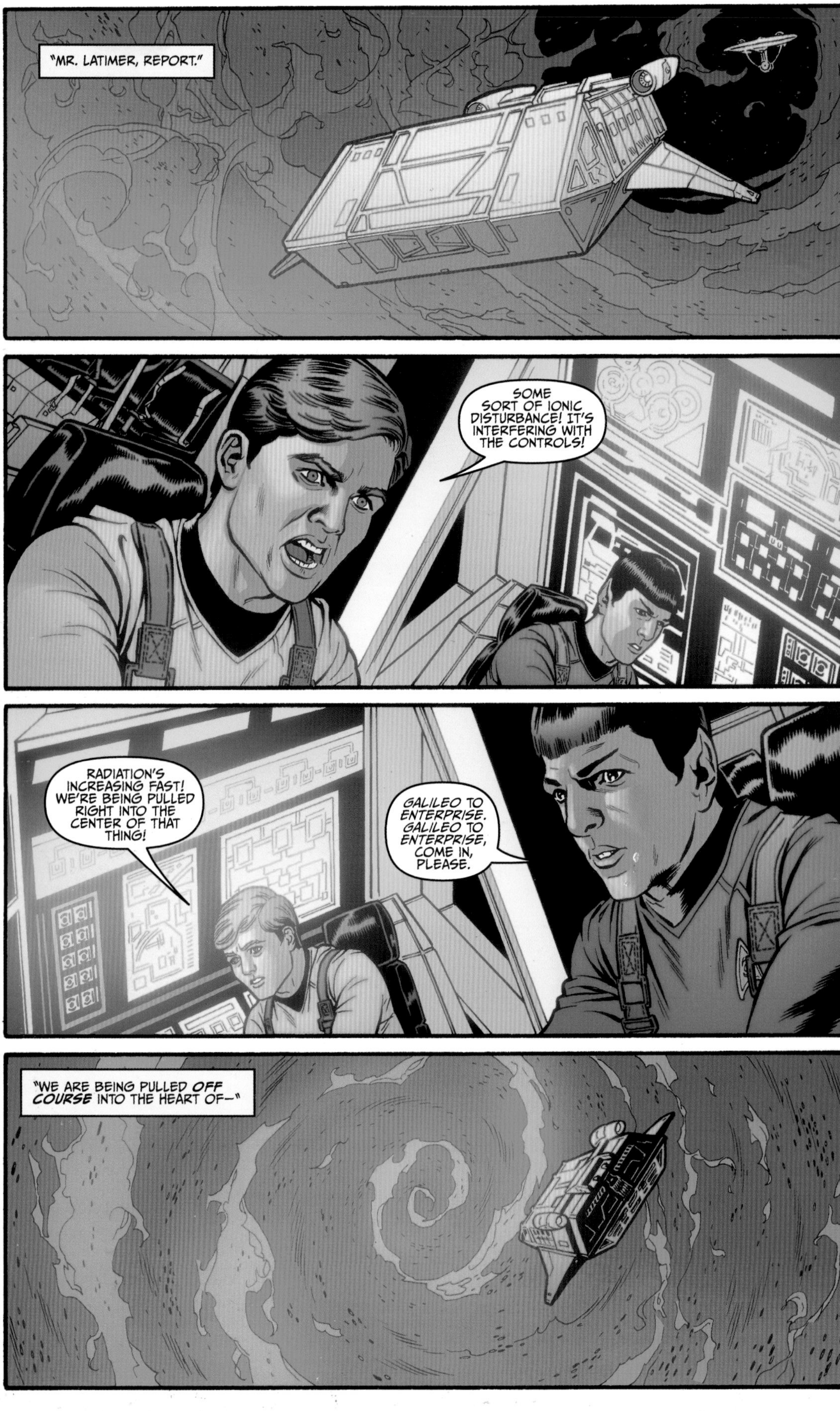
"MR. LATIMER, REPORT."
SOME SORT OF IONIC DISTURBANCE! IT'S INTERFERING WITH THE CONTROLS!
RADIATION'S INCREASING FAST! WE'RE BEING PULLED RIGHT INTO THE CENTER OF THAT THING!
GALILEO TO ENTERPRISE. GALILEO TO ENTERPRISE, COME IN, PLEASE.
"WE ARE BEING PULLED *OFF COURSE* INTO THE HEART OF—"

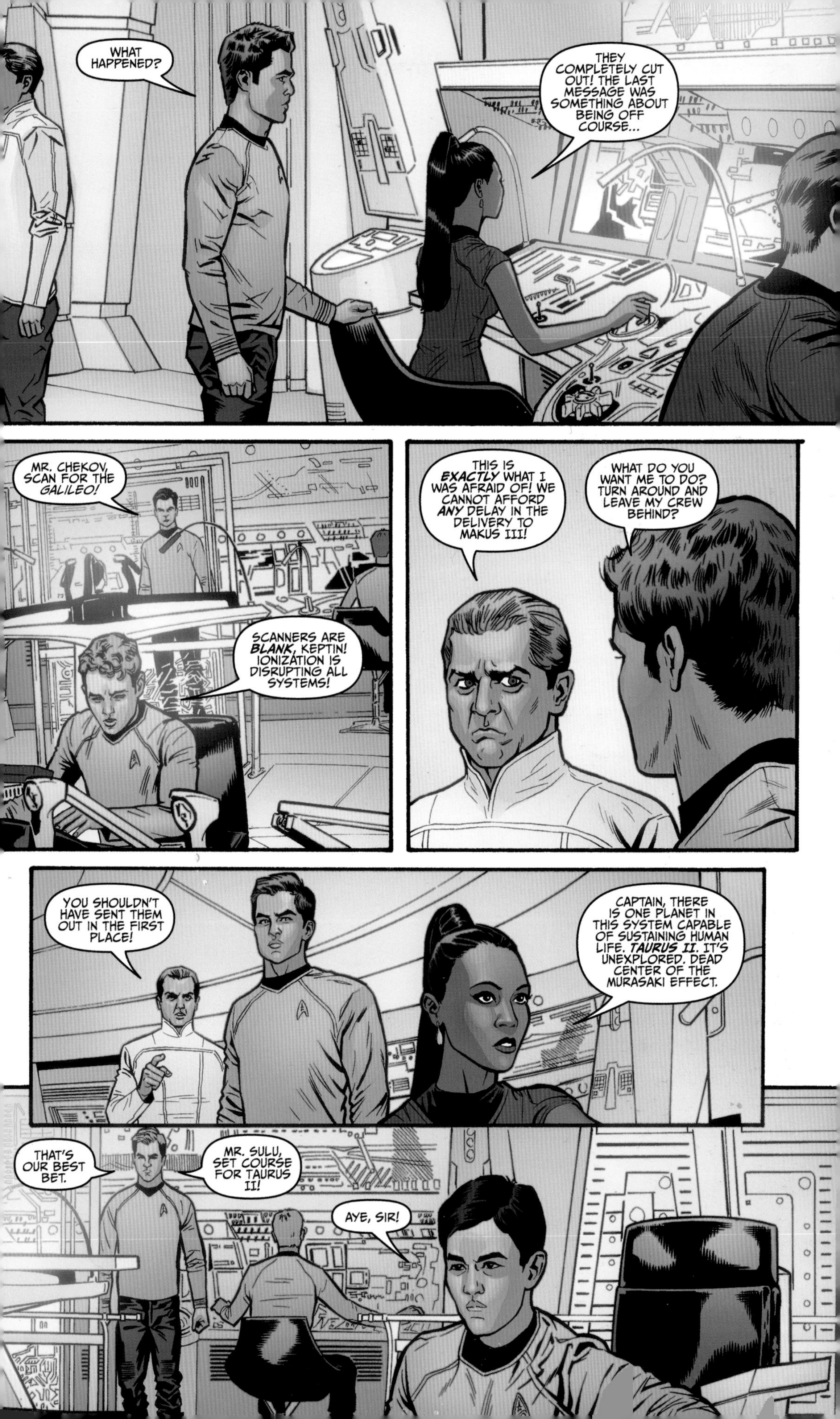
WHAT HAPPENED?
THEY COMPLETELY CUT OUT! THE LAST MESSAGE WAS SOMETHING ABOUT BEING OFF COURSE...
MR. CHEKOV, SCAN FOR THE *GALILEO!*
SCANNERS ARE ***BLANK***, KEPTIN! IONIZATION IS DISRUPTING ALL SYSTEMS!
THIS IS ***EXACTLY*** WHAT I WAS AFRAID OF! WE CANNOT AFFORD ***ANY*** DELAY IN THE DELIVERY TO MAKUS III!
WHAT DO YOU WANT ME TO DO? TURN AROUND AND LEAVE MY CREW BEHIND?
YOU SHOULDN'T HAVE SENT THEM OUT IN THE FIRST PLACE!
CAPTAIN, THERE IS ONE PLANET IN THIS SYSTEM CAPABLE OF SUSTAINING HUMAN LIFE. ***TAURUS II***. IT'S UNEXPLORED. DEAD CENTER OF THE MURASAKI EFFECT.
THAT'S OUR BEST BET.
MR. SULU, SET COURSE FOR TAURUS II!
AYE, SIR!

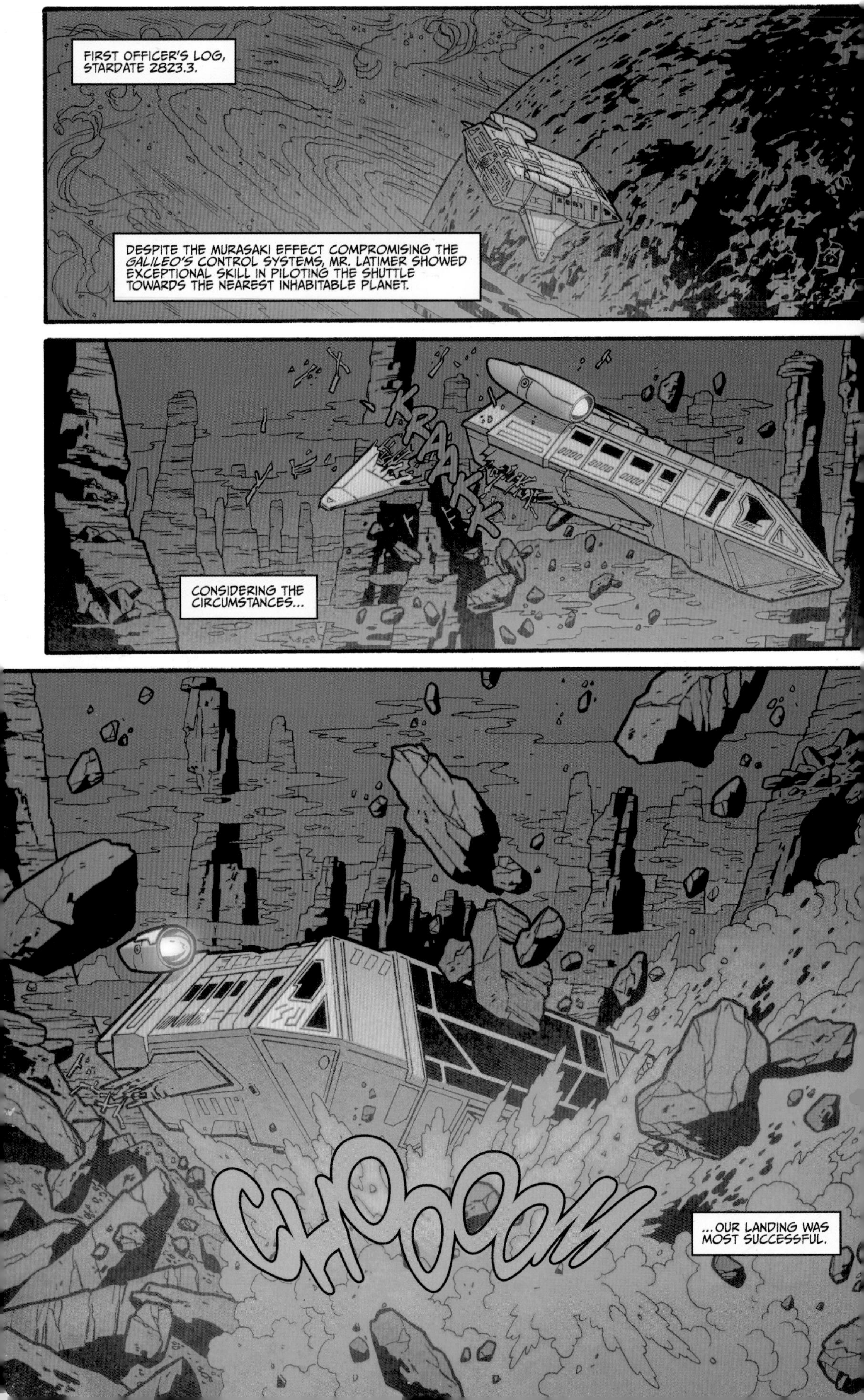
FIRST OFFICER'S LOG, STARDATE 2823.3.
DESPITE THE MURASAKI EFFECT COMPROMISING THE *GALILEO'S* CONTROL SYSTEMS, MR. LATIMER SHOWED EXCEPTIONAL SKILL IN PILOTING THE SHUTTLE TOWARDS THE NEAREST INHABITABLE PLANET.
KRAAKK
CONSIDERING THE CIRCUMSTANCES...
CHOOOOM
...OUR LANDING WAS MOST SUCCESSFUL.

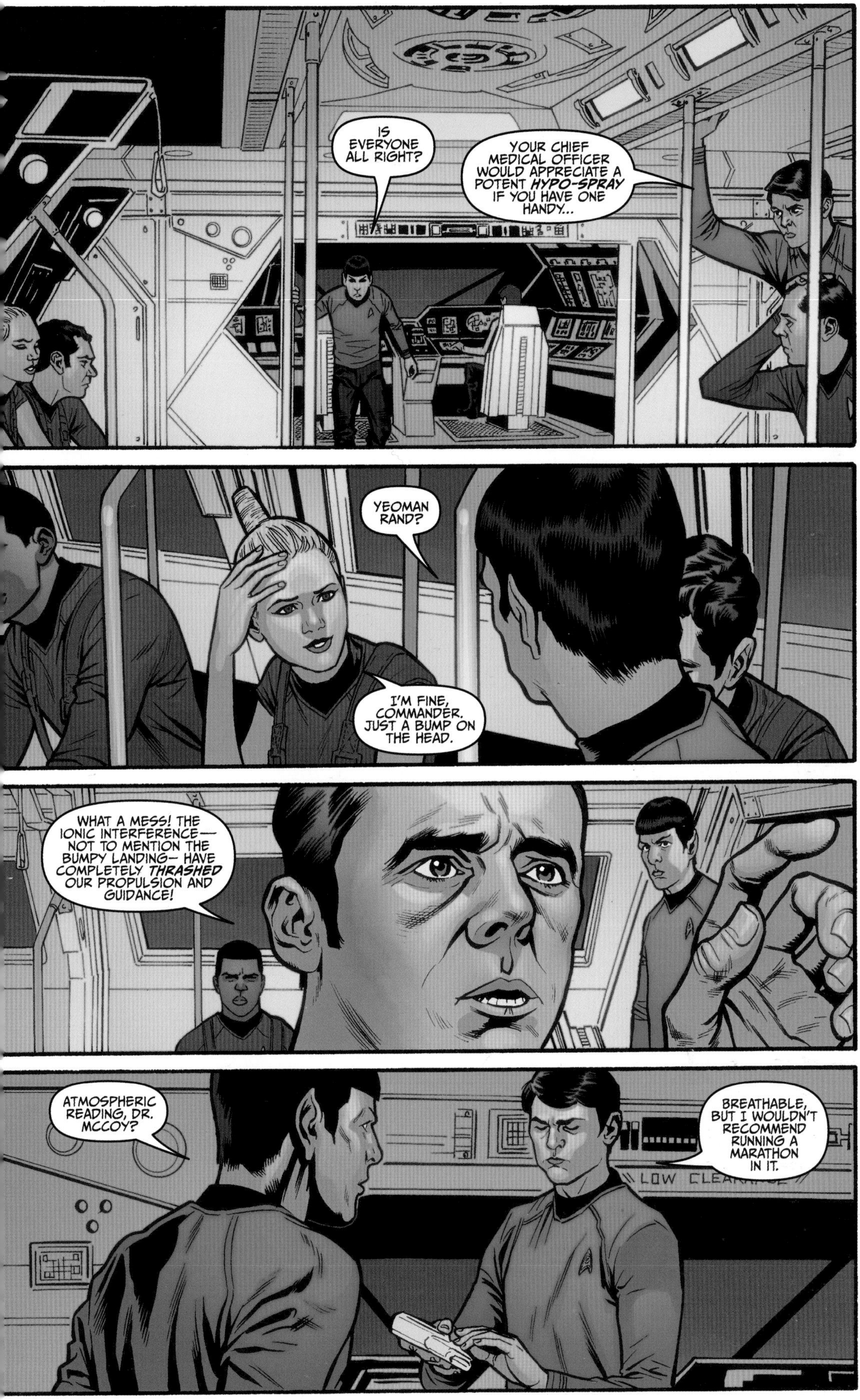
IS EVERYONE ALL RIGHT?
YOUR CHIEF MEDICAL OFFICER WOULD APPRECIATE A POTENT HYPO-SPRAY IF YOU HAVE ONE HANDY...
YEOMAN RAND?
I'M FINE, COMMANDER. JUST A BUMP ON THE HEAD.
WHAT A MESS! THE IONIC INTERFERENCE— NOT TO MENTION THE BUMPY LANDING— HAVE COMPLETELY THRASHED OUR PROPULSION AND GUIDANCE!
ATMOSPHERIC READING, DR. MCCOY?
BREATHABLE, BUT I WOULDN'T RECOMMEND RUNNING A MARATHON IN IT.

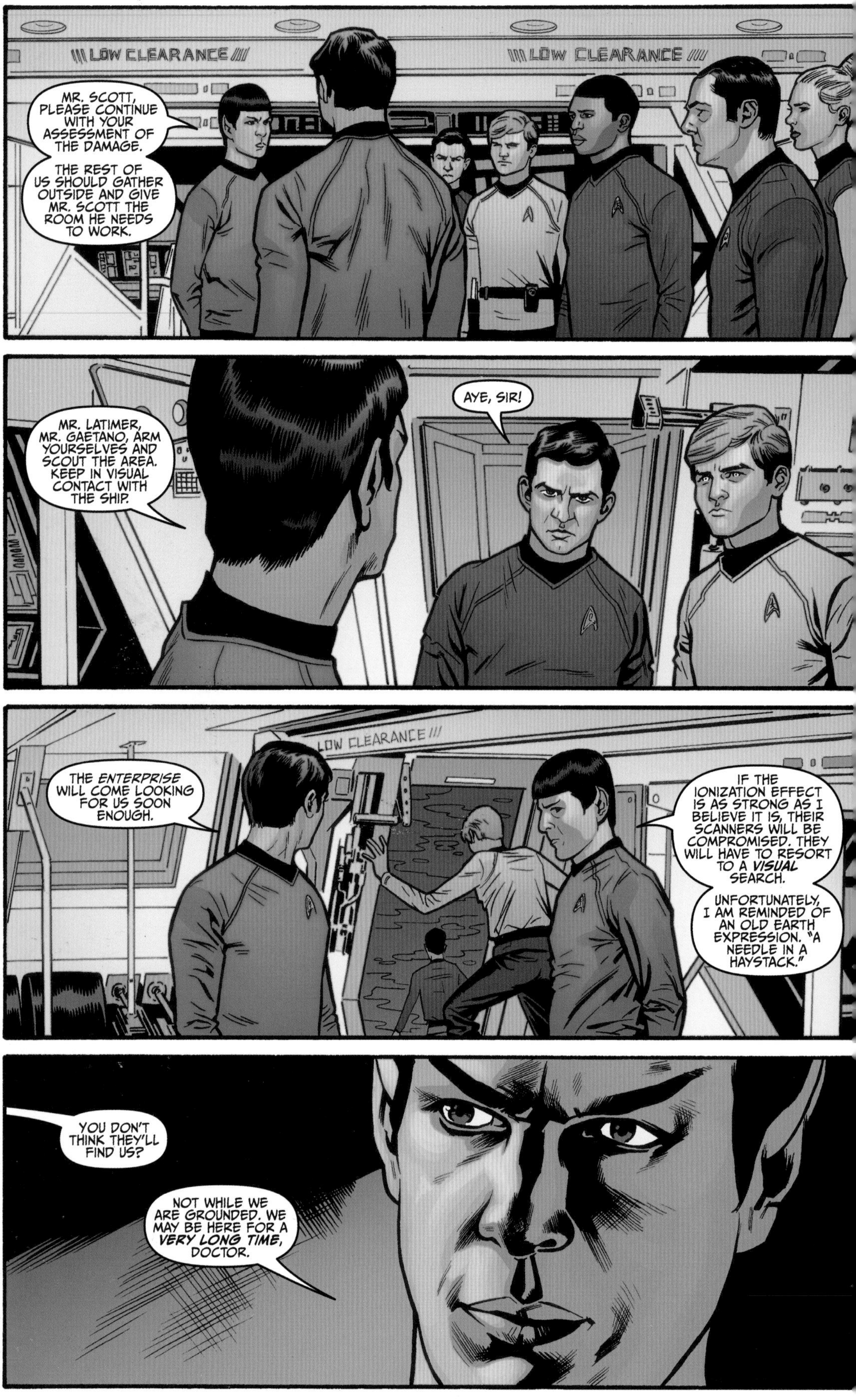
LOW CLEARANCE
LOW CLEARANCE
MR. SCOTT, PLEASE CONTINUE WITH YOUR ASSESSMENT OF THE DAMAGE.
THE REST OF US SHOULD GATHER OUTSIDE AND GIVE MR. SCOTT THE ROOM HE NEEDS TO WORK.
MR. LATIMER, MR. GAETANO, ARM YOURSELVES AND SCOUT THE AREA. KEEP IN VISUAL CONTACT WITH THE SHIP.
AYE, SIR!
LOW CLEARANCE
THE *ENTERPRISE* WILL COME LOOKING FOR US SOON ENOUGH.
IF THE IONIZATION EFFECT IS AS STRONG AS I BELIEVE IT IS, THEIR SCANNERS WILL BE COMPROMISED. THEY WILL HAVE TO RESORT TO A ***VISUAL*** SEARCH.
UNFORTUNATELY, I AM REMINDED OF AN OLD EARTH EXPRESSION. "A NEEDLE IN A HAYSTACK."
YOU DON'T THINK THEY'LL FIND US?
NOT WHILE WE ARE GROUNDED. WE MAY BE HERE FOR A ***VERY LONG TIME***, DOCTOR.

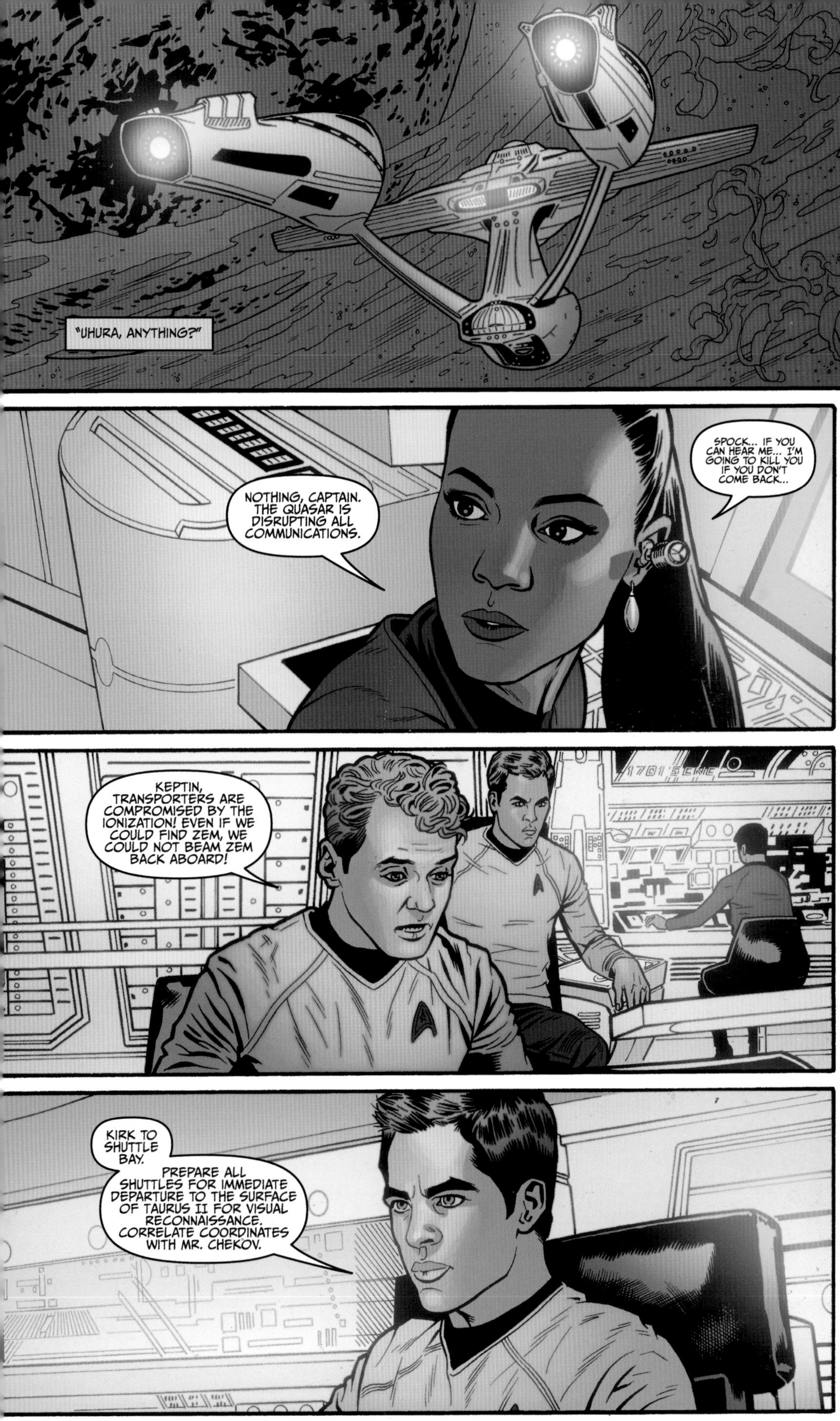
"UHURA, ANYTHING?"
NOTHING, CAPTAIN. THE QUASAR IS DISRUPTING ALL COMMUNICATIONS.
SPOCK... IF YOU CAN HEAR ME... I'M GOING TO KILL YOU IF YOU DON'T COME BACK...
KEPTIN, TRANSPORTERS ARE COMPROMISED BY THE IONIZATION! EVEN IF WE COULD FIND ZEM, WE COULD NOT BEAM ZEM BACK ABOARD!
KIRK TO SHUTTLE BAY.
PREPARE ALL SHUTTLES FOR IMMEDIATE DEPARTURE TO THE SURFACE OF TAURUS II FOR VISUAL RECONNAISSANCE. CORRELATE COORDINATES WITH MR. CHEKOV.

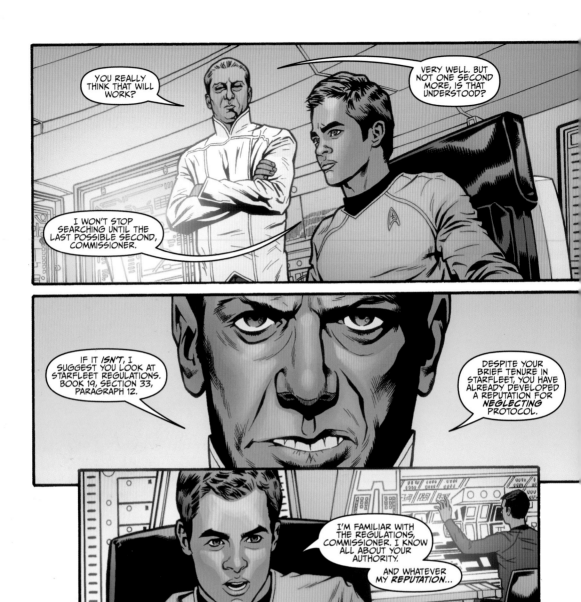

YOU REALLY THINK THAT WILL WORK?

VERY WELL. BUT NOT ONE SECOND MORE, IS THAT UNDERSTOOD?

I WON'T STOP SEARCHING UNTIL THE LAST POSSIBLE SECOND, COMMISSIONER.

IF IT *ISN'T*, I SUGGEST YOU LOOK AT STARFLEET REGULATIONS. BOOK 19, SECTION 33, PARAGRAPH 12.

DESPITE YOUR BRIEF TENURE IN STARFLEET, YOU HAVE ALREADY DEVELOPED A REPUTATION FOR *NEGLECTING* PROTOCOL.

I'M FAMILIAR WITH THE REGULATIONS, COMMISSIONER. I KNOW ALL ABOUT YOUR AUTHORITY.

AND WHATEVER MY *REPUTATION*...

"...I WON'T GIVE UP ON MY *CREW*."

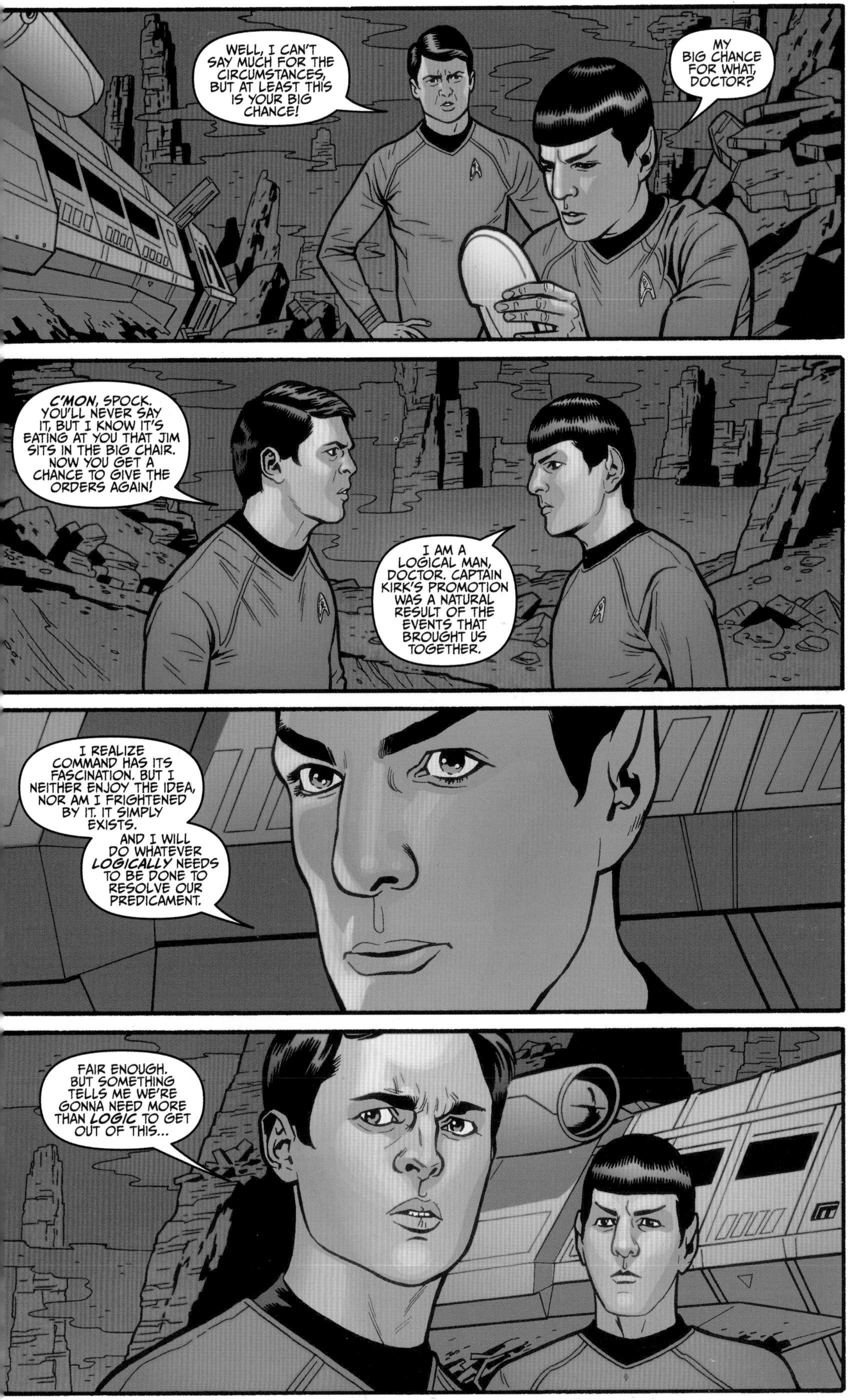
WELL, I CAN'T SAY MUCH FOR THE CIRCUMSTANCES, BUT AT LEAST THIS IS YOUR BIG CHANCE!
MY BIG CHANCE FOR WHAT, DOCTOR?
C'MON, SPOCK. YOU'LL NEVER SAY IT, BUT I KNOW IT'S EATING AT YOU THAT JIM SITS IN THE BIG CHAIR. NOW YOU GET A CHANCE TO GIVE THE ORDERS AGAIN!
I AM A LOGICAL MAN, DOCTOR. CAPTAIN KIRK'S PROMOTION WAS A NATURAL RESULT OF THE EVENTS THAT BROUGHT US TOGETHER.
I REALIZE COMMAND HAS ITS FASCINATION. BUT I NEITHER ENJOY THE IDEA, NOR AM I FRIGHTENED BY IT. IT SIMPLY EXISTS.
AND I WILL DO WHATEVER LOGICALLY NEEDS TO BE DONE TO RESOLVE OUR PREDICAMENT.
FAIR ENOUGH. BUT SOMETHING TELLS ME WE'RE GONNA NEED MORE THAN LOGIC TO GET OUT OF THIS...

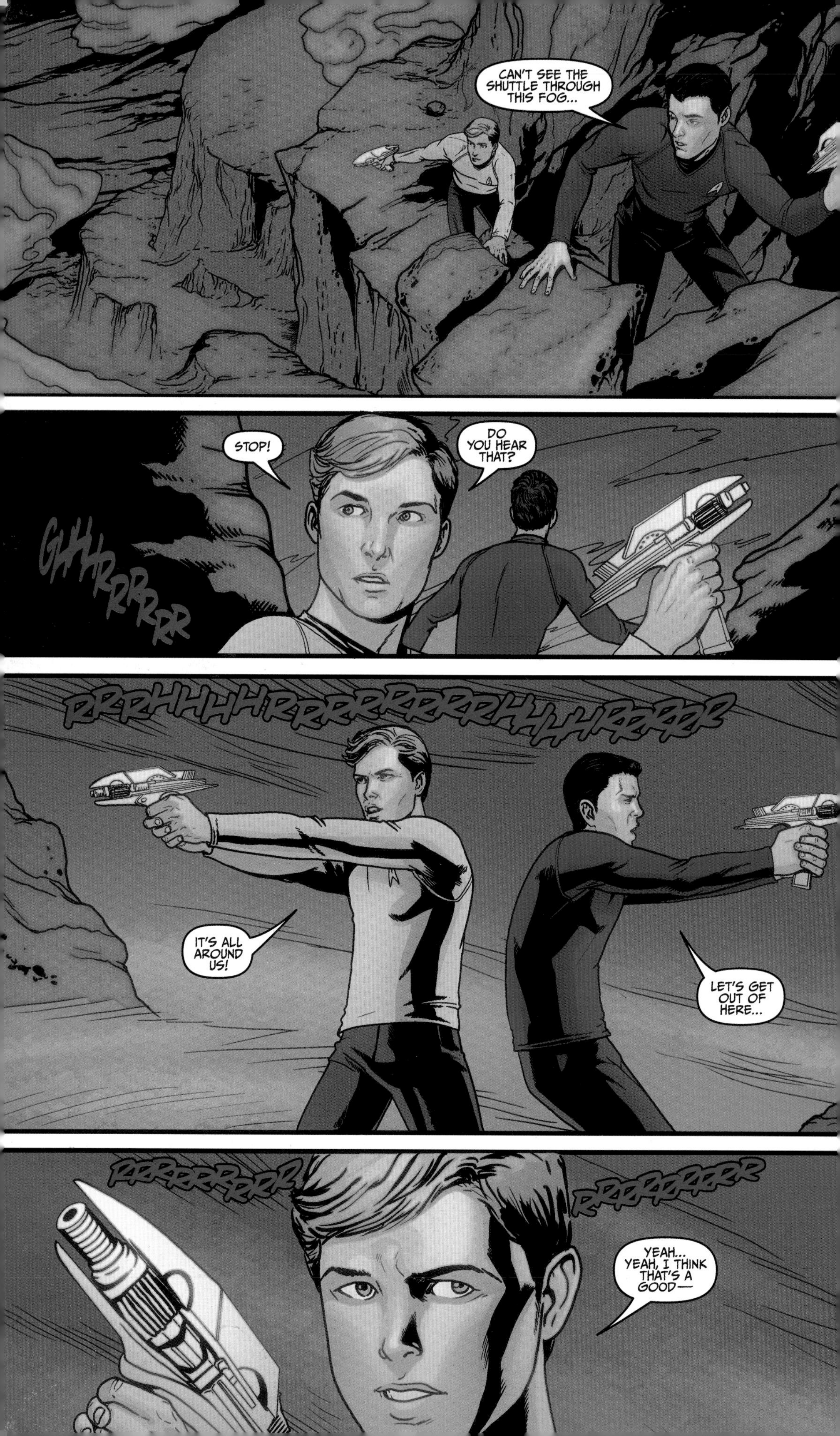
CAN'T SEE THE SHUTTLE THROUGH THIS FOG...
STOP!
DO YOU HEAR THAT?
GHHRRRRRR
RRRHHHHRRRRRRRRHHHHRRRRR
IT'S ALL AROUND US!
LET'S GET OUT OF HERE...
RRRRRRRRRR
RRRRRRRRRR
YEAH... YEAH, I THINK THAT'S A GOOD—

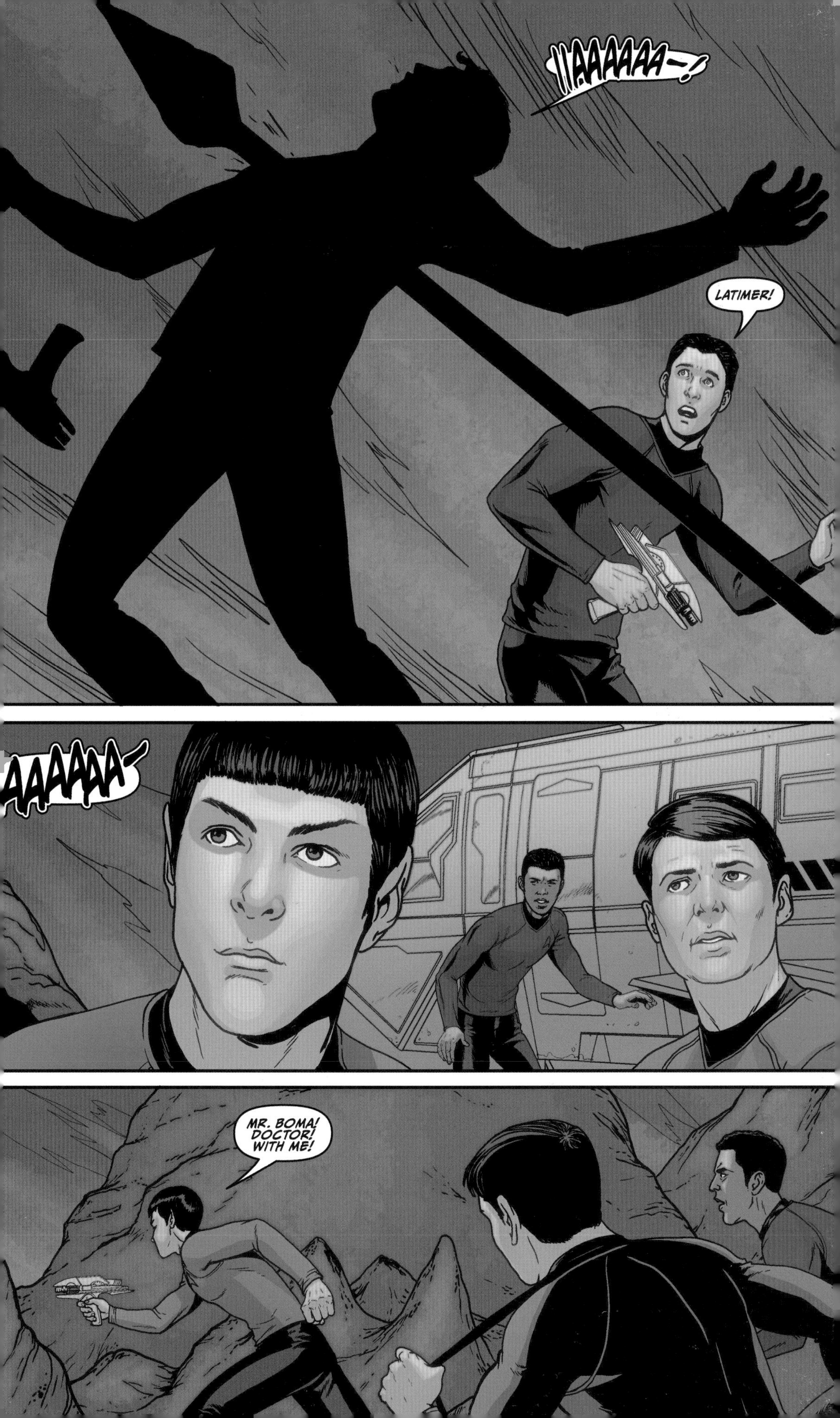

AAAAAA--!
LATIMER!
AAAAAA-
MR. BOMA! DOCTOR! WITH ME!

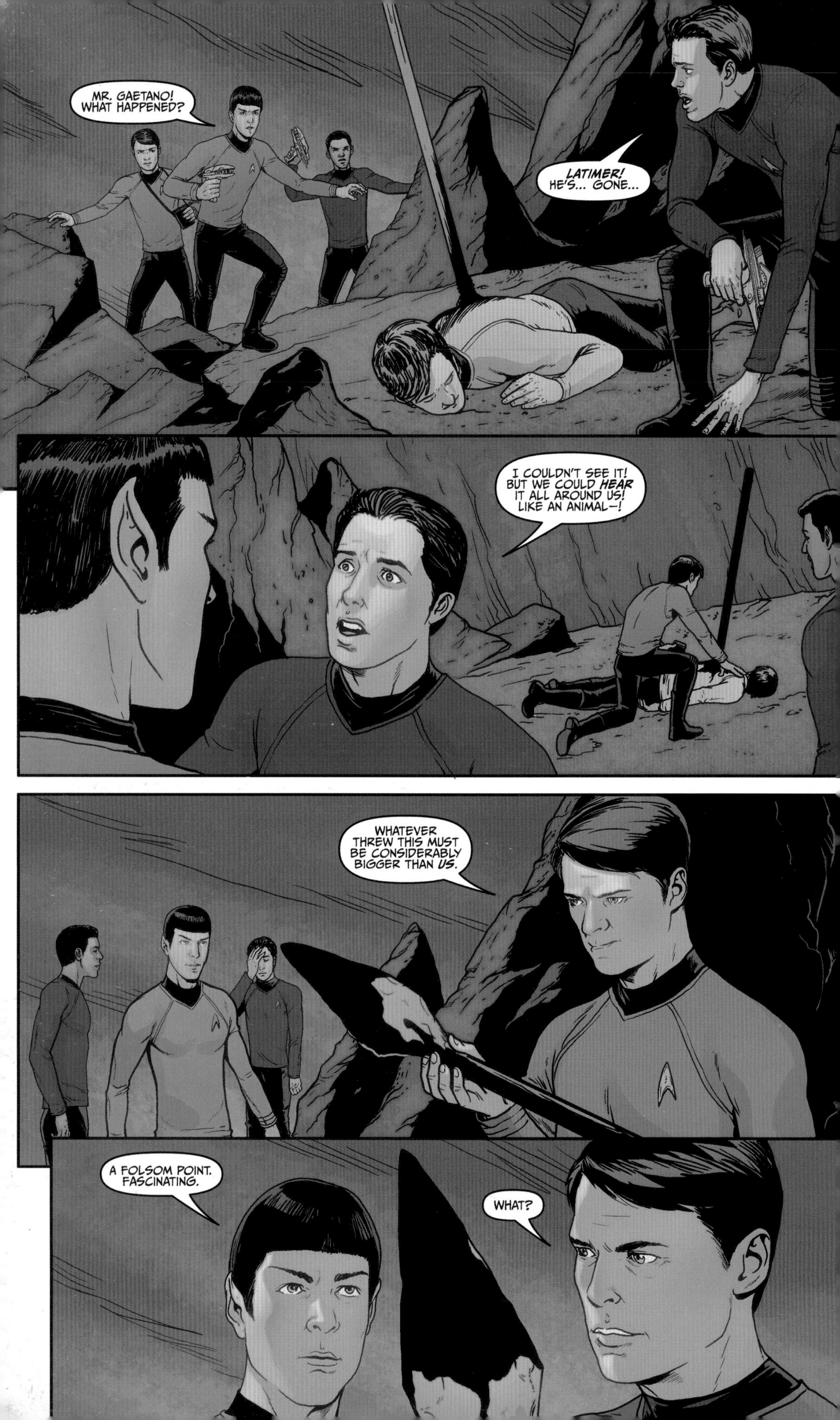
MR. GAETANO! WHAT HAPPENED?
LATIMER! HE'S... GONE...
I COULDN'T SEE IT! BUT WE COULD HEAR IT ALL AROUND US! LIKE AN ANIMAL—!
WHATEVER THREW THIS MUST BE CONSIDERABLY BIGGER THAN US.
A FOLSOM POINT. FASCINATING.
WHAT?

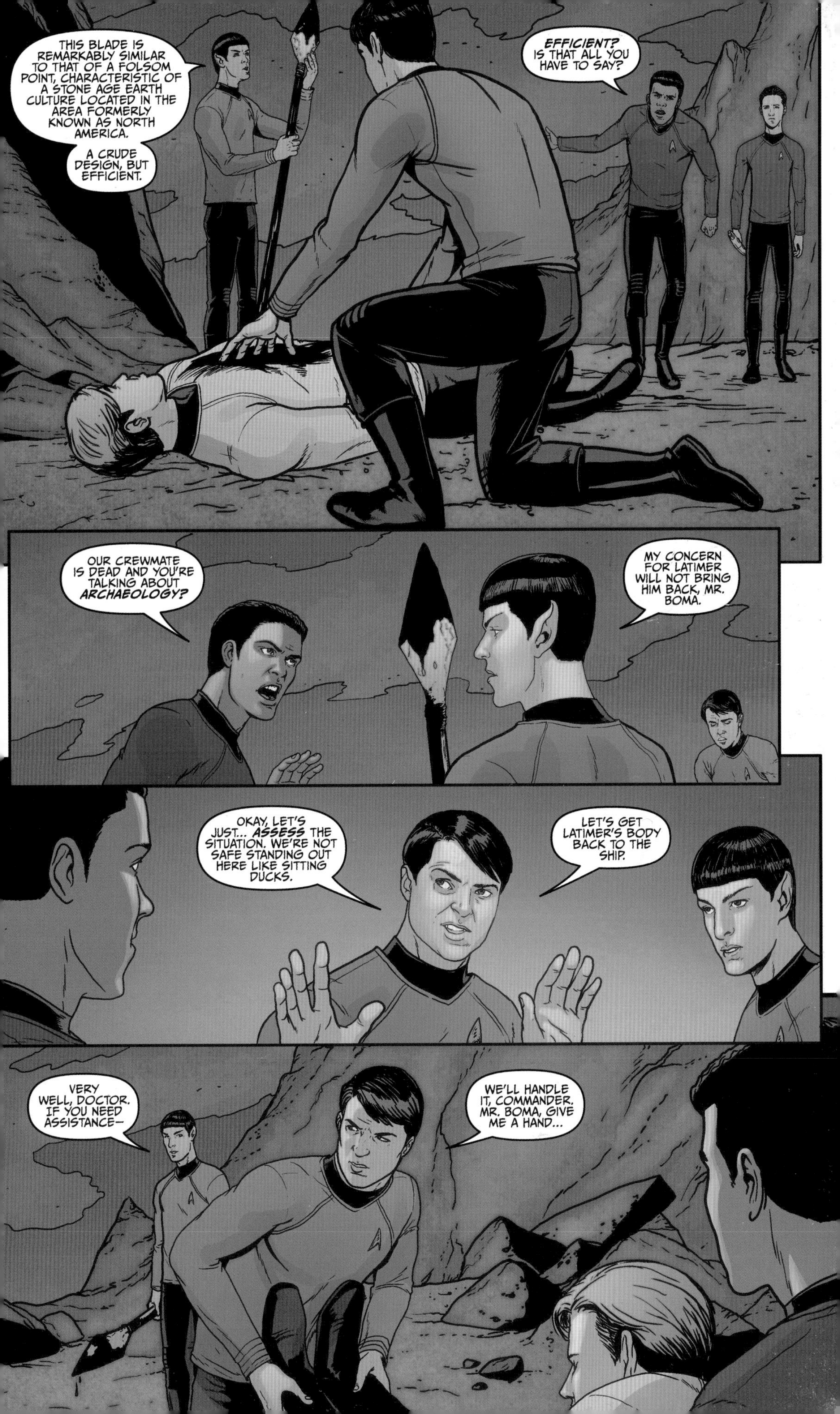

THIS BLADE IS REMARKABLY SIMILAR TO THAT OF A FOLSOM POINT, CHARACTERISTIC OF A STONE AGE EARTH CULTURE LOCATED IN THE AREA FORMERLY KNOWN AS NORTH AMERICA.
A CRUDE DESIGN, BUT EFFICIENT.
EFFICIENT? IS THAT ALL YOU HAVE TO SAY?
OUR CREWMATE IS DEAD AND YOU'RE TALKING ABOUT *ARCHAEOLOGY?*
MY CONCERN FOR LATIMER WILL NOT BRING HIM BACK, MR. BOMA.
OKAY, LET'S JUST... *ASSESS* THE SITUATION. WE'RE NOT SAFE STANDING OUT HERE LIKE SITTING DUCKS.
LET'S GET LATIMER'S BODY BACK TO THE SHIP.
VERY WELL, DOCTOR. IF YOU NEED ASSISTANCE–
WE'LL HANDLE IT, COMMANDER. MR. BOMA, GIVE ME A HAND...

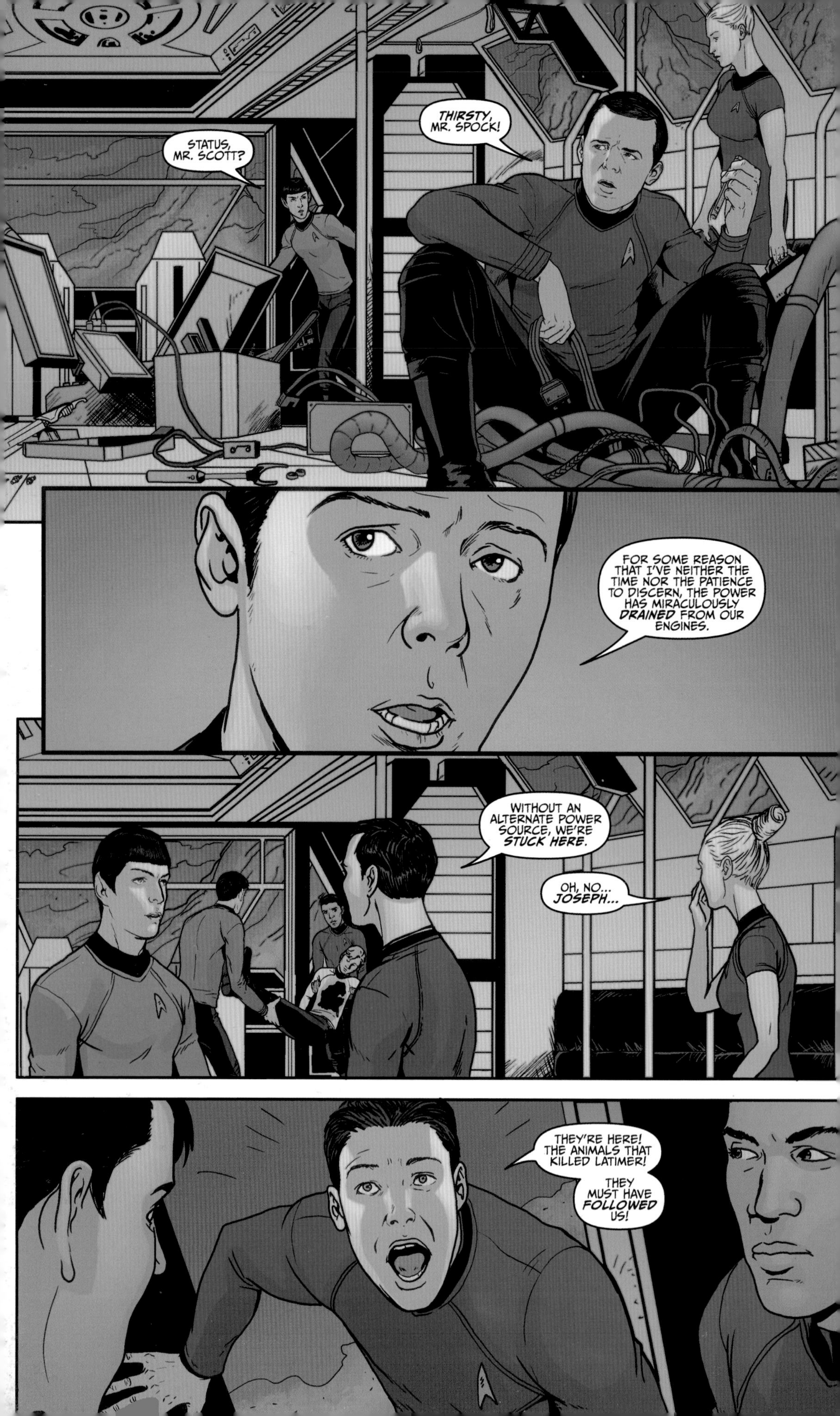
STATUS, MR. SCOTT?
THIRSTY, MR. SPOCK!
FOR SOME REASON THAT I'VE NEITHER THE TIME NOR THE PATIENCE TO DISCERN, THE POWER HAS MIRACULOUSLY DRAINED FROM OUR ENGINES.
WITHOUT AN ALTERNATE POWER SOURCE, WE'RE STUCK HERE.
OH, NO... JOSEPH...
THEY'RE HERE! THE ANIMALS THAT KILLED LATIMER!
THEY MUST HAVE FOLLOWED US!

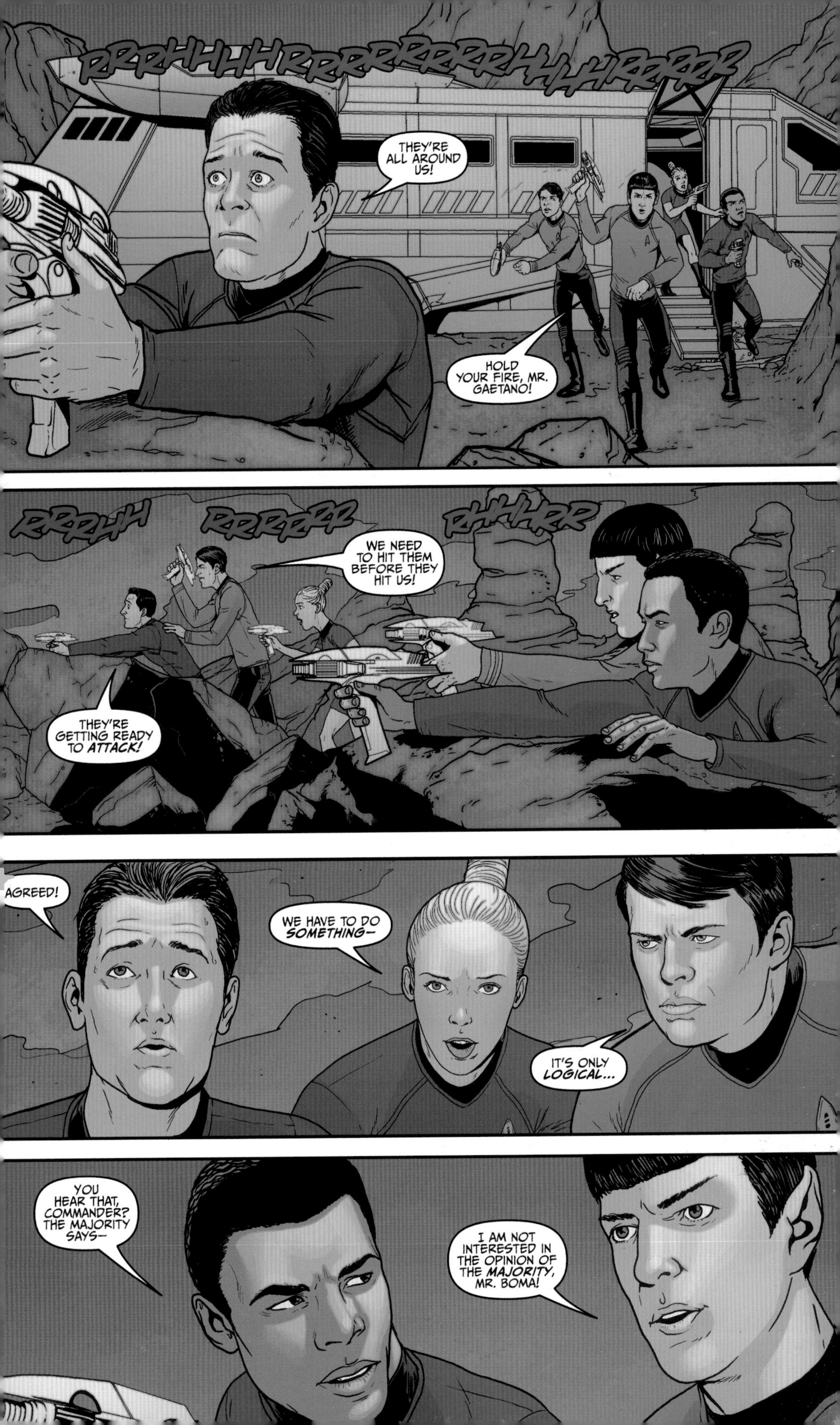
RRRHHHHRRRRRRRRRHHHHRRRRR
THEY'RE ALL AROUND US!
HOLD YOUR FIRE, MR. GAETANO!
RRRRHH
RRRRRR
RHHHRR
WE NEED TO HIT THEM BEFORE THEY HIT US!
THEY'RE GETTING READY TO ATTACK!
AGREED!
WE HAVE TO DO SOMETHING—
IT'S ONLY LOGICAL...
YOU HEAR THAT, COMMANDER? THE MAJORITY SAYS—
I AM NOT INTERESTED IN THE OPINION OF THE MAJORITY, MR. BOMA!

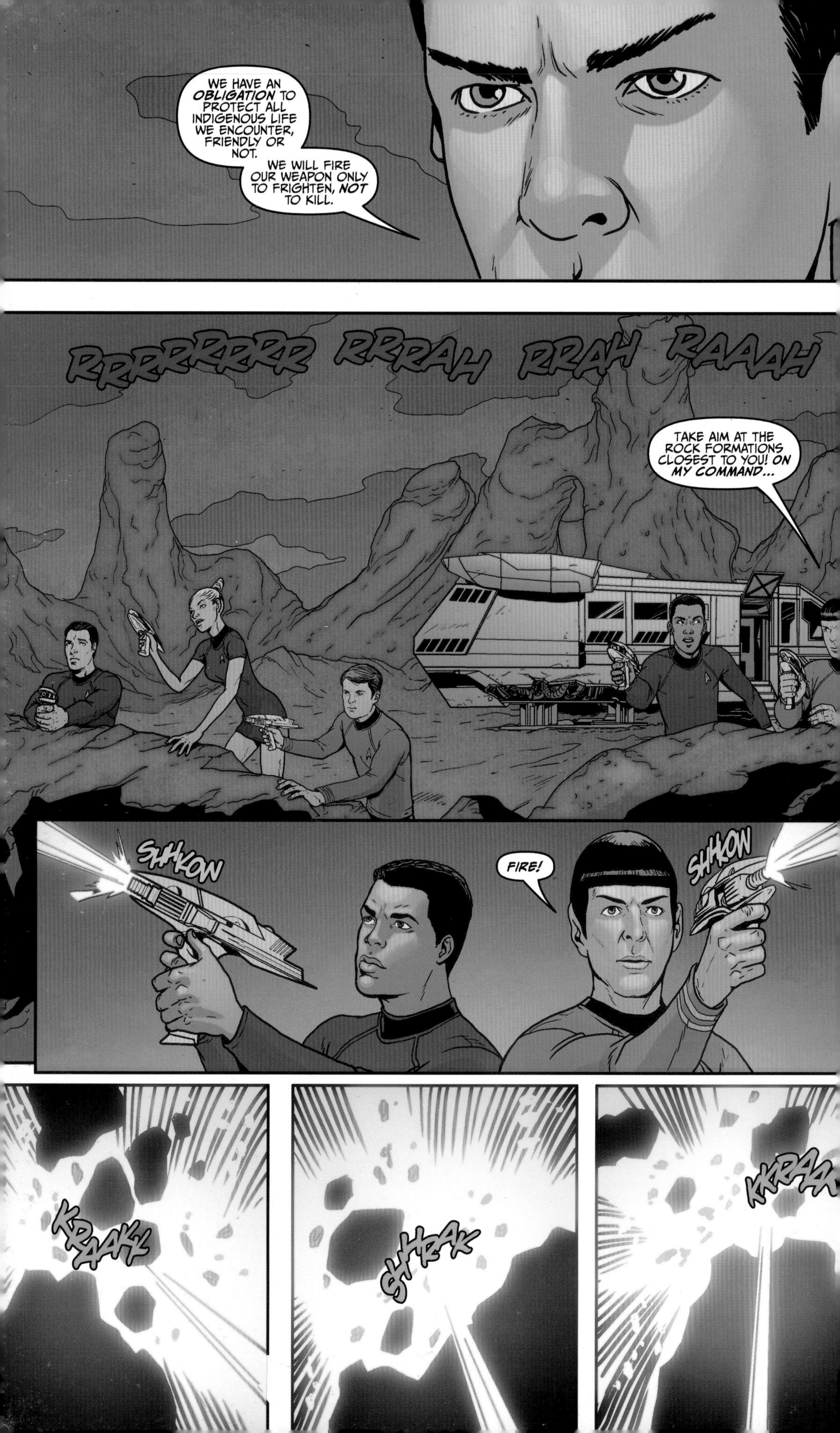
WE HAVE AN *OBLIGATION* TO PROTECT ALL INDIGENOUS LIFE WE ENCOUNTER, FRIENDLY OR NOT.
WE WILL FIRE OUR WEAPON ONLY TO FRIGHTEN, *NOT* TO KILL.
RRRRRRRR RRRAH RRAH RAAAH
TAKE AIM AT THE ROCK FORMATIONS CLOSEST TO YOU! *ON MY COMMAND...*
SHHKOW
FIRE!
SHHKOW
KRAAK
SHRAK
KKRAA

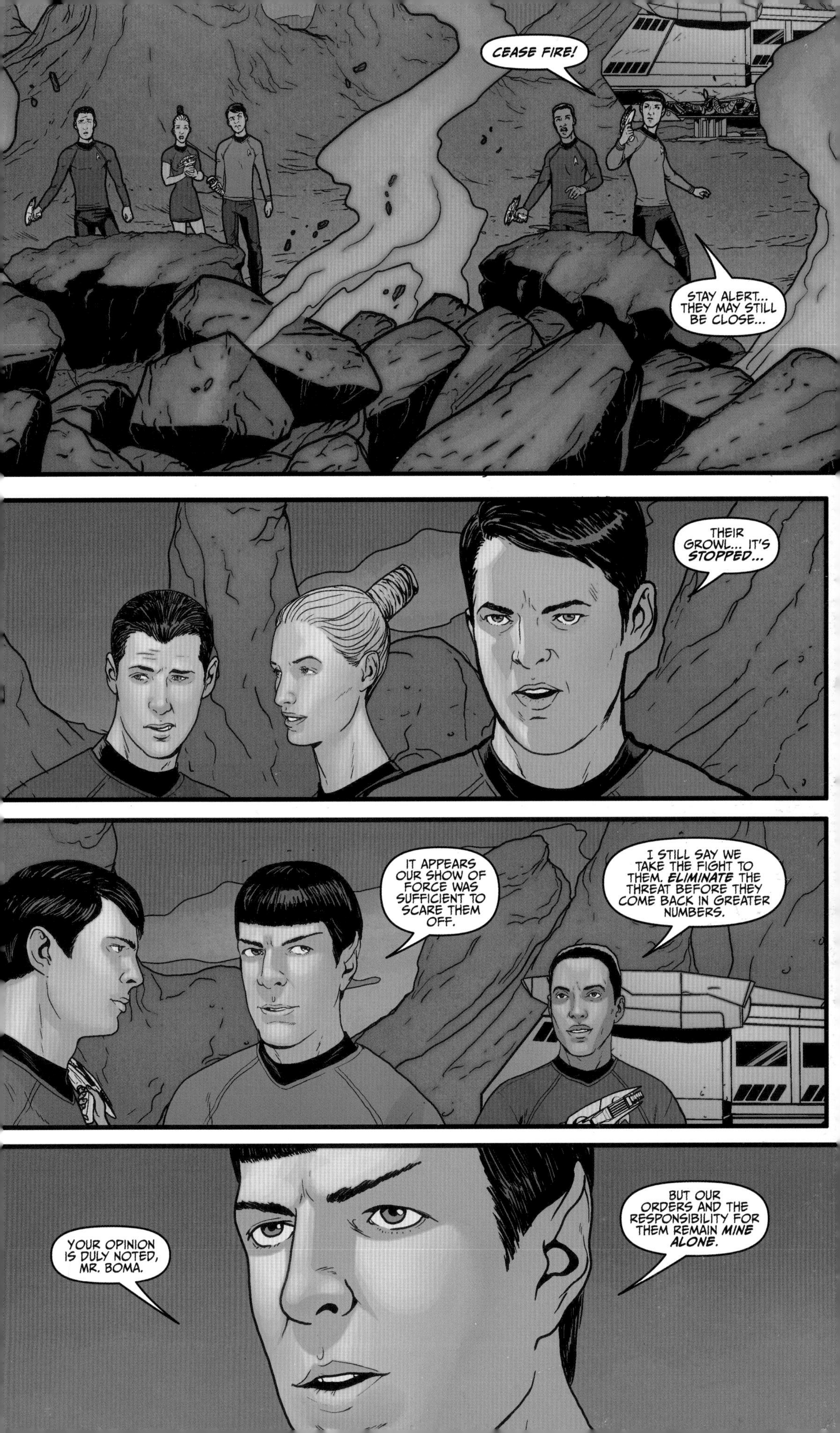
CEASE FIRE!
STAY ALERT... THEY MAY STILL BE CLOSE...
THEIR GROWL... IT'S STOPPED...
IT APPEARS OUR SHOW OF FORCE WAS SUFFICIENT TO SCARE THEM OFF.
I STILL SAY WE TAKE THE FIGHT TO THEM. ELIMINATE THE THREAT BEFORE THEY COME BACK IN GREATER NUMBERS.
YOUR OPINION IS DULY NOTED, MR. BOMA.
BUT OUR ORDERS AND THE RESPONSIBILITY FOR THEM REMAIN MINE ALONE.

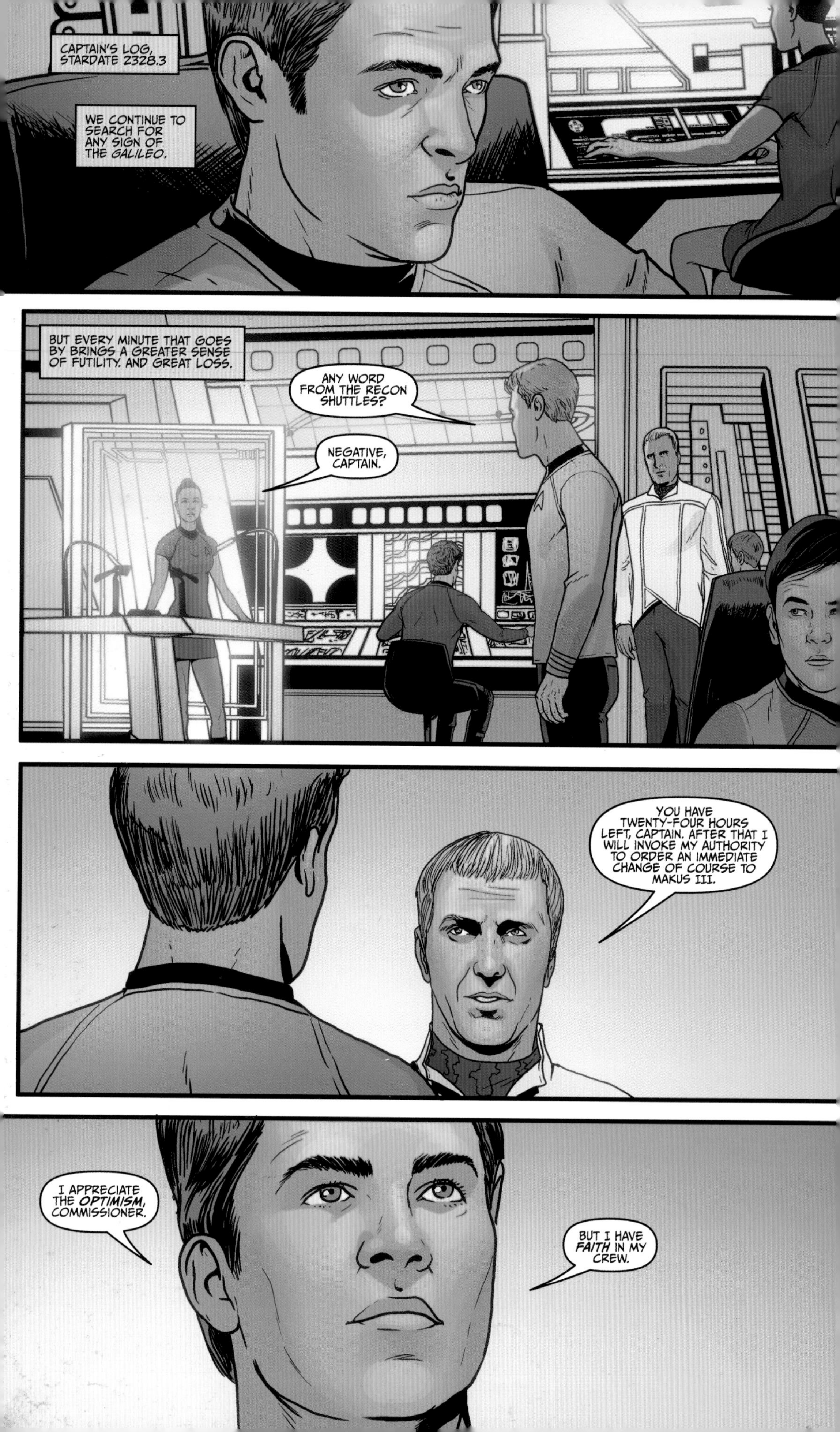
CAPTAIN'S LOG, STARDATE 2328.3
WE CONTINUE TO SEARCH FOR ANY SIGN OF THE GALILEO.
BUT EVERY MINUTE THAT GOES BY BRINGS A GREATER SENSE OF FUTILITY. AND GREAT LOSS.
ANY WORD FROM THE RECON SHUTTLES?
NEGATIVE, CAPTAIN.
YOU HAVE TWENTY-FOUR HOURS LEFT, CAPTAIN. AFTER THAT I WILL INVOKE MY AUTHORITY TO ORDER AN IMMEDIATE CHANGE OF COURSE TO MAKUS III.
I APPRECIATE THE OPTIMISM, COMMISSIONER.
BUT I HAVE FAITH IN MY CREW.

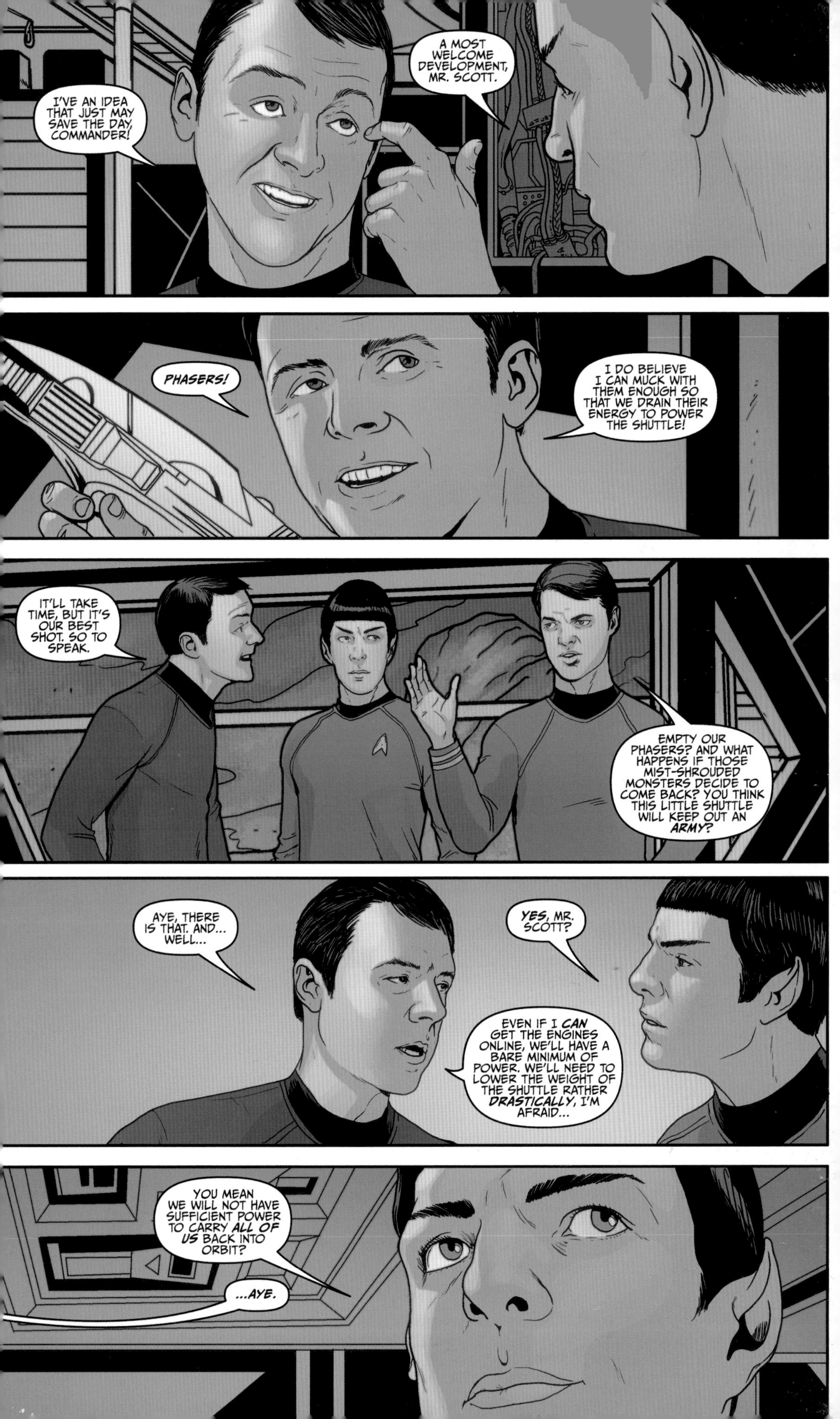
I'VE AN IDEA THAT JUST MAY SAVE THE DAY, COMMANDER!
A MOST WELCOME DEVELOPMENT, MR. SCOTT.
PHASERS!
I DO BELIEVE I CAN MUCK WITH THEM ENOUGH SO THAT WE DRAIN THEIR ENERGY TO POWER THE SHUTTLE!
IT'LL TAKE TIME, BUT IT'S OUR BEST SHOT. SO TO SPEAK.
EMPTY OUR PHASERS? AND WHAT HAPPENS IF THOSE MIST-SHROUDED MONSTERS DECIDE TO COME BACK? YOU THINK THIS LITTLE SHUTTLE WILL KEEP OUT AN ARMY?
AYE, THERE IS THAT. AND... WELL...
YES, MR. SCOTT?
EVEN IF I CAN GET THE ENGINES ONLINE, WE'LL HAVE A BARE MINIMUM OF POWER. WE'LL NEED TO LOWER THE WEIGHT OF THE SHUTTLE RATHER DRASTICALLY, I'M AFRAID...
YOU MEAN WE WILL NOT HAVE SUFFICIENT POWER TO CARRY ALL OF US BACK INTO ORBIT?
...AYE.

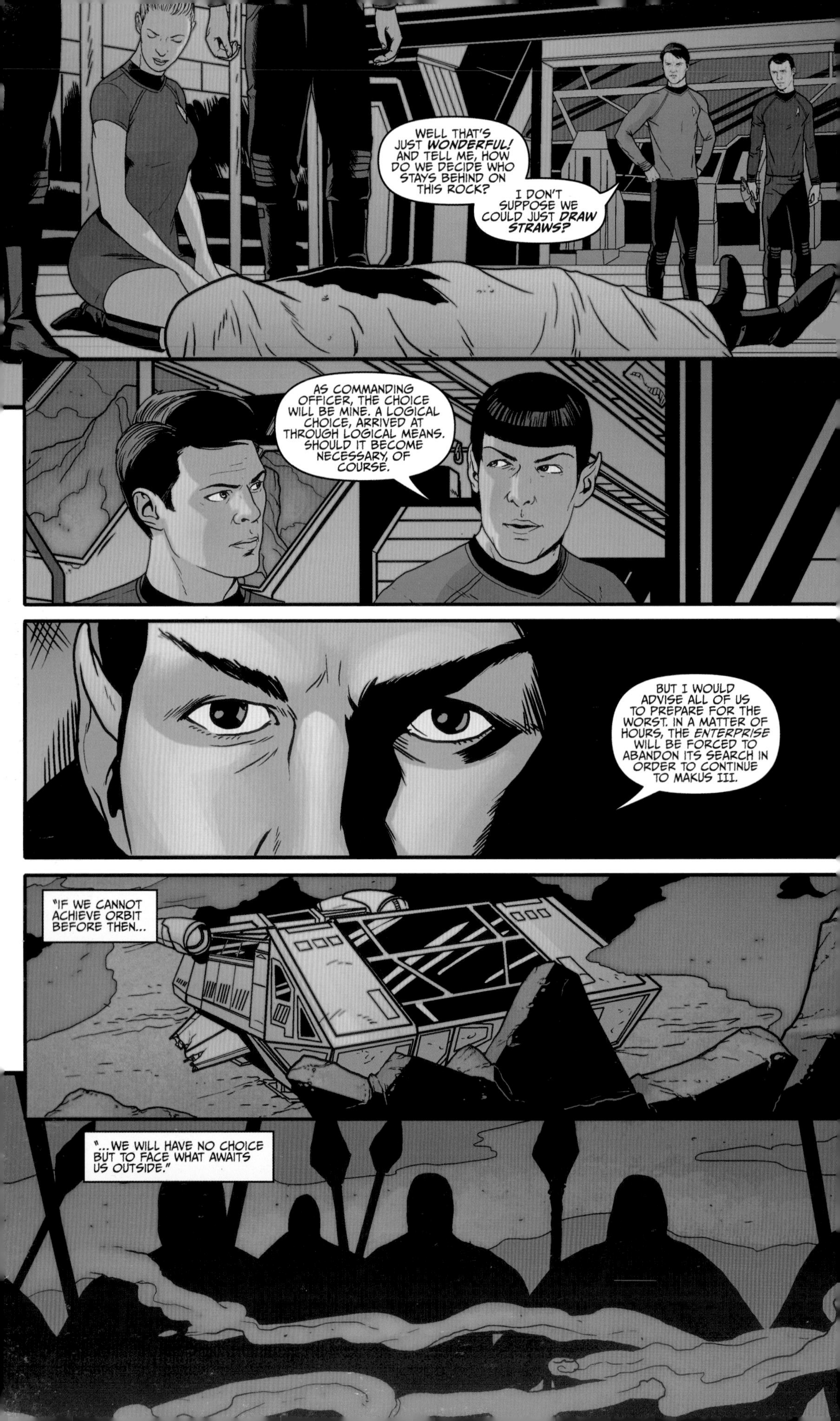

WELL THAT'S JUST WONDERFUL! AND TELL ME, HOW DO WE DECIDE WHO STAYS BEHIND ON THIS ROCK?
I DON'T SUPPOSE WE COULD JUST DRAW STRAWS?
AS COMMANDING OFFICER, THE CHOICE WILL BE MINE. A LOGICAL CHOICE, ARRIVED AT THROUGH LOGICAL MEANS. SHOULD IT BECOME NECESSARY, OF COURSE.
BUT I WOULD ADVISE ALL OF US TO PREPARE FOR THE WORST. IN A MATTER OF HOURS, THE ENTERPRISE WILL BE FORCED TO ABANDON ITS SEARCH IN ORDER TO CONTINUE TO MAKUS III.
"IF WE CANNOT ACHIEVE ORBIT BEFORE THEN...
"...WE WILL HAVE NO CHOICE BUT TO FACE WHAT AWAITS US OUTSIDE."

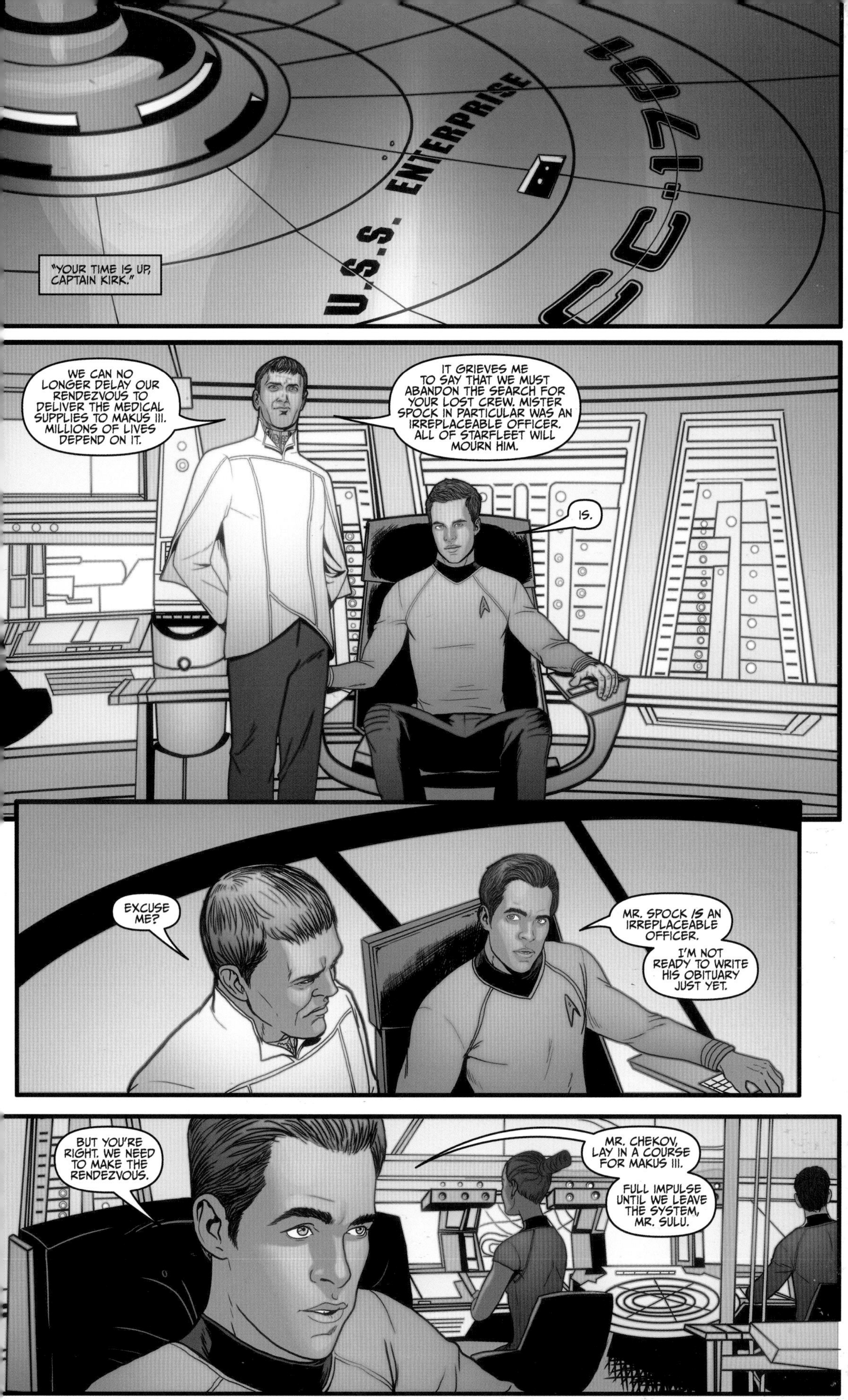
"YOUR TIME IS UP, CAPTAIN KIRK."
U.S.S. ENTERPRISE
NCC-1701
WE CAN NO LONGER DELAY OUR RENDEZVOUS TO DELIVER THE MEDICAL SUPPLIES TO MAKUS III. MILLIONS OF LIVES DEPEND ON IT.
IT GRIEVES ME TO SAY THAT WE MUST ABANDON THE SEARCH FOR YOUR LOST CREW. MISTER SPOCK IN PARTICULAR WAS AN IRREPLACEABLE OFFICER. ALL OF STARFLEET WILL MOURN HIM.
IS.
EXCUSE ME?
MR. SPOCK *IS* AN IRREPLACEABLE OFFICER.
I'M NOT READY TO WRITE HIS OBITUARY JUST YET.
BUT YOU'RE RIGHT. WE NEED TO MAKE THE RENDEZVOUS.
MR. CHEKOV, LAY IN A COURSE FOR MAKUS III.
FULL IMPULSE UNTIL WE LEAVE THE SYSTEM, MR. SULU.

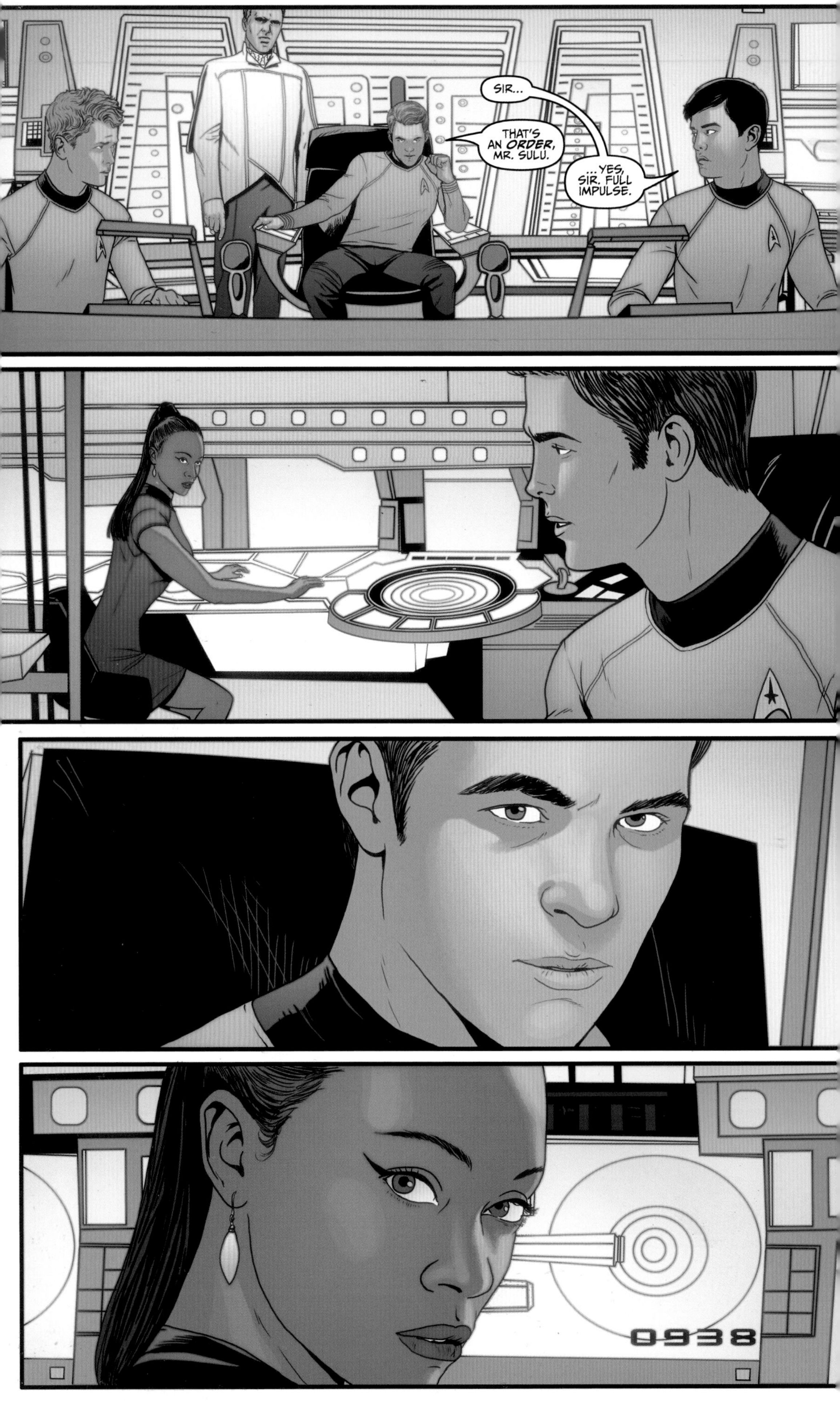
SIR...
THAT'S AN ORDER, MR. SULU.
...YES, SIR. FULL IMPULSE.
0938

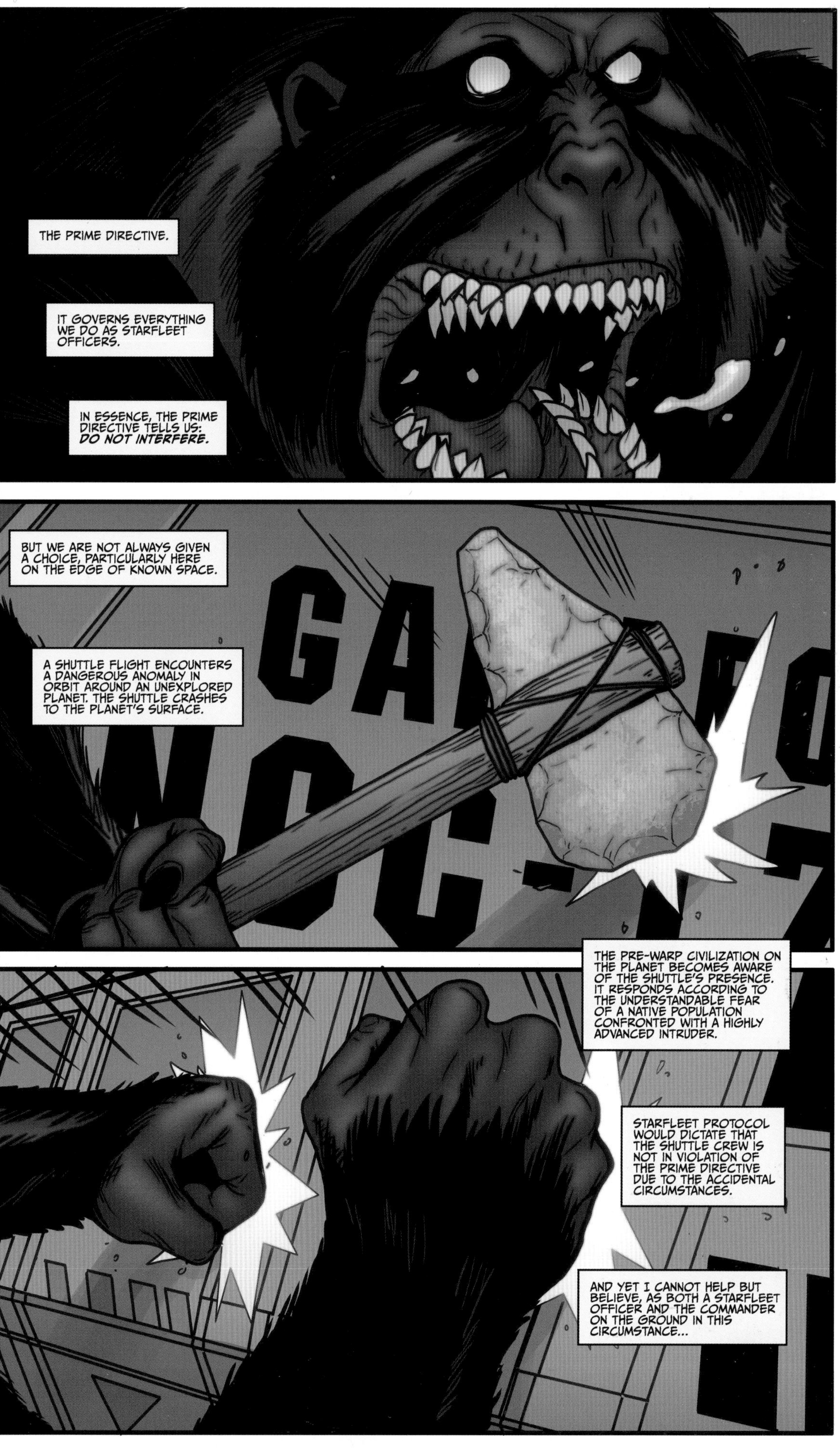
THE PRIME DIRECTIVE.
IT GOVERNS EVERYTHING WE DO AS STARFLEET OFFICERS.
IN ESSENCE, THE PRIME DIRECTIVE TELLS US: *DO NOT INTERFERE.*
BUT WE ARE NOT ALWAYS GIVEN A CHOICE, PARTICULARLY HERE ON THE EDGE OF KNOWN SPACE.
A SHUTTLE FLIGHT ENCOUNTERS A DANGEROUS ANOMALY IN ORBIT AROUND AN UNEXPLORED PLANET. THE SHUTTLE CRASHES TO THE PLANET'S SURFACE.
THE PRE-WARP CIVILIZATION ON THE PLANET BECOMES AWARE OF THE SHUTTLE'S PRESENCE. IT RESPONDS ACCORDING TO THE UNDERSTANDABLE FEAR OF A NATIVE POPULATION CONFRONTED WITH A HIGHLY ADVANCED INTRUDER.
STARFLEET PROTOCOL WOULD DICTATE THAT THE SHUTTLE CREW IS NOT IN VIOLATION OF THE PRIME DIRECTIVE DUE TO THE ACCIDENTAL CIRCUMSTANCES.
AND YET I CANNOT HELP BUT BELIEVE, AS BOTH A STARFLEET OFFICER AND THE COMMANDER ON THE GROUND IN THIS CIRCUMSTANCE...

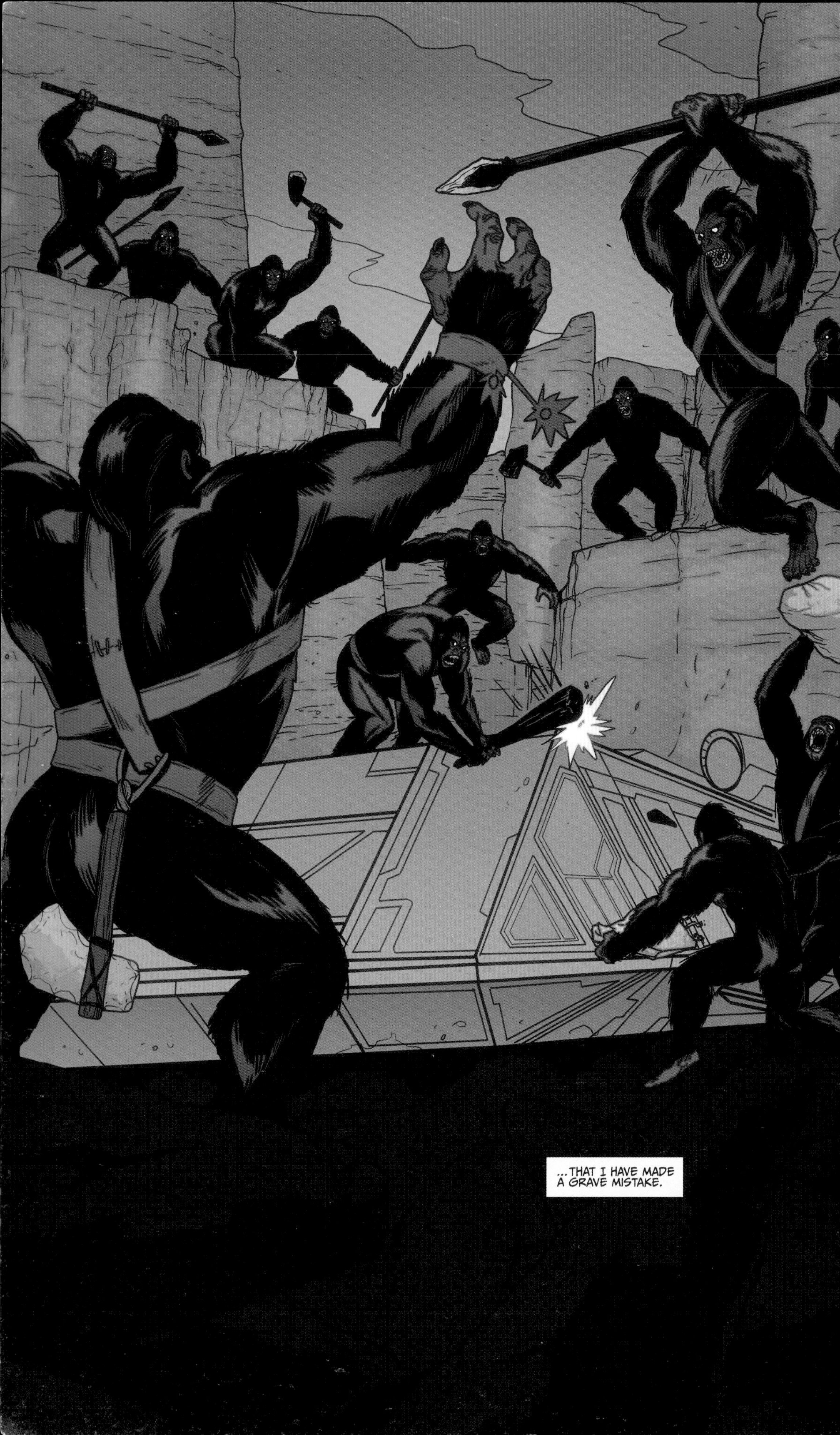

...THAT I HAVE MADE A GRAVE MISTAKE.

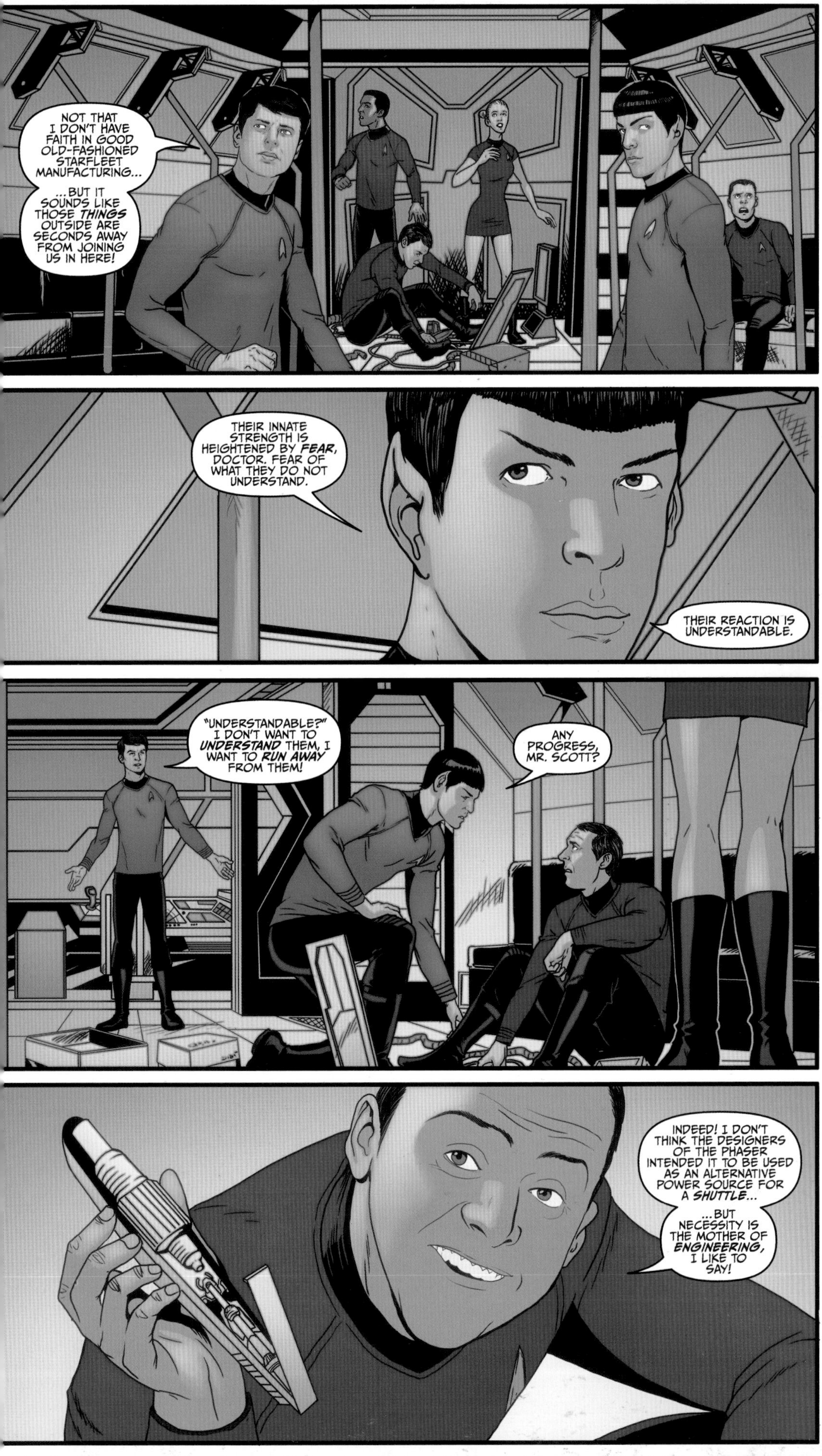
NOT THAT I DON'T HAVE FAITH IN GOOD OLD-FASHIONED STARFLEET MANUFACTURING...
...BUT IT SOUNDS LIKE THOSE THINGS OUTSIDE ARE SECONDS AWAY FROM JOINING US IN HERE!
THEIR INNATE STRENGTH IS HEIGHTENED BY FEAR, DOCTOR. FEAR OF WHAT THEY DO NOT UNDERSTAND.
THEIR REACTION IS UNDERSTANDABLE.
"UNDERSTANDABLE?" I DON'T WANT TO UNDERSTAND THEM, I WANT TO RUN AWAY FROM THEM!
ANY PROGRESS, MR. SCOTT?
INDEED! I DON'T THINK THE DESIGNERS OF THE PHASER INTENDED IT TO BE USED AS AN ALTERNATIVE POWER SOURCE FOR A SHUTTLE...
...BUT NECESSITY IS THE MOTHER OF ENGINEERING, I LIKE TO SAY!

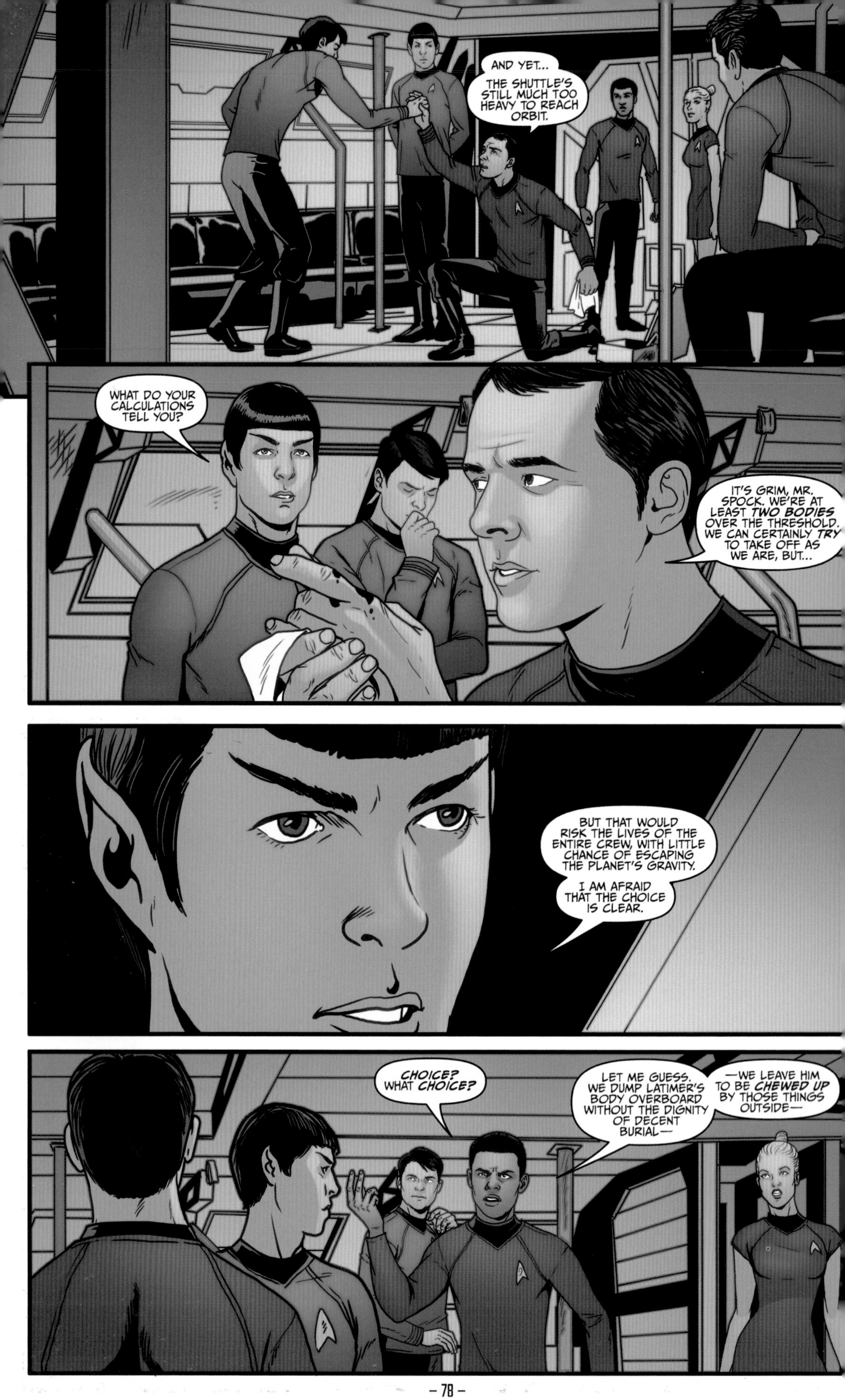
AND YET... THE SHUTTLE'S STILL MUCH TOO HEAVY TO REACH ORBIT.
WHAT DO YOUR CALCULATIONS TELL YOU?
IT'S GRIM, MR. SPOCK. WE'RE AT LEAST *TWO BODIES* OVER THE THRESHOLD. WE CAN CERTAINLY *TRY* TO TAKE OFF AS WE ARE, BUT...
BUT THAT WOULD RISK THE LIVES OF THE ENTIRE CREW, WITH LITTLE CHANCE OF ESCAPING THE PLANET'S GRAVITY.
I AM AFRAID THAT THE CHOICE IS CLEAR.
CHOICE? WHAT *CHOICE?*
LET ME GUESS. WE DUMP LATIMER'S BODY OVERBOARD WITHOUT THE DIGNITY OF DECENT BURIAL—
—WE LEAVE HIM TO BE *CHEWED UP* BY THOSE THINGS OUTSIDE—

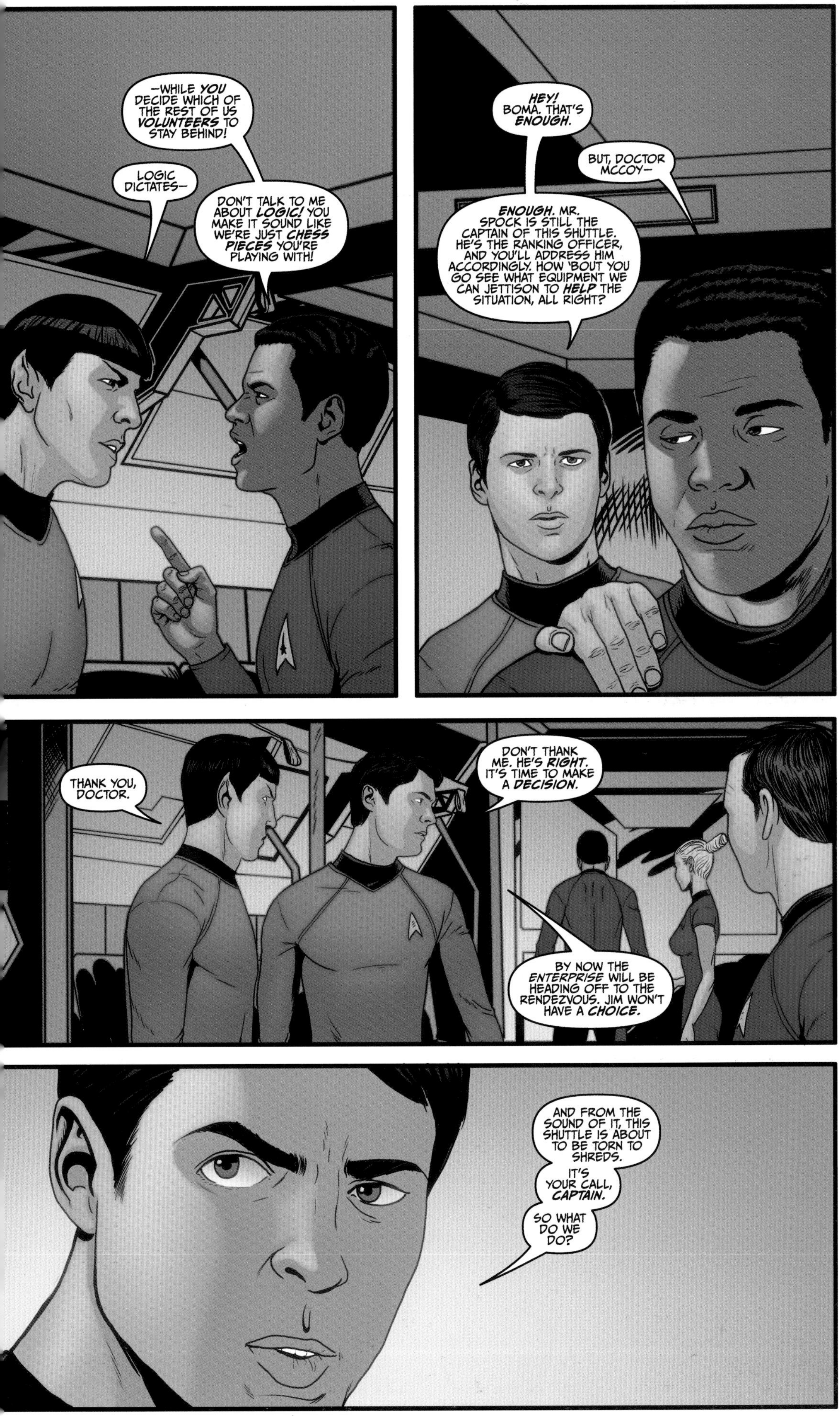

—WHILE YOU DECIDE WHICH OF THE REST OF US VOLUNTEERS TO STAY BEHIND!
LOGIC DICTATES—
DON'T TALK TO ME ABOUT LOGIC! YOU MAKE IT SOUND LIKE WE'RE JUST CHESS PIECES YOU'RE PLAYING WITH!
HEY! BOMA. THAT'S ENOUGH.
BUT, DOCTOR MCCOY—
ENOUGH. MR. SPOCK IS STILL THE CAPTAIN OF THIS SHUTTLE. HE'S THE RANKING OFFICER, AND YOU'LL ADDRESS HIM ACCORDINGLY. HOW 'BOUT YOU GO SEE WHAT EQUIPMENT WE CAN JETTISON TO HELP THE SITUATION, ALL RIGHT?
THANK YOU, DOCTOR.
DON'T THANK ME. HE'S RIGHT. IT'S TIME TO MAKE A DECISION.
BY NOW THE ENTERPRISE WILL BE HEADING OFF TO THE RENDEZVOUS. JIM WON'T HAVE A CHOICE.
AND FROM THE SOUND OF IT, THIS SHUTTLE IS ABOUT TO BE TORN TO SHREDS.
IT'S YOUR CALL, CAPTAIN.
SO WHAT DO WE DO?

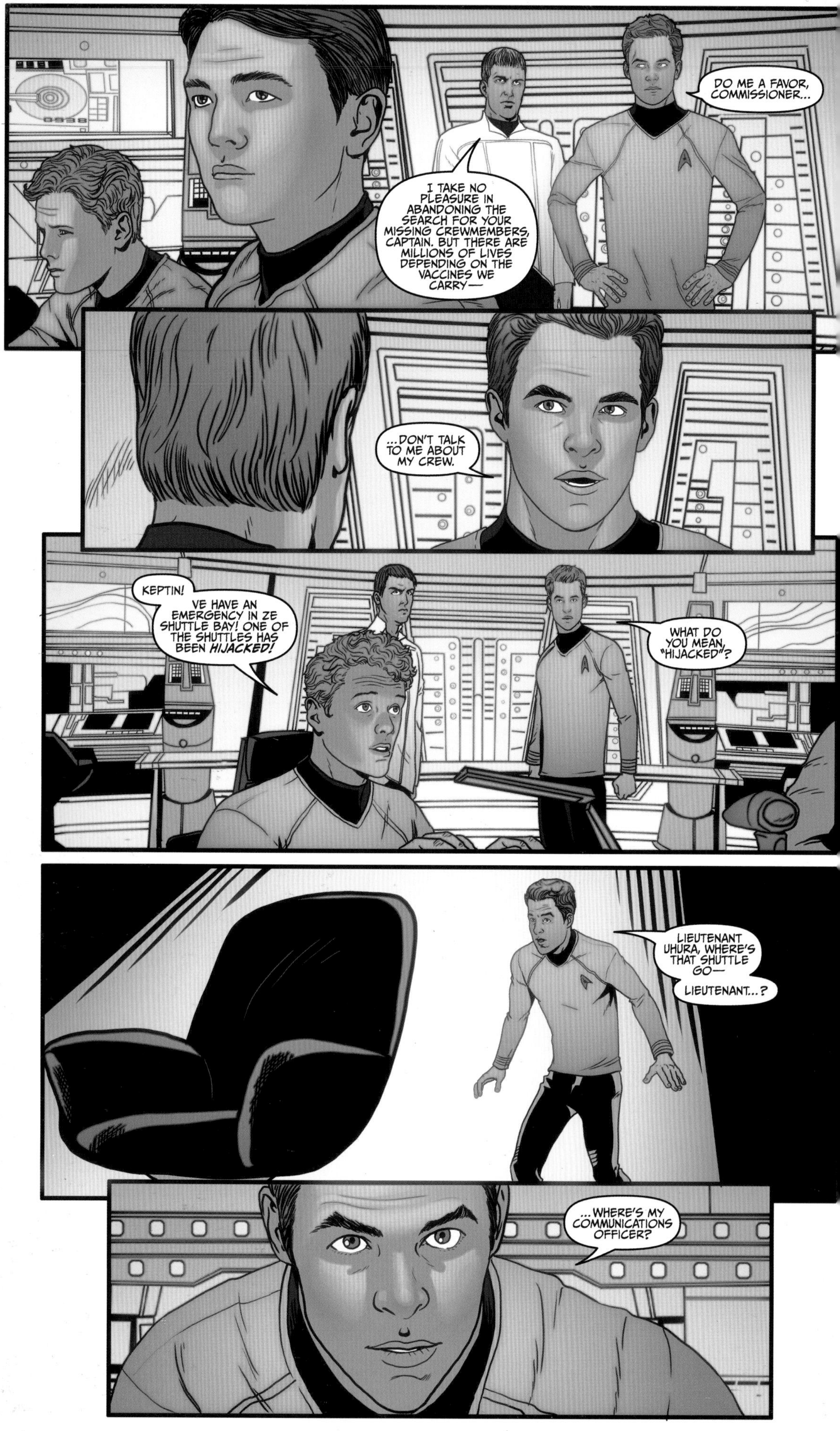
DO ME A FAVOR, COMMISSIONER...
I TAKE NO PLEASURE IN ABANDONING THE SEARCH FOR YOUR MISSING CREWMEMBERS, CAPTAIN. BUT THERE ARE MILLIONS OF LIVES DEPENDING ON THE VACCINES WE CARRY—
...DON'T TALK TO ME ABOUT MY CREW.
KEPTIN!
VE HAVE AN EMERGENCY IN ZE SHUTTLE BAY! ONE OF THE SHUTTLES HAS BEEN *HIJACKED!*
WHAT DO YOU MEAN, "HIJACKED"?
LIEUTENANT UHURA, WHERE'S THAT SHUTTLE GO—
LIEUTENANT...?
...WHERE'S MY COMMUNICATIONS OFFICER?

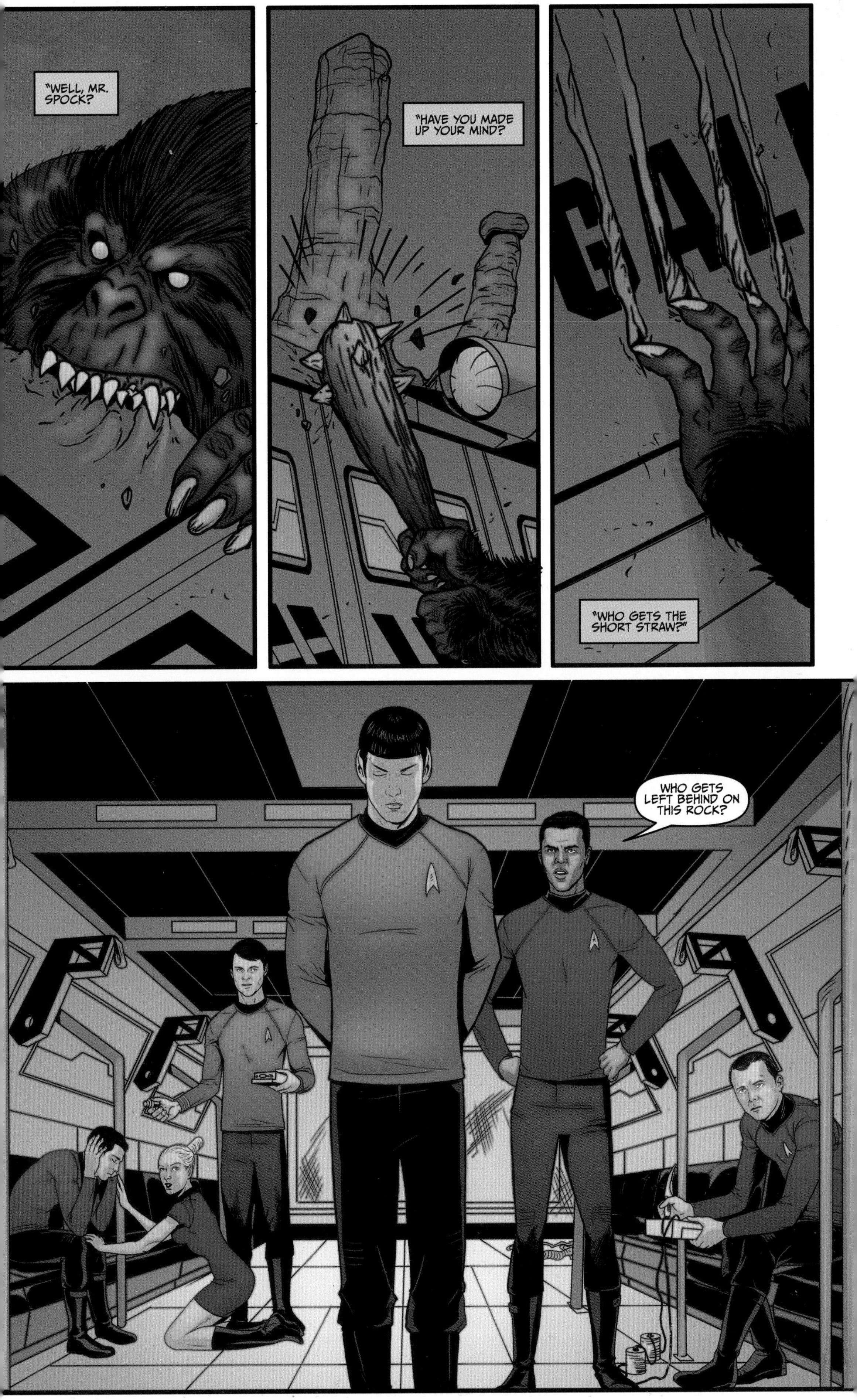
"WELL, MR. SPOCK?
"HAVE YOU MADE UP YOUR MIND?
"WHO GETS THE SHORT STRAW?"
WHO GETS LEFT BEHIND ON THIS ROCK?

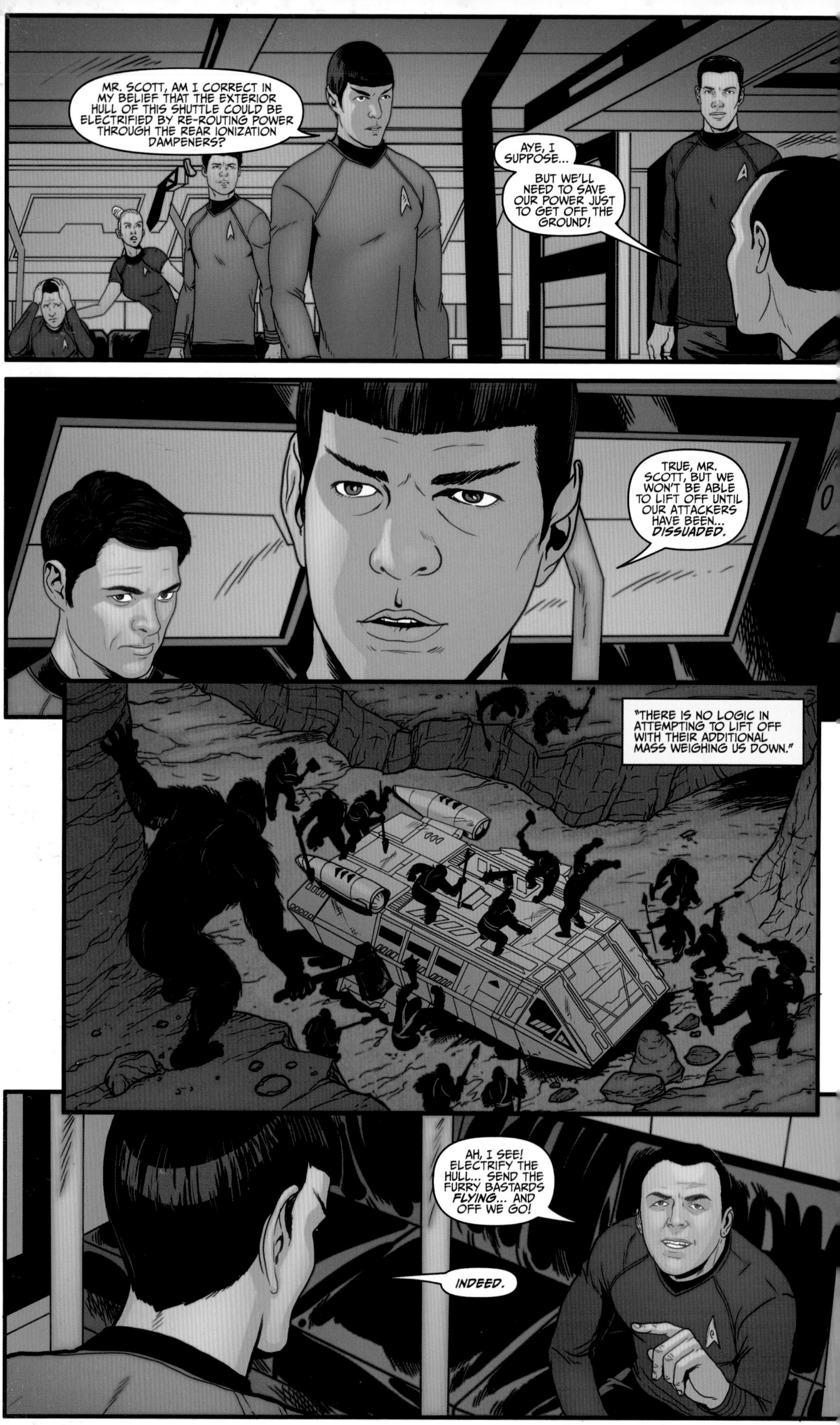
MR. SCOTT, AM I CORRECT IN MY BELIEF THAT THE EXTERIOR HULL OF THIS SHUTTLE COULD BE ELECTRIFIED BY RE-ROUTING POWER THROUGH THE REAR IONIZATION DAMPENERS?
AYE, I SUPPOSE...
BUT WE'LL NEED TO SAVE OUR POWER JUST TO GET OFF THE GROUND!
TRUE, MR. SCOTT, BUT WE WON'T BE ABLE TO LIFT OFF UNTIL OUR ATTACKERS HAVE BEEN... DISSUADED.
"THERE IS NO LOGIC IN ATTEMPTING TO LIFT OFF WITH THEIR ADDITIONAL MASS WEIGHING US DOWN."
AH, I SEE! ELECTRIFY THE HULL... SEND THE FURRY BASTARDS FLYING... AND OFF WE GO!
INDEED.

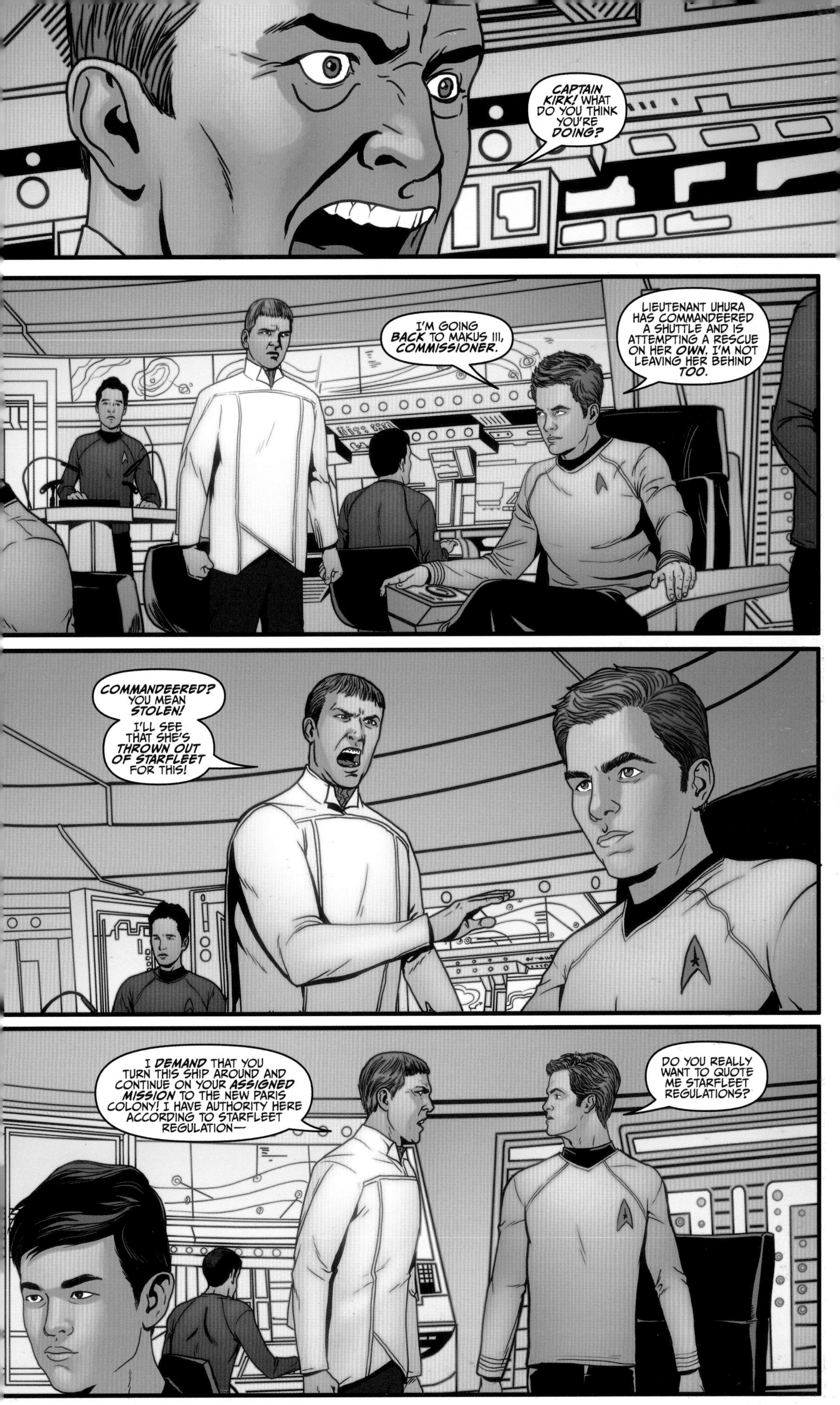
CAPTAIN KIRK! WHAT DO YOU THINK YOU'RE DOING?
I'M GOING BACK TO MAKUS III, COMMISSIONER.
LIEUTENANT UHURA HAS COMMANDEERED A SHUTTLE AND IS ATTEMPTING A RESCUE ON HER OWN. I'M NOT LEAVING HER BEHIND TOO.
COMMANDEERED? YOU MEAN STOLEN!
I'LL SEE THAT SHE'S THROWN OUT OF STARFLEET FOR THIS!
I DEMAND THAT YOU TURN THIS SHIP AROUND AND CONTINUE ON YOUR ASSIGNED MISSION TO THE NEW PARIS COLONY! I HAVE AUTHORITY HERE ACCORDING TO STARFLEET REGULATION—
DO YOU REALLY WANT TO QUOTE ME STARFLEET REGULATIONS?

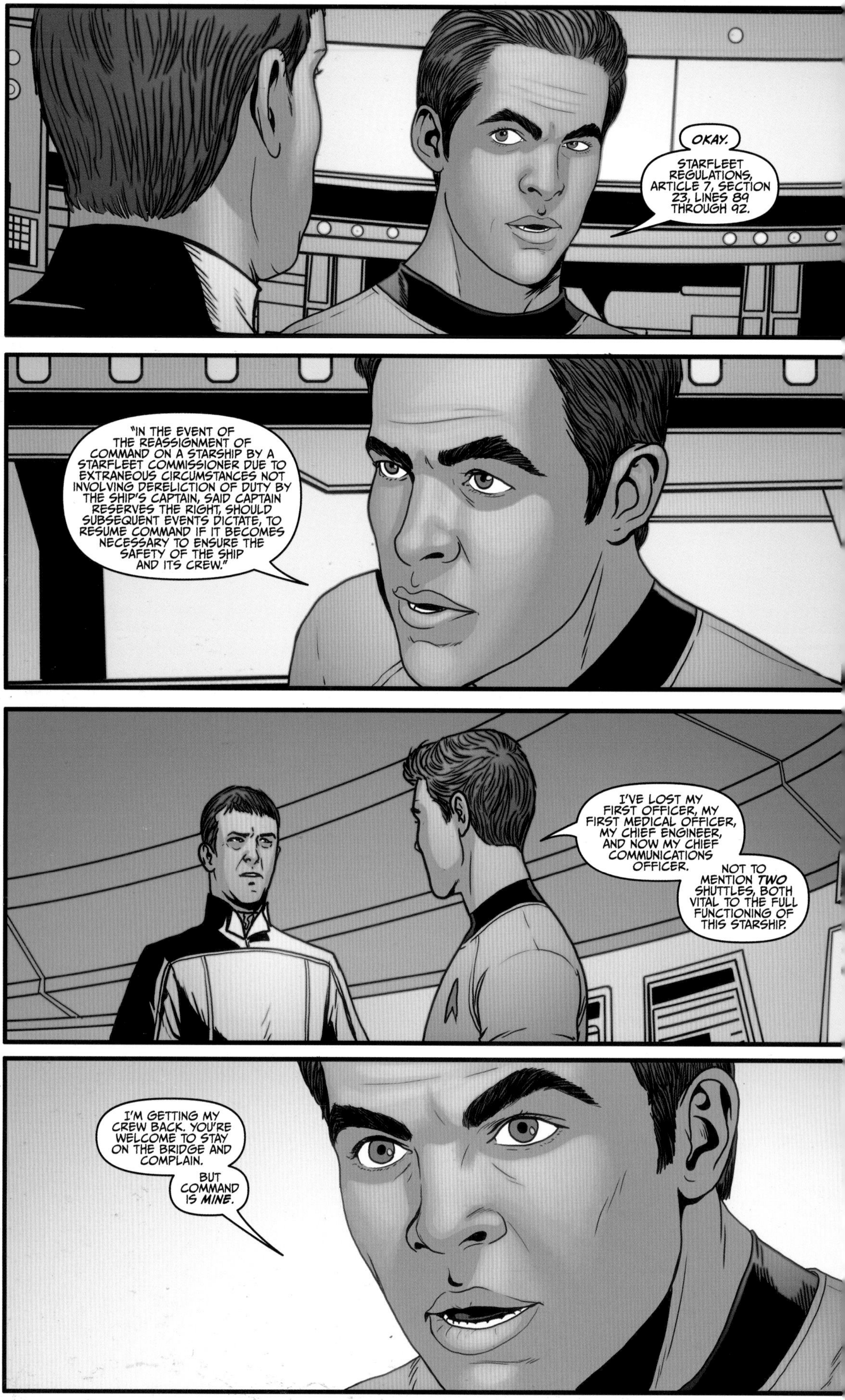
OKAY.
STARFLEET REGULATIONS, ARTICLE 7, SECTION 23, LINES 89 THROUGH 92.
"IN THE EVENT OF THE REASSIGNMENT OF COMMAND ON A STARSHIP BY A STARFLEET COMMISSIONER DUE TO EXTRANEOUS CIRCUMSTANCES NOT INVOLVING DERELICTION OF DUTY BY THE SHIP'S CAPTAIN, SAID CAPTAIN RESERVES THE RIGHT, SHOULD SUBSEQUENT EVENTS DICTATE, TO RESUME COMMAND IF IT BECOMES NECESSARY TO ENSURE THE SAFETY OF THE SHIP AND ITS CREW."
I'VE LOST MY FIRST OFFICER, MY FIRST MEDICAL OFFICER, MY CHIEF ENGINEER, AND NOW MY CHIEF COMMUNICATIONS OFFICER.
NOT TO MENTION TWO SHUTTLES, BOTH VITAL TO THE FULL FUNCTIONING OF THIS STARSHIP.
I'M GETTING MY CREW BACK. YOU'RE WELCOME TO STAY ON THE BRIDGE AND COMPLAIN.
BUT COMMAND IS MINE.

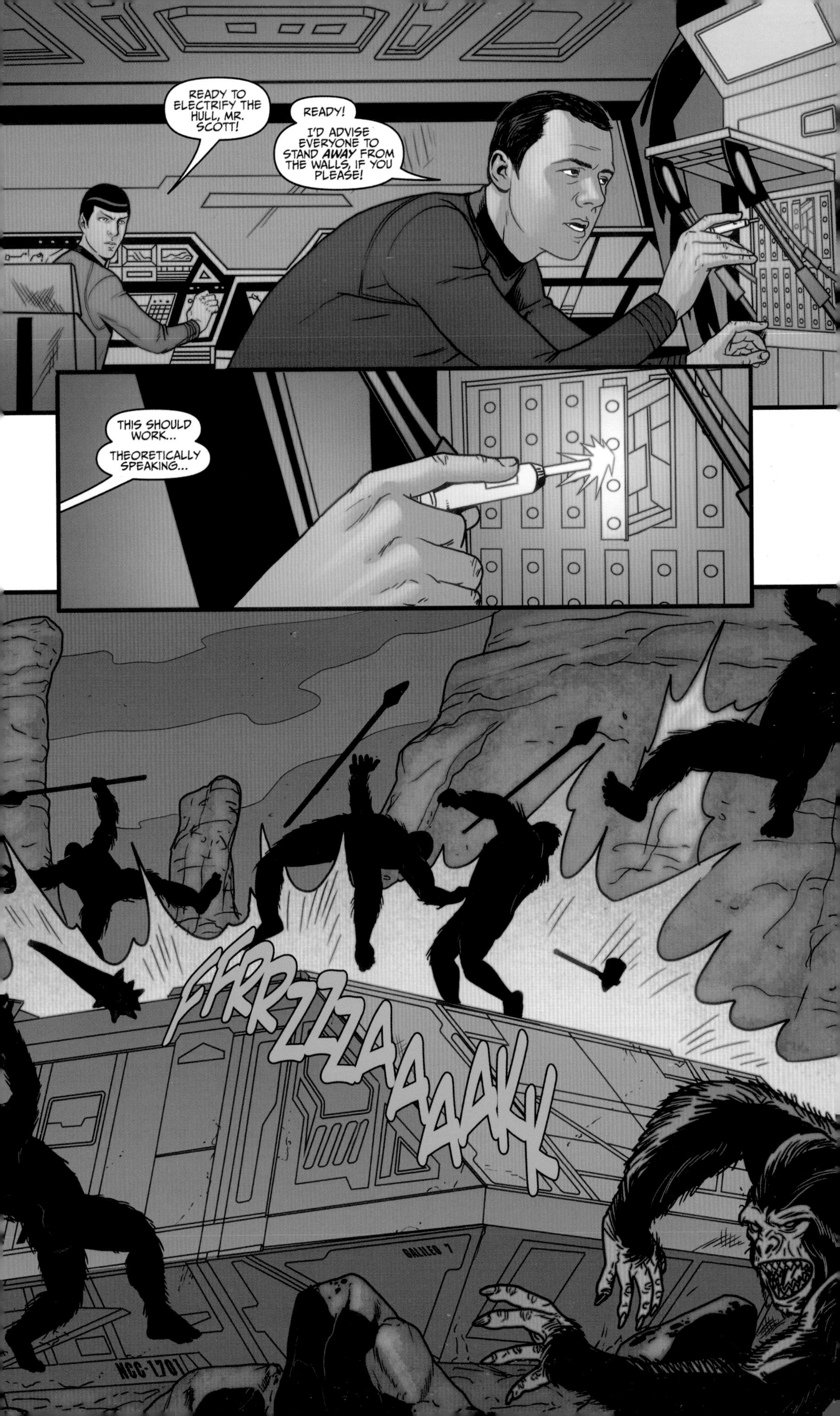
READY TO ELECTRIFY THE HULL, MR. SCOTT!
READY!
I'D ADVISE EVERYONE TO STAND **AWAY** FROM THE WALLS, IF YOU PLEASE!
THIS SHOULD WORK...
THEORETICALLY SPEAKING...
FFRRZZZAAAAKK
GALILEO 7
NCC-1701

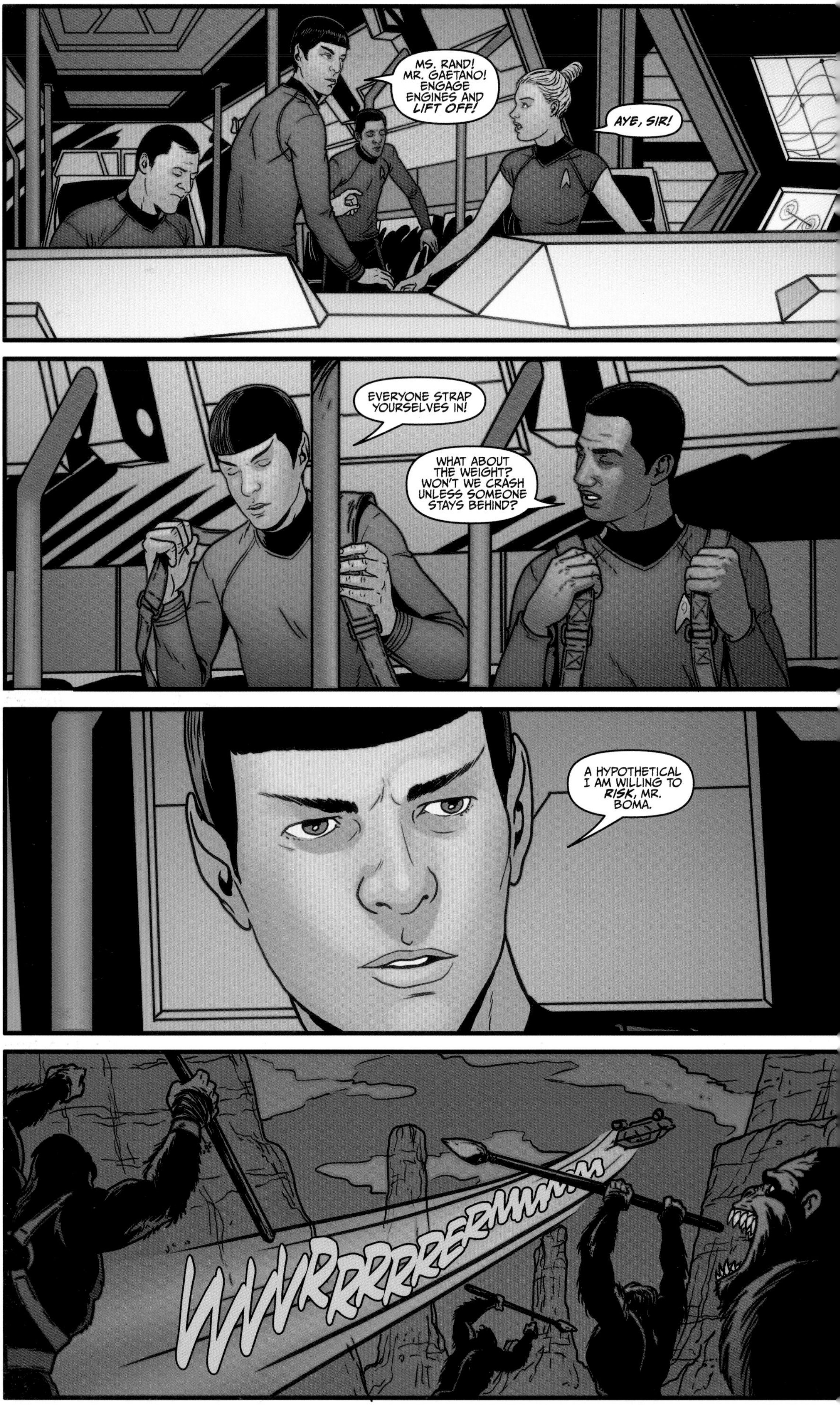
MS. RAND! MR. GAETANO! ENGAGE ENGINES AND LIFT OFF!
AYE, SIR!
EVERYONE STRAP YOURSELVES IN!
WHAT ABOUT THE WEIGHT? WON'T WE CRASH UNLESS SOMEONE STAYS BEHIND?
A HYPOTHETICAL I AM WILLING TO RISK, MR. BOMA.
WWRRRRRERMMMM

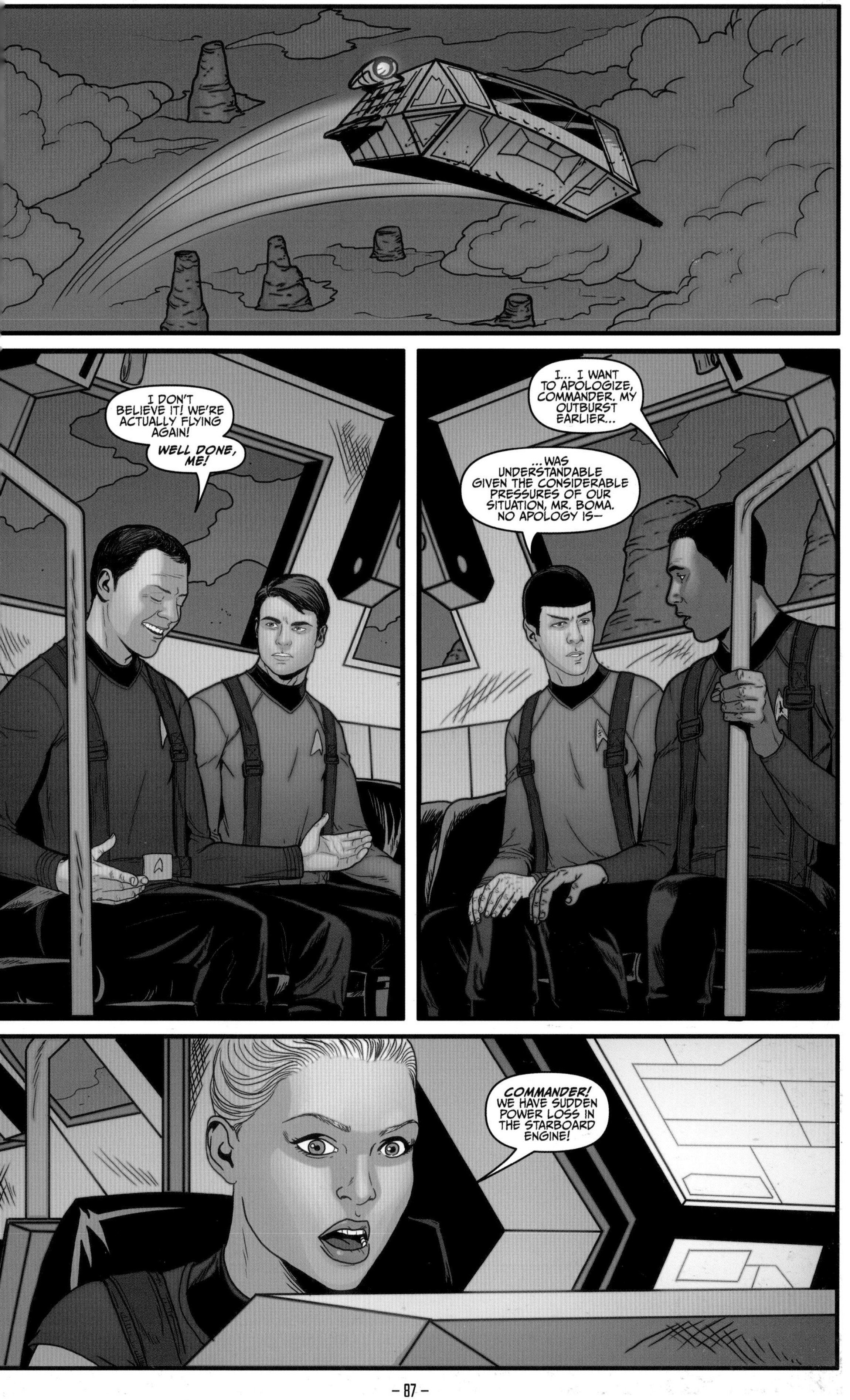
I DON'T BELIEVE IT! WE'RE ACTUALLY FLYING AGAIN!
WELL DONE, ME!
I... I WANT TO APOLOGIZE, COMMANDER. MY OUTBURST EARLIER...
...WAS UNDERSTANDABLE GIVEN THE CONSIDERABLE PRESSURES OF OUR SITUATION, MR. BOMA. NO APOLOGY IS—
COMMANDER! WE HAVE SUDDEN POWER LOSS IN THE STARBOARD ENGINE!

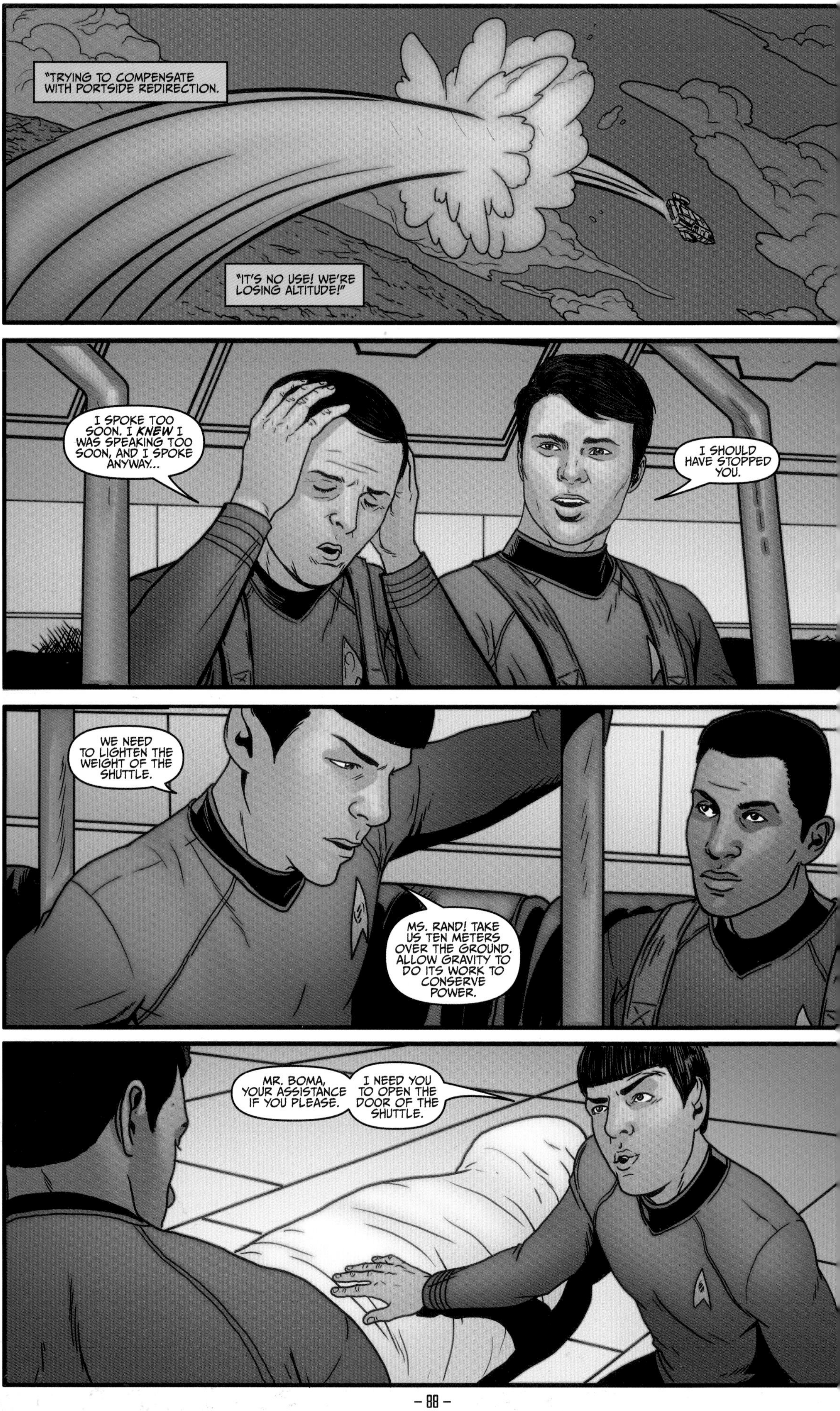
"TRYING TO COMPENSATE WITH PORTSIDE REDIRECTION.
"IT'S NO USE! WE'RE LOSING ALTITUDE!"
I SPOKE TOO SOON. I *KNEW* I WAS SPEAKING TOO SOON, AND I SPOKE ANYWAY...
I SHOULD HAVE STOPPED YOU.
WE NEED TO LIGHTEN THE WEIGHT OF THE SHUTTLE.
MS. RAND! TAKE US TEN METERS OVER THE GROUND. ALLOW GRAVITY TO DO ITS WORK TO CONSERVE POWER.
MR. BOMA, YOUR ASSISTANCE IF YOU PLEASE.
I NEED YOU TO OPEN THE DOOR OF THE SHUTTLE.

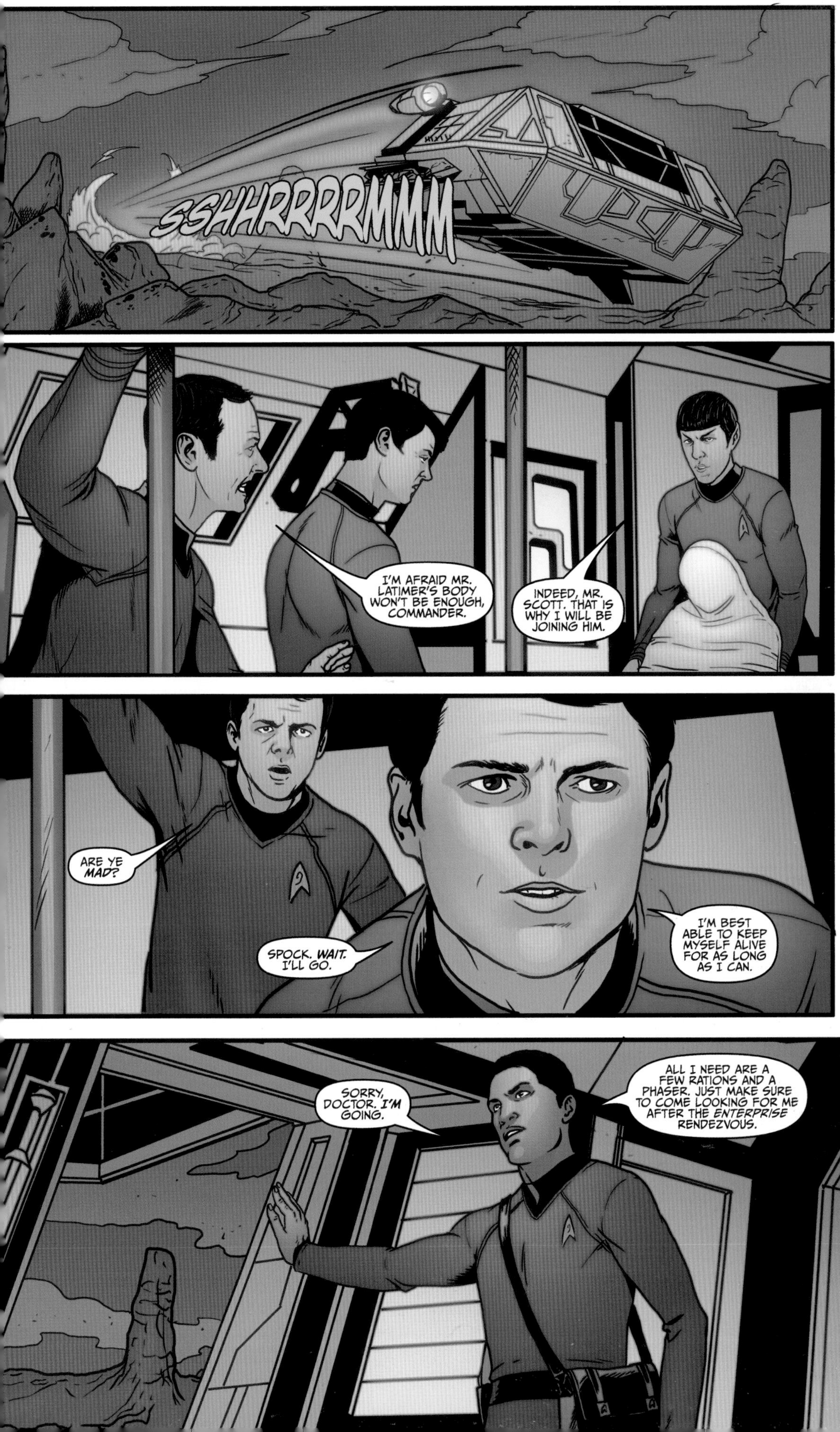
SSHHRRRRMMM
I'M AFRAID MR. LATIMER'S BODY WON'T BE ENOUGH, COMMANDER.
INDEED, MR. SCOTT. THAT IS WHY I WILL BE JOINING HIM.
ARE YE *MAD*?
SPOCK. *WAIT.* I'LL GO.
I'M BEST ABLE TO KEEP MYSELF ALIVE FOR AS LONG AS I CAN.
SORRY, DOCTOR. *I'M* GOING.
ALL I NEED ARE A FEW RATIONS AND A PHASER. JUST MAKE SURE TO COME LOOKING FOR ME AFTER THE *ENTERPRISE* RENDEZVOUS.

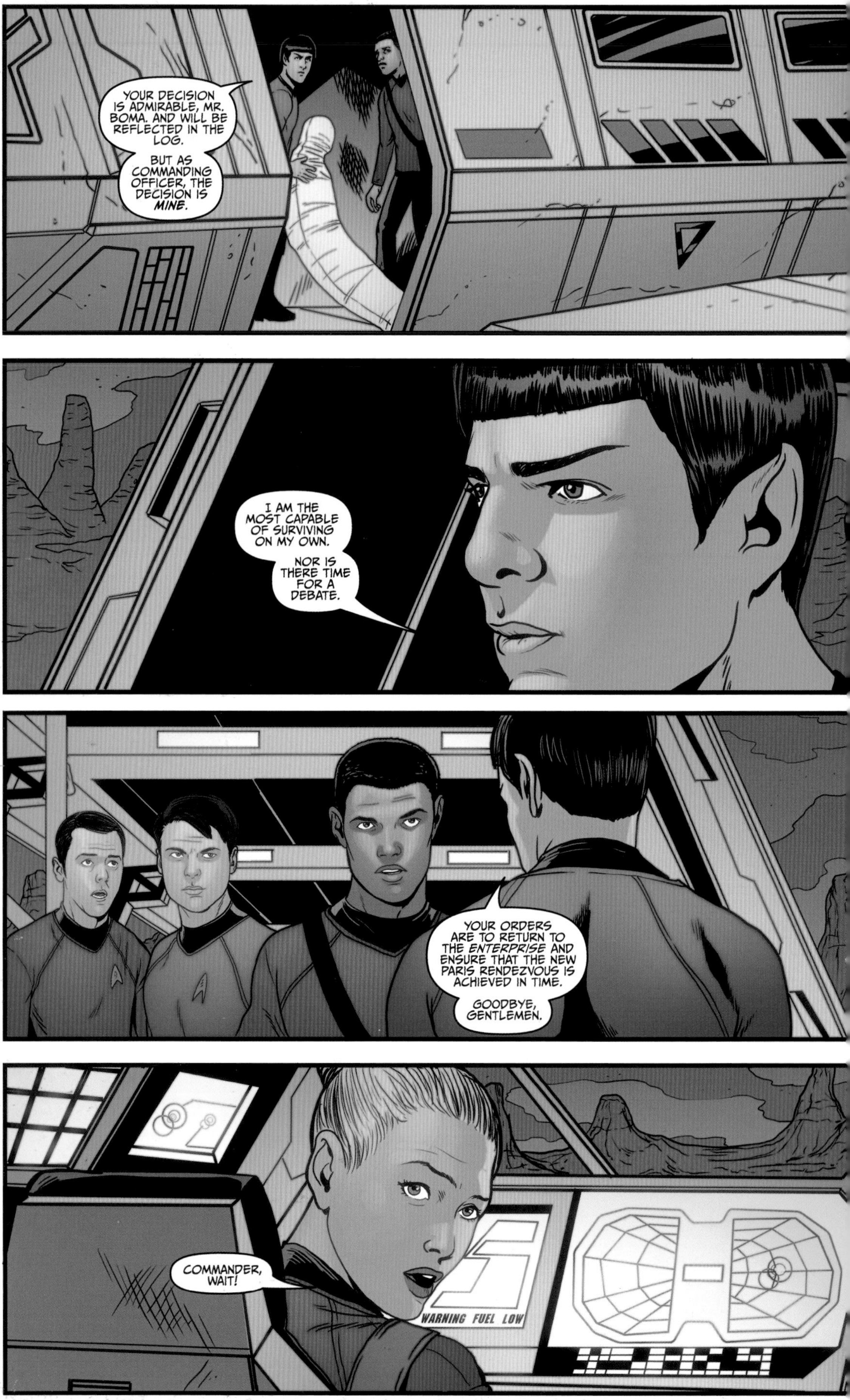
YOUR DECISION IS ADMIRABLE, MR. BOMA. AND WILL BE REFLECTED IN THE LOG.
BUT AS COMMANDING OFFICER, THE DECISION IS *MINE*.
I AM THE MOST CAPABLE OF SURVIVING ON MY OWN.
NOR IS THERE TIME FOR A DEBATE.
YOUR ORDERS ARE TO RETURN TO THE *ENTERPRISE* AND ENSURE THAT THE NEW PARIS RENDEZVOUS IS ACHIEVED IN TIME.
GOODBYE, GENTLEMEN.
COMMANDER, WAIT!
WARNING FUEL LOW

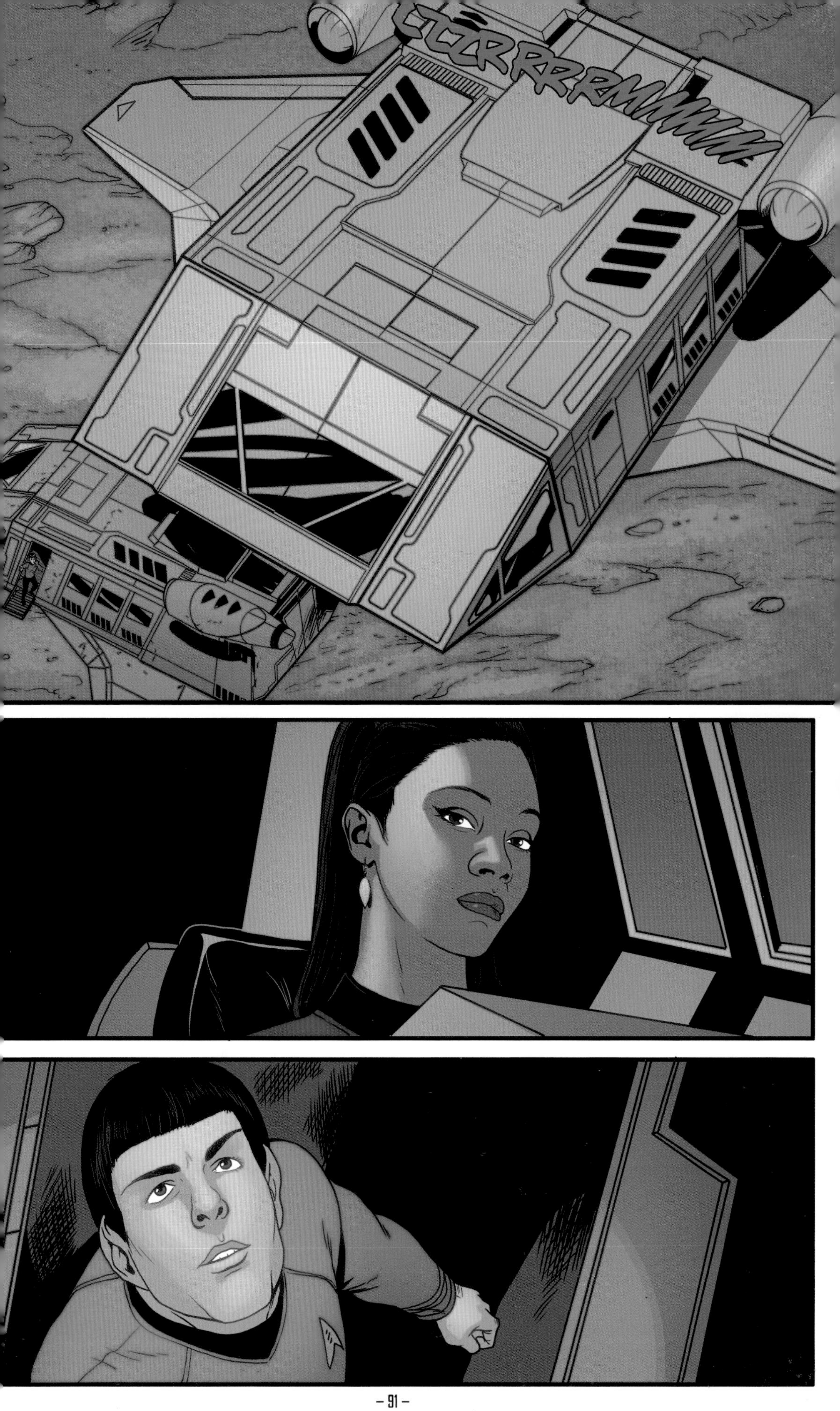
CZRRRRMMMMM

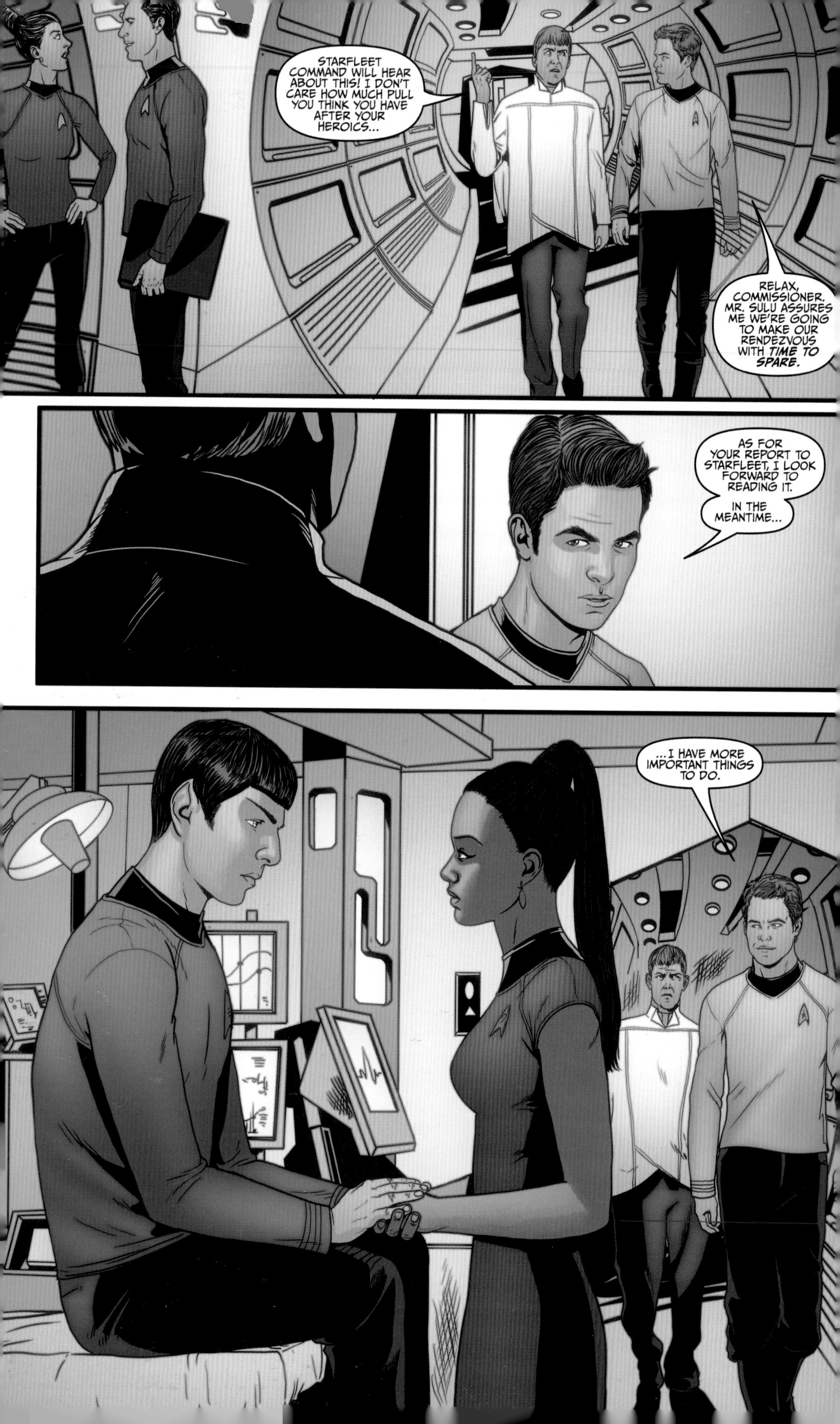
STARFLEET COMMAND WILL HEAR ABOUT THIS! I DON'T CARE HOW MUCH PULL YOU THINK YOU HAVE AFTER YOUR HEROICS...
RELAX, COMMISSIONER. MR. SULU ASSURES ME WE'RE GOING TO MAKE OUR RENDEZVOUS WITH *TIME TO SPARE.*
AS FOR YOUR REPORT TO STARFLEET, I LOOK FORWARD TO READING IT.
IN THE MEANTIME...
...I HAVE MORE IMPORTANT THINGS TO DO.

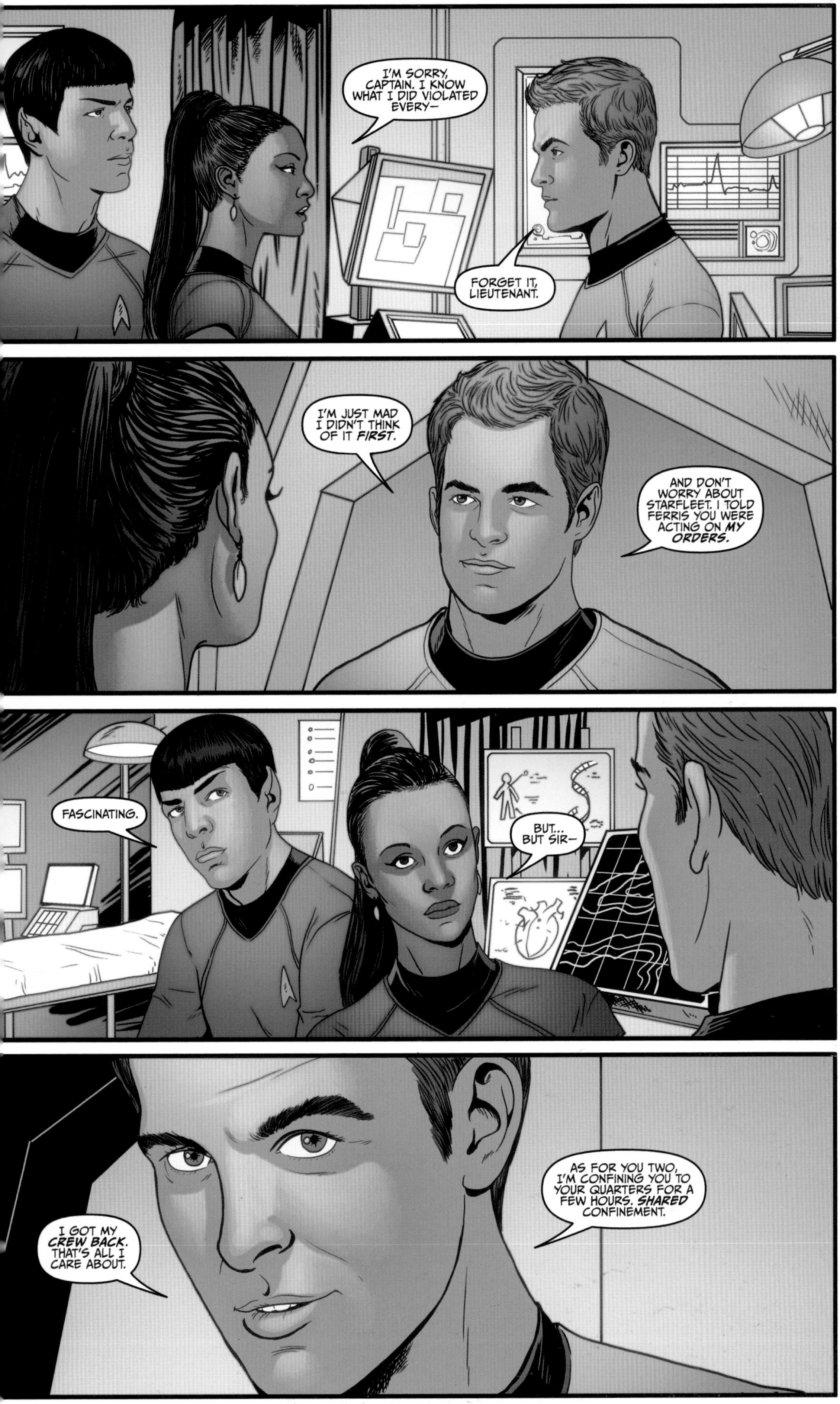

I'M SORRY, CAPTAIN. I KNOW WHAT I DID VIOLATED EVERY—
FORGET IT, LIEUTENANT.
I'M JUST MAD I DIDN'T THINK OF IT *FIRST*.
AND DON'T WORRY ABOUT STARFLEET. I TOLD FERRIS YOU WERE ACTING ON *MY ORDERS*.
FASCINATING.
BUT... BUT SIR—
I GOT MY *CREW BACK*. THAT'S ALL I CARE ABOUT.
AS FOR YOU TWO, I'M CONFINING YOU TO YOUR QUARTERS FOR A FEW HOURS. *SHARED* CONFINEMENT.

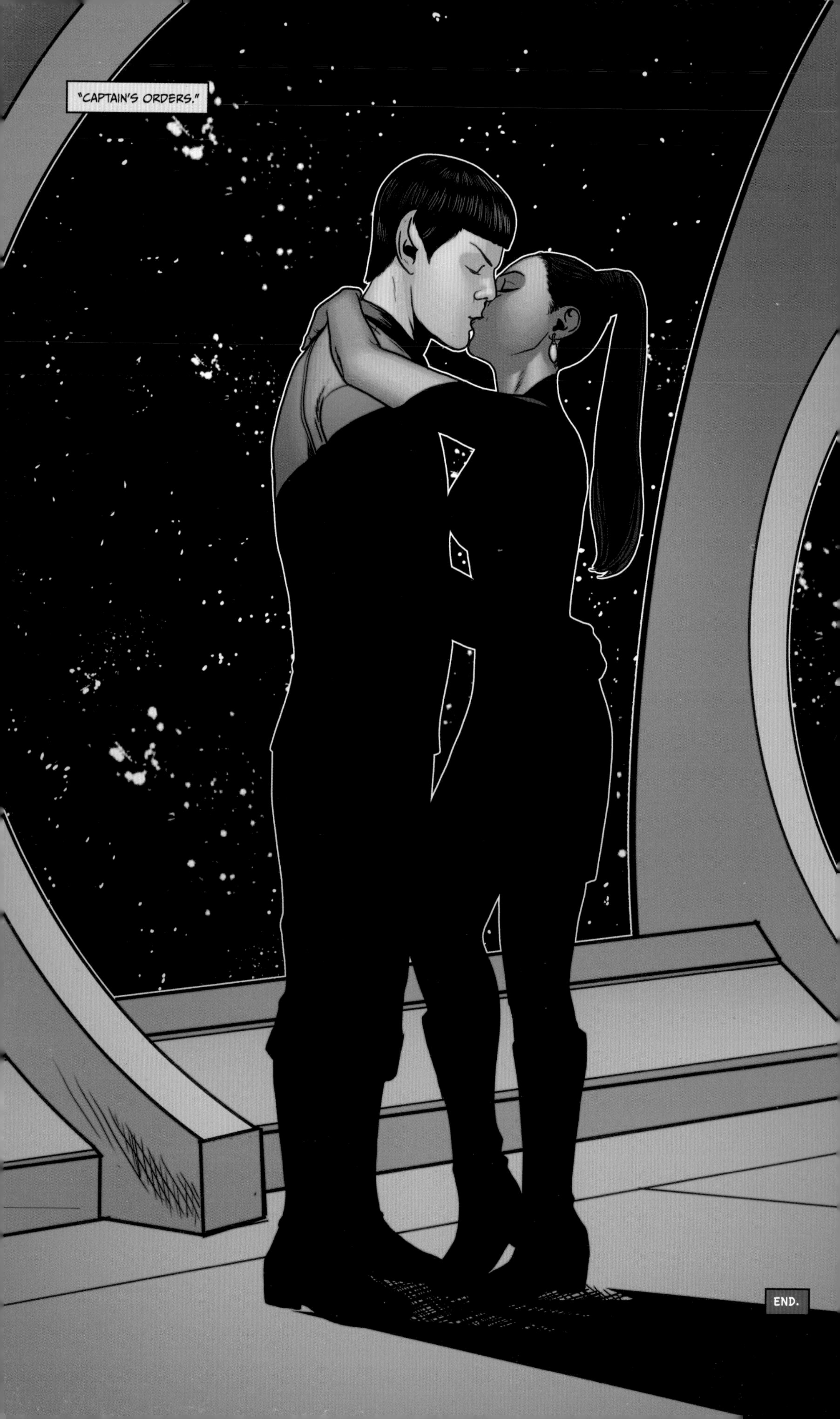
"CAPTAIN'S ORDERS."
END.

ART GALLERY

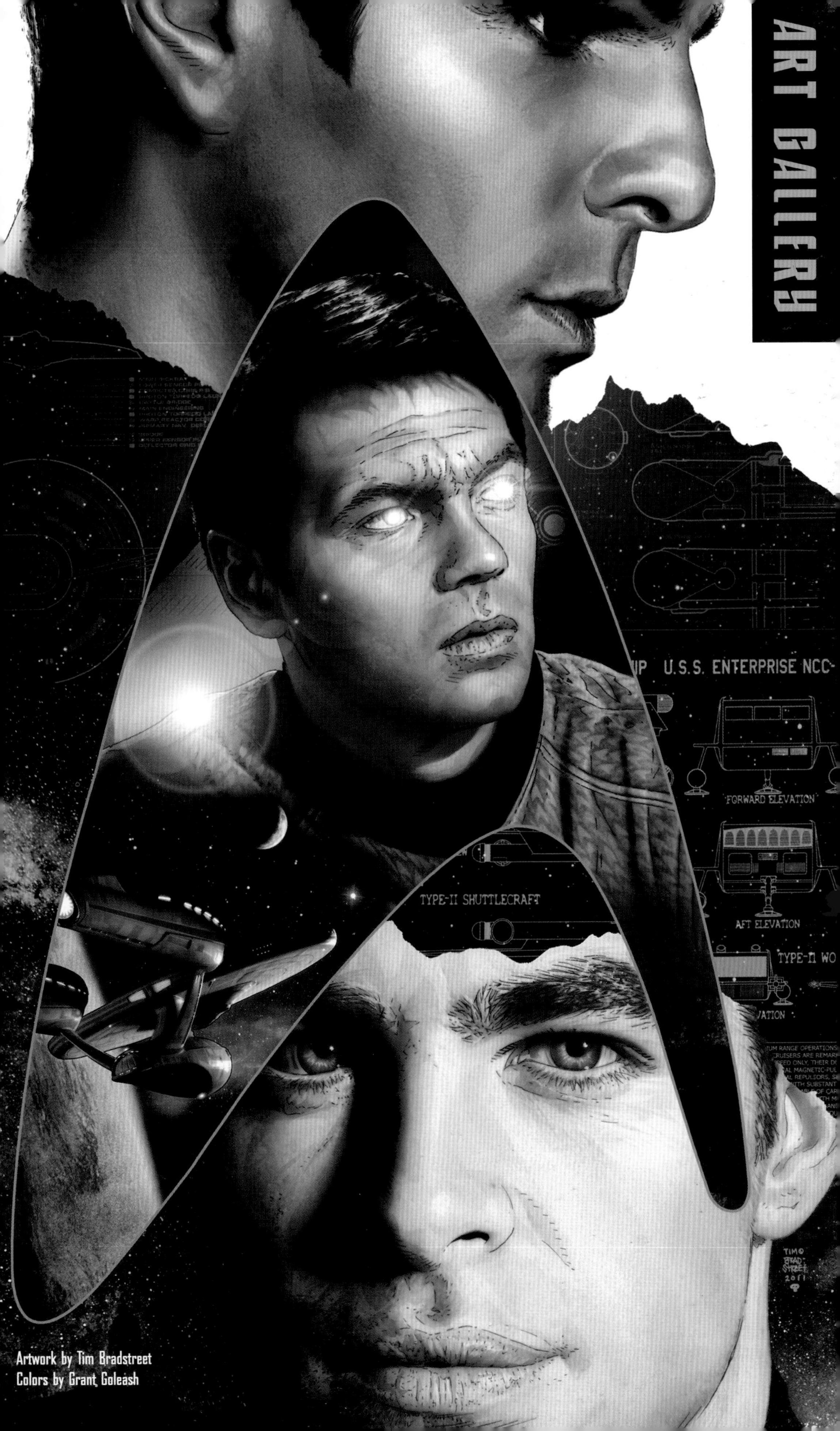
U.S.S. ENTERPRISE NCC-
FORWARD ELEVATION
AFT ELEVATION
TYPE-II SHUTTLECRAFT
TYPE-II WO
TIMO BRADSTREET 2011

Artwork by Tim Bradstreet
Colors by Grant Goleash

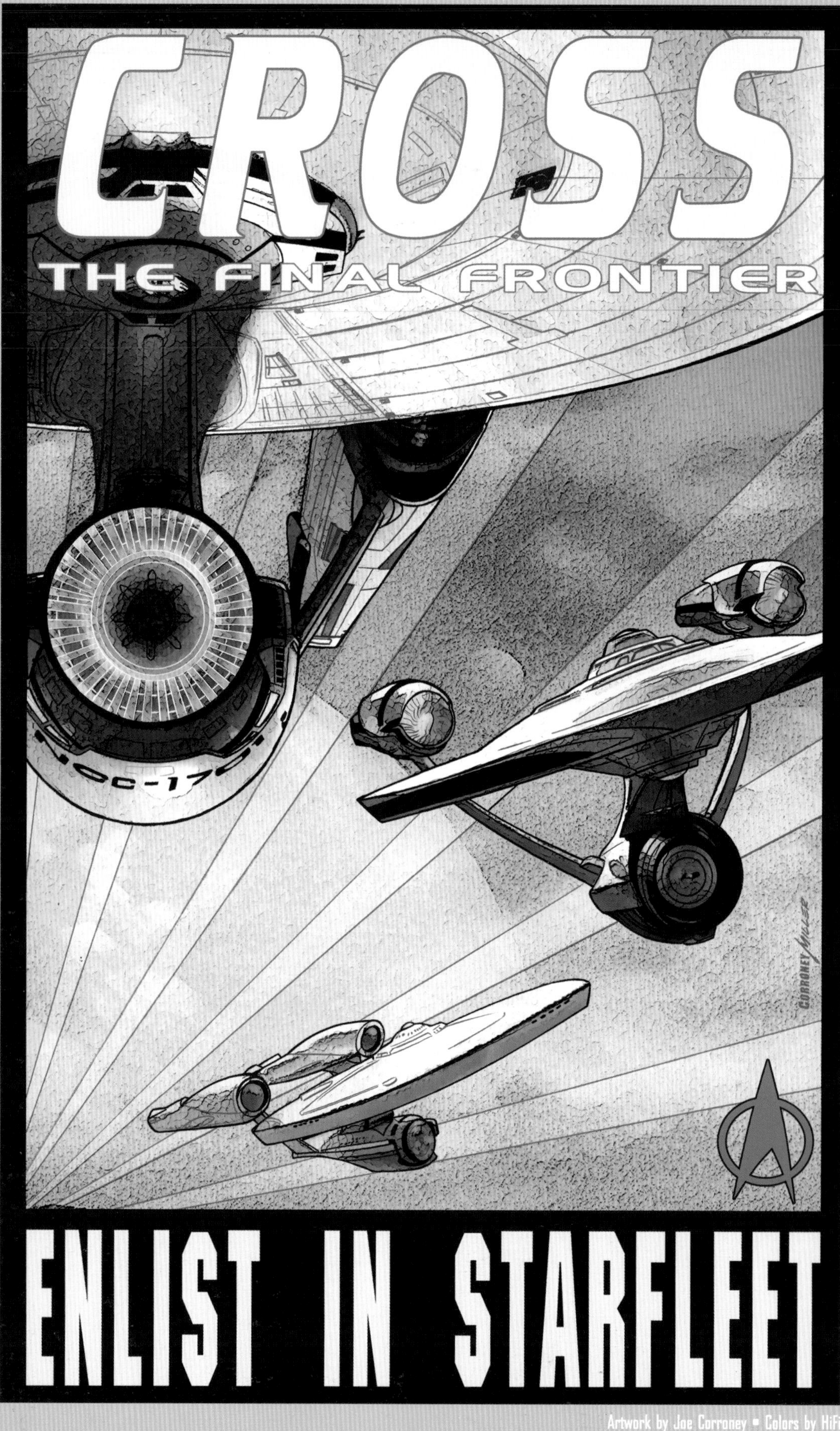
CROSS
THE FINAL FRONTIER
CORRONEY/MILLER
ENLIST IN STARFLEET

Artwork by Joe Corroney ■ Colors by HiFi

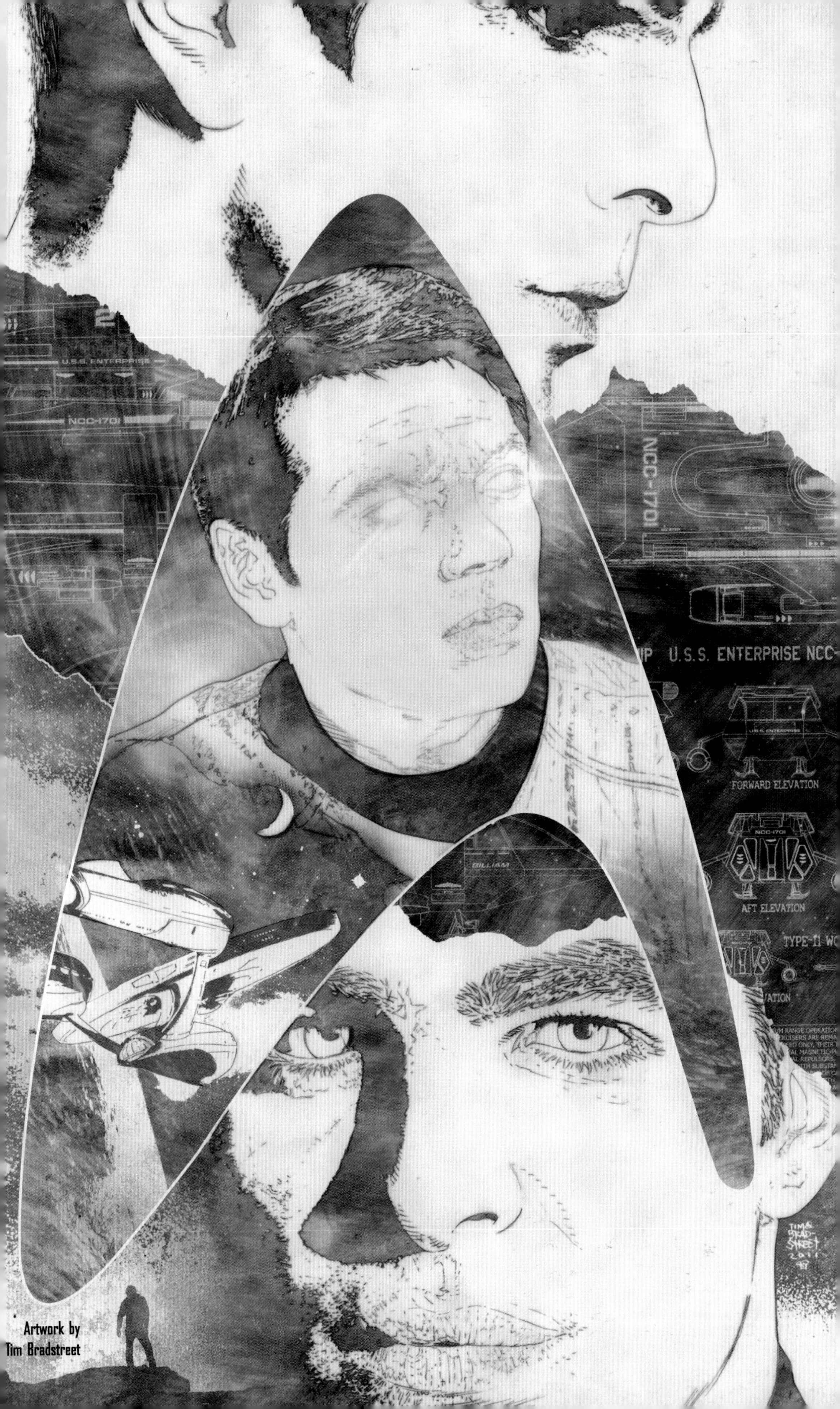
U.S.S. ENTERPRISE
NCC-1701
NCC-1701
U.S.S. ENTERPRISE NCC-
FORWARD ELEVATION
AFT ELEVATION
TYPE-II
GILLIAM
TIM BRADSTREET 2011

Artwork by
Tim Bradstreet

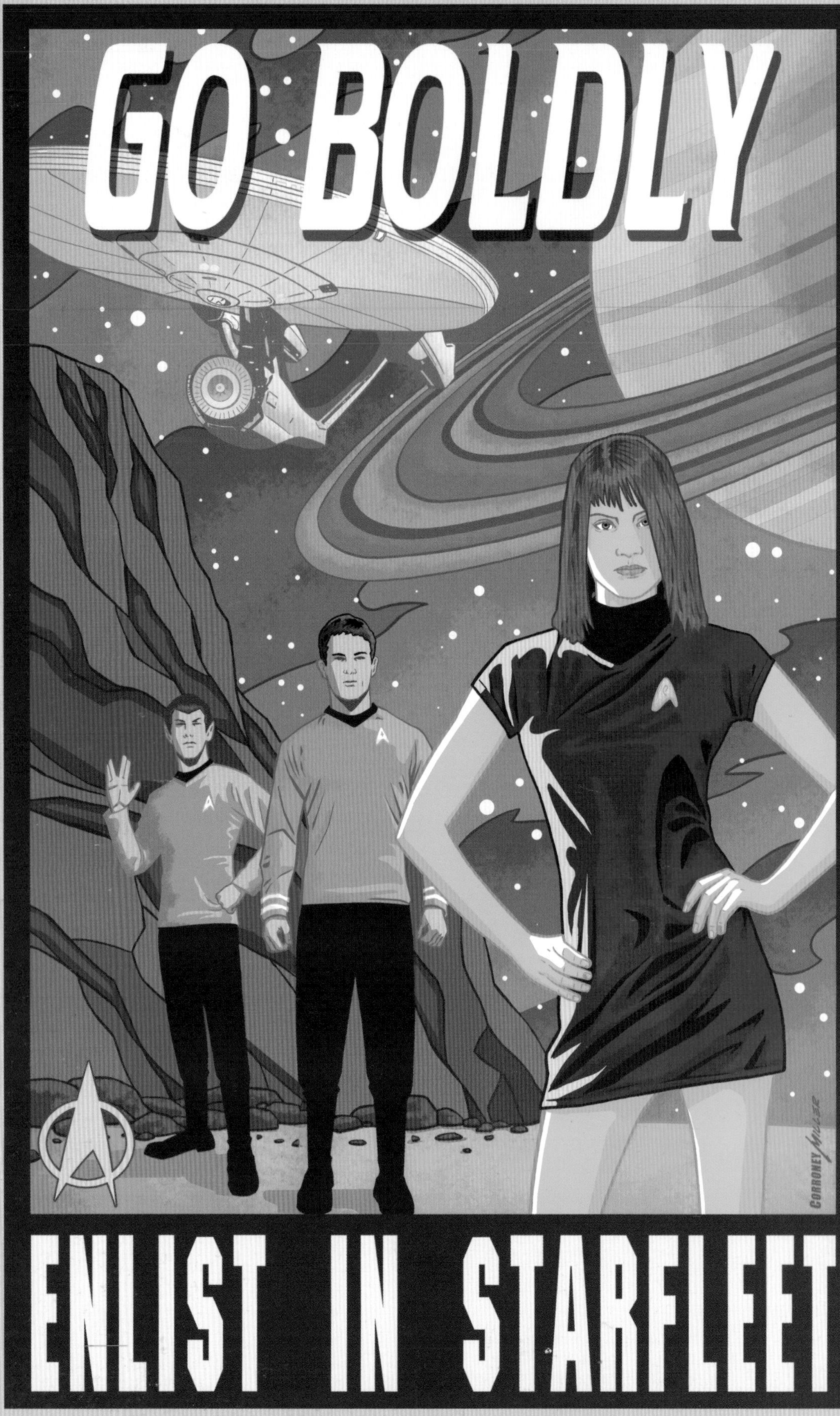
GO BOLDLY
CORRONEY MILLER
ENLIST IN STARFLEET

Artwork by Joe Corroney • Colors by HiFi

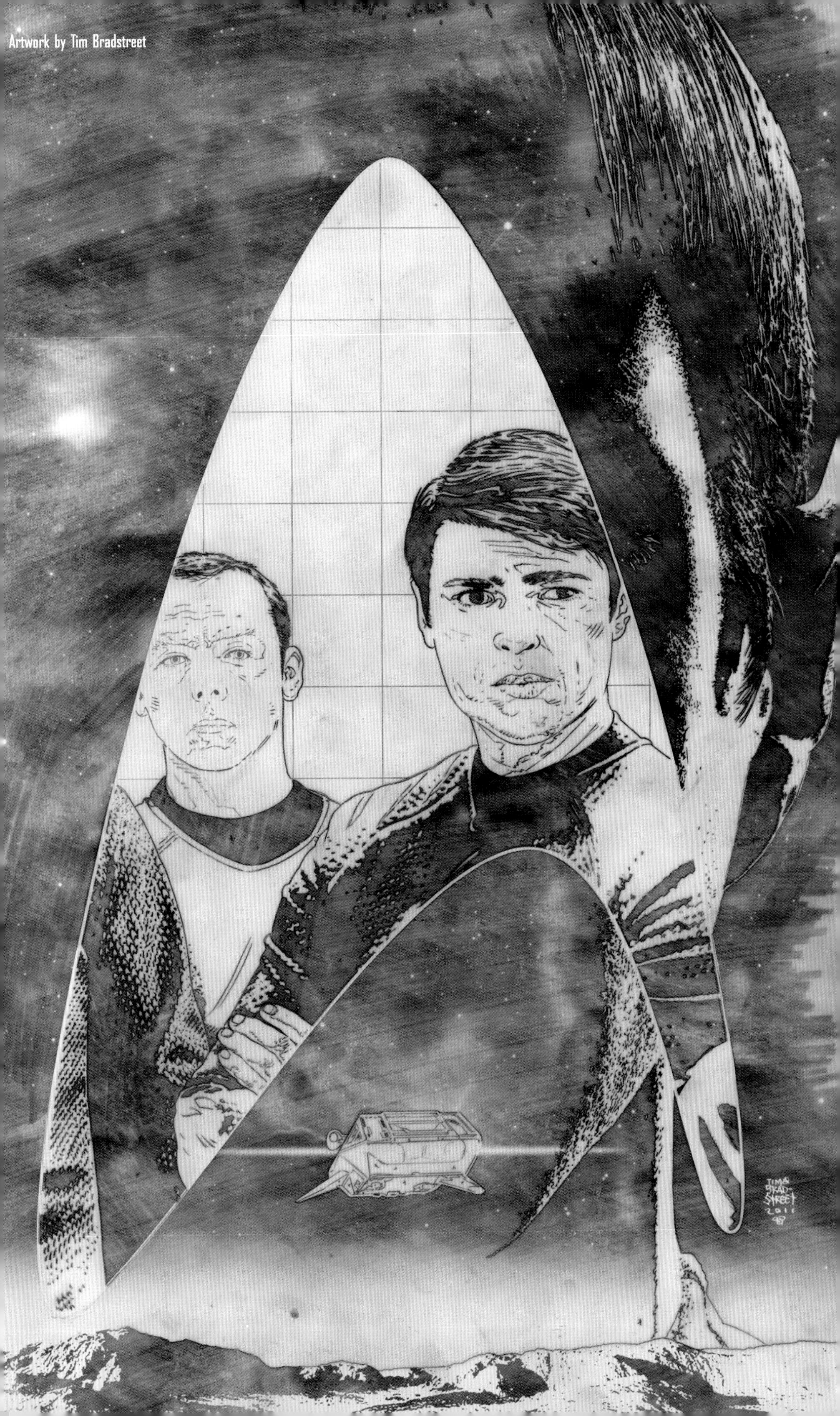
TIM BRAD-STREET 2011

Artwork by Tim Bradstreet

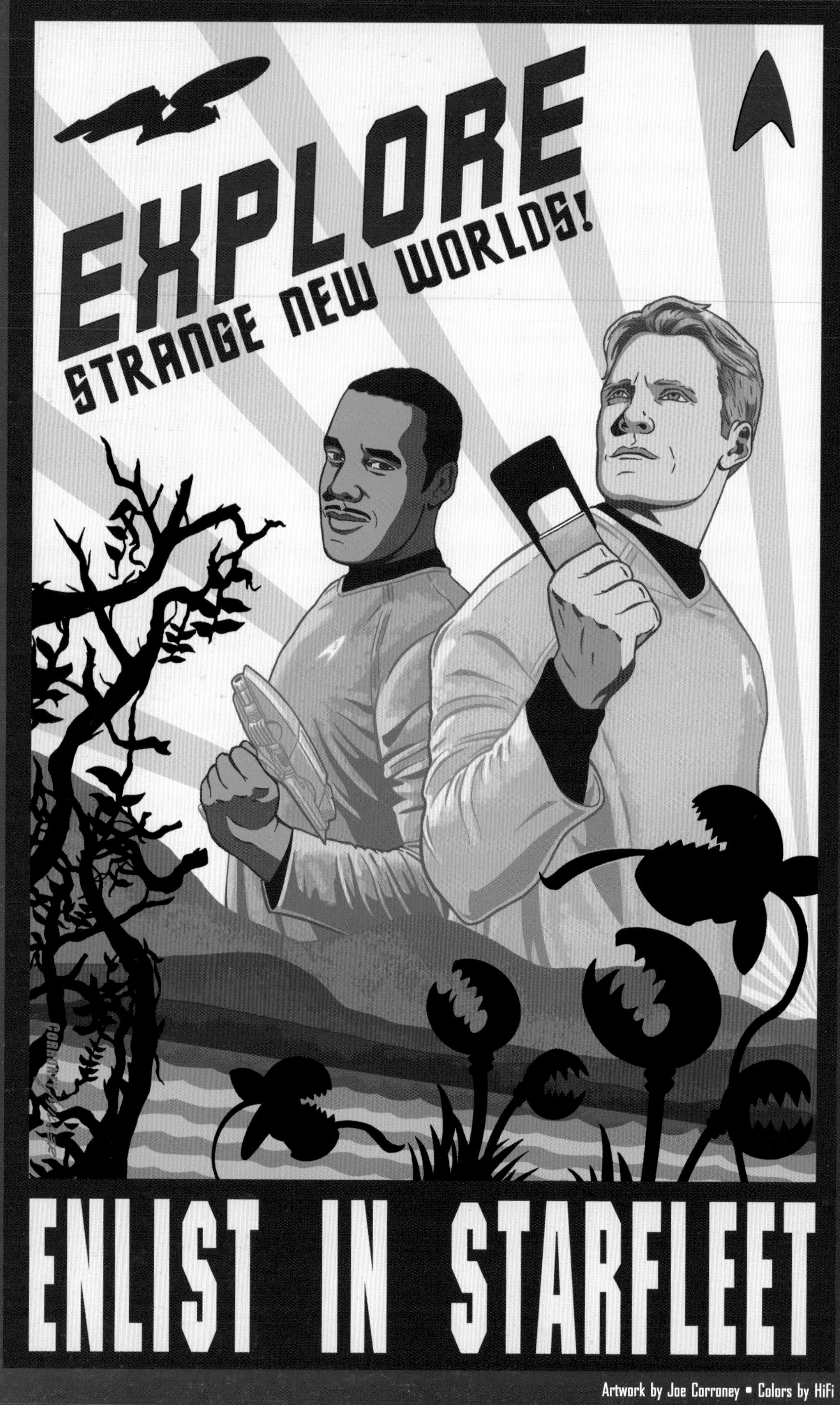
EXPLORE
STRANGE NEW WORLDS!
ENLIST IN STARFLEET

Artwork by Joe Corroney • Colors by HiFi

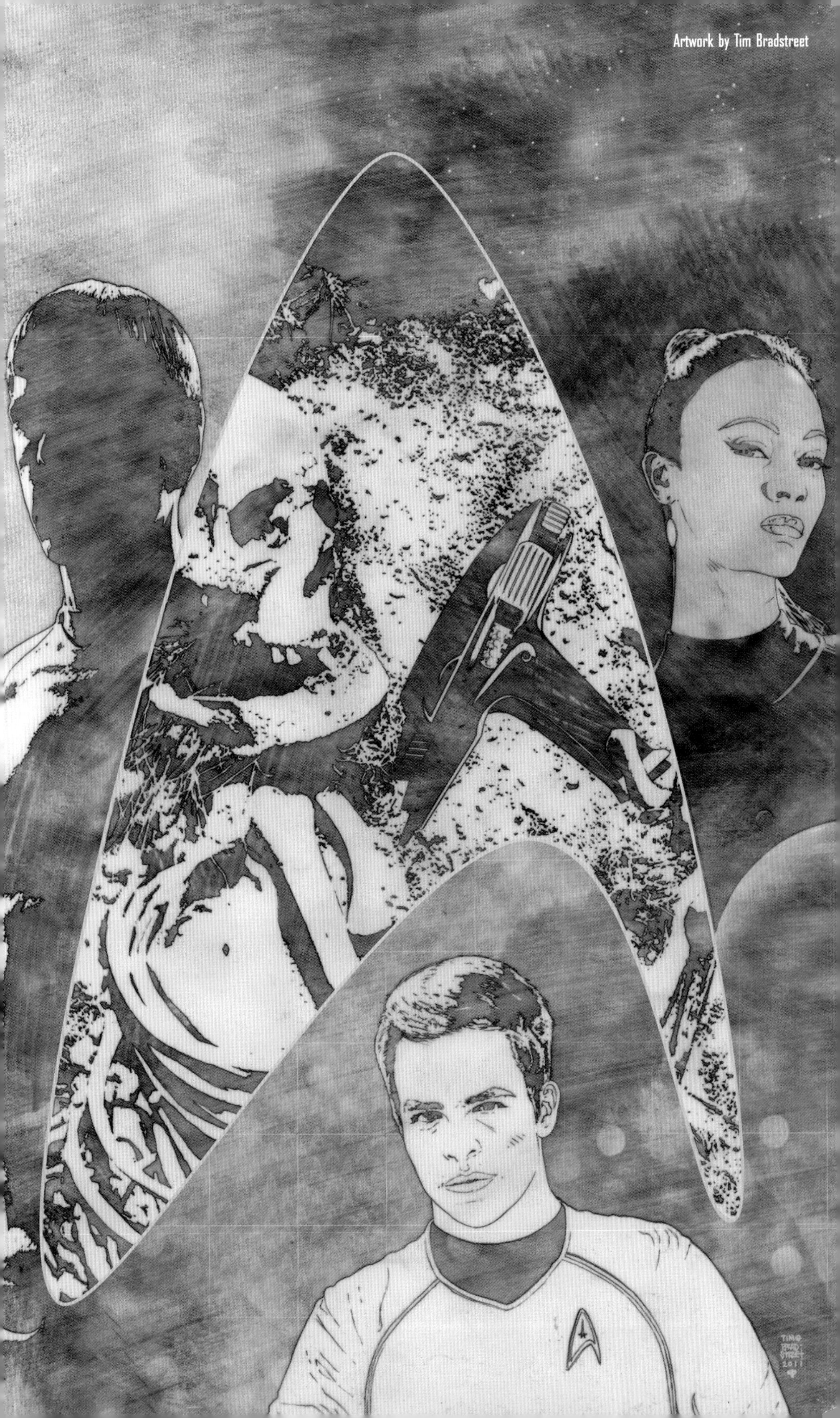

Artwork by Tim Bradstreet

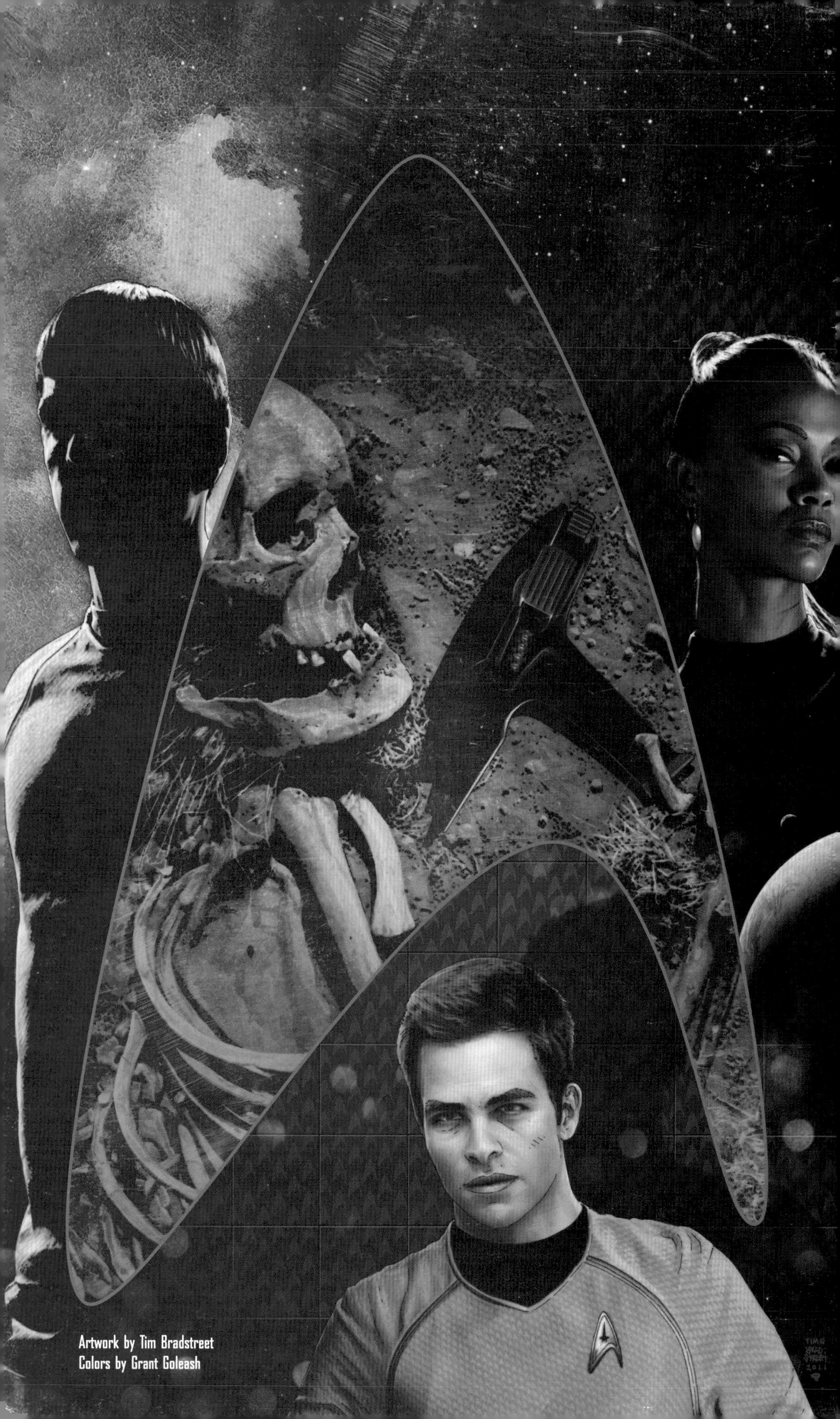
TIM BRAD-STREET 2011

Artwork by Tim Bradstreet
Colors by Grant Goleash

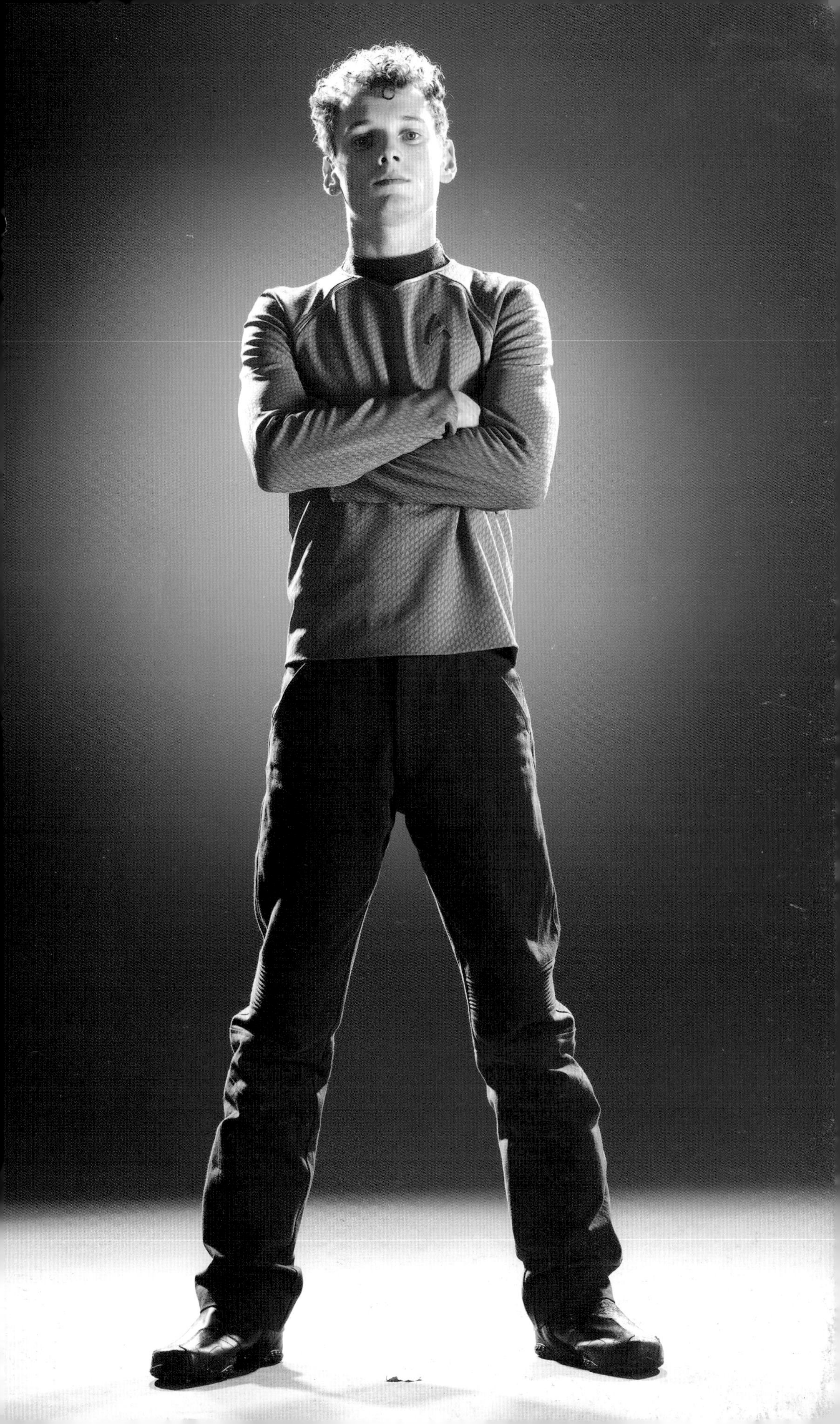

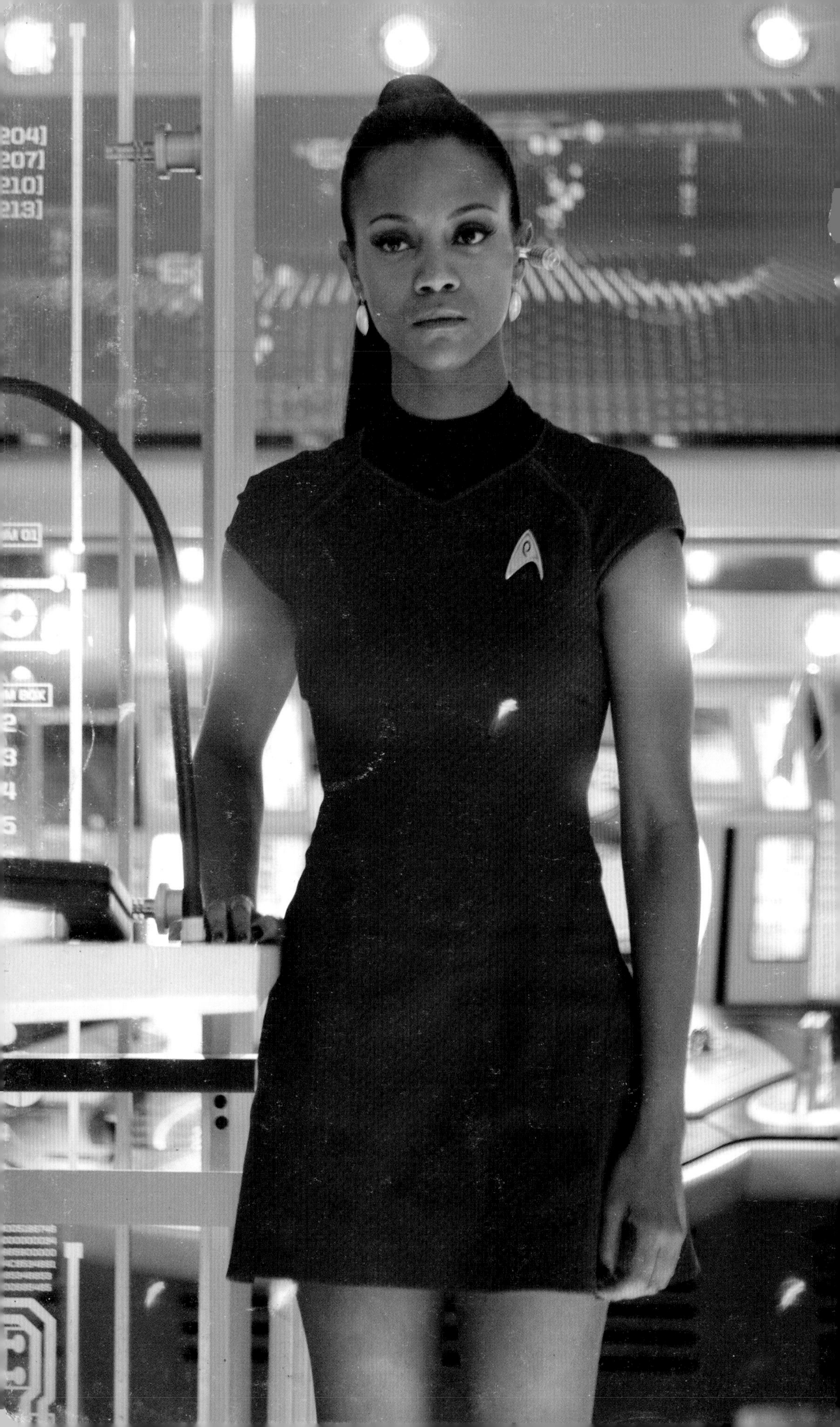